THE PAINTED WOMAN

BOOK I

VICTORIA PARRA

PARRA PUBLISHING

Cover design: Faera Lane

Editing: Ronan Sadler, Hanna Richards, Kim Halstead

ISBN (print): 979-8-9851557-0-9

ISBN (ebook): 979-8-9851557-1-6

This book is dedicated to every sex worker who was made
to feel like they couldn't be the main character.

CHAPTER ONE

Sigrid did not have to think about what she did. Her mind was on the next day's shopping, where she'd use the money the man beneath her had spent. He was her second visitor of the day, and he'd brought coin aplenty. She laughed at a joke, the punchline immediately forgotten, and wondered if she'd find apples at the market. Shifting in his lap, she brought her watered-down beer up to her lips and sipped as the man beneath her took yet another shot of rum. He was becoming sloppy, and if she didn't stop him, he'd likely not remember the evening. But he was there for a good time, and she wasn't his mother.

"My dear Evangeline," he slurred.

She flashed him a smile. It wasn't her name, it wasn't even the name she'd given him, but he could call her whatever he wanted. She didn't care. Mostly, she was counting down the minutes to when the man would pass out and be escorted out of the Golden Pearl by his manservant.

A full tankard of mead later, the lord passed out in the chaise. His cheeks were rosy, and a bit of drool wet his chin.

Sigrid frowned in disgust before leaving the room to fetch his servant from the waiting room.

"He's too drunk to remember the ride home," she said flatly. "May want to get him some water."

The man, clearly well used to such antics, slunk off to lift his rather heavy master into their waiting carriage.

Once the door was firmly locked behind them, Sigrid let out a yawn she'd been stifling and rambled toward her bedroom. She didn't remember going to bed.

When she woke the next morning, her silk scarf half unraveled and her hair a flattened mess, just the thought of painting her face and coddling the feelings of men made her want to pull the covers back over her body. Still, she did not wish to be alone, so she crept out of bed and headed down the hall. Pressing the thin door open, Sigrid's eyes landed on the dark-skinned girl bundled in sheets and blankets.

"I don't want to work today," Sigrid groaned as she tumbled into Brigid's bed.

The woman beneath the covers grunted as Sigrid's body fell atop her. "So, take the day off. It was a good weekend." Brigid poked her head out from beneath the crimson blanket, her thick, coarse hair wrapped in a silk scarf that had, unlike Sigrid's, not come loose and let her hair become frizzy and messy.

"I should," came Sigrid's reply as she scooted off her friend to wrap her arms around the smaller woman's frame. "I suppose we don't have to open our doors today unless someone comes with extra coin. It has been a few days since I've been able to escape to the gymnasium."

Brigid rolled out of the bed and stomped rather ungracefully to her vanity, where Sigrid had placed a bowl of water. She dipped a bit of soft cotton cloth into the warm bowl and gently washed her face. From the bed, Sigrid wrapped the sheets around her body. With only marginally more grace than her tired friend, Sigrid strolled toward the window that overlooked Copper City. The morning was bright as the sun shone down on the city as it began to wake. Summer was around the corner, but the air was hot even so early.

"Then we could go to the bathhouse," Brigid said as she dried her face and dipped her fingers into a small pot of oil. Looking into her mirror, she massaged the oil into her face and dabbed it around her eyes with a single finger. "Last night was particularly warm, and I could use a dip in some water."

Sigrid nodded, taking a seat just next to the window. Below, people began to mill about. "I wouldn't mind a trip to the bathhouse." Her eyes traveled through the crowd below.

Brigid cast a look at her. "Our weekend wasn't so profitable that we can buy too many luxuries. Once our rent is paid, we can have a treat. Now go get ready."

"But we're just going to the bathhouse!"

"And we will be seen en route. You know as well as I do we're never entirely off work."

Feigning a surly disposition, Sigrid rose from her chair and crossed the room. "Fine, fine."

Sigrid was chased from the room and, like a banished child, sulked into her quarters. Taking a seat at her vanity, she cleaned her face and chewed a minty-flavored twig meant to freshen her breath. They were going to get wet, so she did not want to waste much time on makeup that would wash off, but she still rubbed rose hip oil into her face. It was nice not to do the full routine, but it was hard for Sigrid to imagine a day that didn't start like this. Beauty was her currency, and it required upkeep.

She dipped her brush into a pot of turquoise paint and carefully painted the outline of a lotus flower on her forehead. At some point in the more than two centuries that the Heddish had been occupying elven lands, a king passed a law requiring women like Sigrid to mark themselves so that all could see their profession. Now that a painted flower was so unambiguously part of a painted woman's life, Sigrid had difficulty imagining a time when being a painted woman and a woman of the night were not the same thing.

Carefully unwrapping the silk still somehow clinging to her head, she allowed her thick, round curls to release around her shoulders. It was a popular feature of hers, and she took great care of it—or tried to, silk wrapping skills notwithstanding. Smiling into the mirror, she gently fixed stray and unwoven curls, smoothing flyaways with a thick oil that weighed down the strands and kept them from becoming too unruly.

Satisfied with her hair, she stood from her stool and stepped into one of her more casual dresses. It was warm enough to wear a sheerer dress, this one rose-colored and made of layers of nearly transparent fabric. It rested against her skin, moving at the slightest rustle or breeze. It was a little showier than was necessary for the bathhouse, but as Brigid had said, they were never *not* working. It made her feel both regal and carefree.

Draping her bag over her shoulder, she slipped her feet into a pair of leather sandals and glided down the hall to Brigid's room.

The streets were crowded, and Sigrid only managed not to lose Brigid in the crowd by keeping her hand firmly clasped in Brigid's. Copper City had been a hub for many years, but Sigrid could not remember a time it had been so populated. Tired of the chaos of the capital, Hedeby, many humans had begun to migrate to Copper City. Once the main hub of elven life, even after the human conquest of their land, the city had quickly grown into a trendy, quaint place that lacked the overpopulation of Hedeby but had all the luxuries. It was only a matter of years before the city swelled beyond its borders and spilled into surrounding towns.

They passed stall after colorful stall, each with vendors vying for their attention. "Just ten copper," one merchant called out, gesturing to his cart of apples.

"No thank you," Brigid said, waving the man off. Leaning into her friend, she said, "That's too much for apples. A few months ago it was five copper an apple."

Sigrid enjoyed the bustle of crowds and the many artful characters that were drawn to her city, but she found little to love about how expensive even the basics had become. Though the city had long been a quaint vacation destination for wealthy humans, particularly the nobility from Hedeby, it now attracted the nouveau riche and the merchants who followed them.

"It isn't too bad," Sigrid said, casting a glance at the apples as they passed. "We can afford a few overpriced apples."

In some ways, things were better for Sigrid. Money was good, even if prices were steep. The city boasted more to be entertained by, and it had become a haven for artists ready to be patronized by the wealthy. Unfortunately, the humans had their own ideas and customs that often clashed with the locals. Humans had lived in the city long before Sigrid had even been born, but it remained one of the few places in the kingdom that retained its more elven qualities. Now she felt stifled and judged in her own home.

For now, however, Sigrid was determined to enjoy the day. She had no culls to entertain yet, and the weather was nice. The sun shone brightly above them, but it was not quite as hot as it had been the day before, so she counted herself lucky.

Stopping in front of one of the merchant stalls that lined the city street, Sigrid ran her finger over the handle of a jeweled hand mirror.

"Ah, Sigrid," came the voice of a tall, bearded elven man. Silver sparkled in his dark beard, and his lips pulled into a smile. "I haven't seen you in a while. Have you found another purveyor of fine jewelry?"

Sigrid laughed, fluttering her eyelashes at the elder man. "Never! I've simply been saving a bit of money. I promise I'll come by again to see what new things you have to adorn me with."

A younger man exited the home behind the merchant. "I'll tell my mother your well-wishes," the man said, his narrow eyes first setting on the bearded man before sliding forward to Sigrid.

Sigrid smiled at the younger man. He was handsome, she thought. He had high cheekbones, and pin-straight black hair fell over his shoulders. What drew her in were his eyes. They curved into a narrow point that turned up at the outer corners and were lined with dense, black eyelashes. They were set beneath bold brows that gave him an intensity that sparked something in her stomach.

"Go well, Baldr."

The younger man said nothing else before passing by, his eyes lingering on Sigrid for just a moment before disappearing into the crowd.

"Family?" Sigrid asked, motioning toward the door the young man had come through.

"My nephew. Stopped by on an errand for his mother."

Sigrid nodded and briefly browsed through a few of the merchant's necklaces before she felt Brigid's hand on her arm.

"I'll see you later. If any ruby ear cuffs come in, save them for me!" Sigrid said.

The jolly merchant waved at her as she was dragged away.

The stone bathhouse rose above the other buildings and had scenes of women pouring water into baths decorating its roof. Water was freely available in the city thanks to the city's expansive use of aqueducts and pipes, but only the wealthy could afford their own bath in their home. Everyone else relied on copper baths they filled by hand or went to the bathhouse.

Stepping through the entryway, the two women dropped coins in the hand of the attendant and made their way through the building. Different rooms held baths of different sizes and temperatures, and the two made their way to the back where the hottest of the baths awaited them. It was a surprisingly empty day, with just four other people in the large bath. They talked quietly among themselves, leaving Brigid and Sigrid to disrobe in peace.

Sigrid dipped her foot into the hot water and let out a gasp, her lips drawing into a large smile as she slowly inched into the water. Soon she was able to sit along the edge, and she watched as Brigid stepped into the water as if the heat barely registered. Brigid's hair was wrapped in a lovely scarf to keep it protected from the water, but Sigrid's needed no such protection and she was able to dip beneath the water. Coming back up for a deep breath, she swam toward her companion to take the cleansing cloth from Brigid's outstretched hand.

They washed quietly, enjoying the peace. The others in the bath began to leave, and eventually, they were the only two left. They were alone for several minutes before their peace was disrupted by the haughty tones of two human noblemen as they entered the room. Sigrid watched them from across the pool, finding herself annoyed that they were there when they probably had their own baths to pollute.

The men paid no attention to the women present, as noblemen such as they rarely took notice of anyone with pointed ears unless they were visiting the brothel for a bit of fun. Sigrid made a face at her friend and signaled that they should finish, but Brigid was unfazed as she tilted her head back and closed her eyes.

"Remember the fiasco at Queen Hilde's ball?" one nobleman asked the other as he disrobed. Humans were generally far more fearful of nudity than elves, but in the bathhouse even they forgot their hang-ups. "Someone asked me about it today."

"I do. Half the servants simply disappeared. She was able to make it work, but if she finds them, I'm sure they will end up missing a finger or two."

Sigrid did not want to listen, and to ensure they did not catch her eavesdropping, she turned from them and busied herself with washing.

"You would think after they chased off that kitchen boy for putting notions in servants' heads they would have come to their senses, but I suppose madness is contagious." The two noblemen laughed. It was a grating sound that brought goose bumps to Sigrid's arms, and she was forced to rise from the water and make her way toward her belongings. They did not even deign to notice her discomfort. Brigid, giving in to Sigrid's desire to leave, stood and exited the water.

The two made their way into another room where various perfumed oils lined the walls. Sigrid chose her favorite, a blend of rosemary and other earthy-scented herbs, and absently applied the oil to her body as she tried to rub away the feeling of the noblemen's words on her skin. The meaning behind the words was lost on her, but their haughty and entitled attitudes brought up memories of her most irritating culls. Brigid, sensing Sigrid's frustration, settled a hand on her friend's shoulder. "They're pigs, but they're not currently knocking down our front door for a fuck, so enjoy a cull-free day."

"They could at least pretend to be decent people," Sigrid huffed as she took a metal tool from the shelf and began to scrape the oil from her legs. "Sometimes I wish I could actually do something about it."

"Today we aren't fighting the system, we can save that for another day. Today it's our job to charge them as much as we can get away with, then spend their money on ourselves."

Sigrid laughed as she strode naked into the next bath. This one had a few more people, but they were all content to sit alone or with their own groups, which was just as Sigrid preferred it. She didn't mind being around others, but she didn't like being bothered when she wasn't working. It was easy to turn on the social butterfly hidden deep in her personality when there was a promise of money, but it was exhausting, and she simply did not have it in her to pretend when she didn't have to. Fortunately, Brigid loved her as she was, and never forced her to engage with others when she didn't wish to. Sigrid's fierce independence was endearing, and though Brigid did not quite understand Sigrid's desire for solitude, she respected it. In the end, Sigrid always emerged into the light when her spirit was properly rested.

By the time they left the bathhouse, patrons began to stream through the front doors from the street. It was now past noon and the sun shone brightly above them, illuminating the streets and bringing smiles to the city's inhabitants. Sigrid noticed a few more guards in the streets than earlier that day, but lately, it seemed as if there were more and more guards. It was a frustrating development, but they generally left the brothels alone. Their profession was technically not against the law, but it wasn't technically legal either. Guards rarely came to offer help when men got violent, but they also allowed the painted women to conduct business without fear of being shut down.

As they approached their home, they could see two women sitting on the second-story balcony eating lunch. They had recently accepted two new women into their home, and the two had taken to eating their lunches in silken dresses where people on the street could see them. It was a smart way to market themselves—they sat above the street in full view, ignoring calls from men who wanted their attention, only to have those same men in their beds later that night. Cualli and Zuma had come from Hedeby, where as far as the law was concerned, brothels were to be treated just as they were in Copper City, but guards were generally more aggressive. They would bully many varieties of businesses for "protection" fees, which most businesses agreed to at the point of a sword. Sigrid felt lucky that Copper City did not have quite the same problems.

"Hey!" a guard yelled out, his gloved hand pointing toward the same man who had been at the shop. She would have recognized those eyes anywhere, even in a dense crowd.

The man took off between two buildings. Without thinking, Sigrid headed off without Brigid and hurried into the house. Quickly striding through the bottom floor, Sigrid made her way to the kitchen and threw open the door to the alley behind the brothel.

The man skidded as he abruptly changed course, turning down the alley behind the Golden Pearl. The shouts of the guards were growing louder, and there was a panicked look on the man's face. His eyes darted around for anything that might give him the upper hand.

Her eyes locked on his as he ran in the direction of the Pearl. Swallowing hard, Sigrid frantically waved him down. He did not think twice and turned, skidding again on the stone path, and darted through the door.

CHAPTER TWO

Sigrid stood out of the way as the man skirted through the door. His skin was a warm brown, a few shades darker than her own. A few strands of hair had escaped from the rather windswept bun framing his face at the top of his head. He quickly took a seat at the corner breakfast table, bending down so he couldn't be seen from the windows. They could hear the hurried footsteps and agitated yells of the guards as they ran past the door, not even thinking to stop and check. There were a few tense moments before he finally exhaled a breath and shot Sigrid an apologetic grin. "I didn't clear out when they told me to. My mistake!"

The heavy tapestry that divided the kitchen from the rest of the house was pushed open to reveal Brigid, her eyebrow raised high at the sight of a man in their kitchen. "I thought you weren't working today. Should I fetch wine?"

"He's not a cull," Sigrid said, turning her head to look at the newcomer. "Seems some guards were trying to take their aggression out on him today, if that's what I'm gathering."

"You gathered correctly," he said.

Brigid's lips pursed, and her eyes narrowed as she looked the strange man over. "What's your name?"

He hesitated, looking between the two women before shrugging his shoulders. "Baldr," he replied simply. "The guards and I aren't on good terms, so I hope you don't mind that your friend gave me refuge."

"We aren't known to seek their company," Brigid said plainly. "I hope you don't bring unwanted attention down on our home. That would be an unkind gift for Sigrid's generosity."

"Sigrid, is it?" He looked between the two women. "You've done me a great service. Can I repay your kindness?"

Brigid swiftly strode across the wooden floor, the delicate fabric of her dress catching the wind in her step. She pulled a bottle of wine from a shelf and three glasses. Handing the strange gentleman a glass of wine, Brigid took a seat next to the small table and crossed her dark arms across the pale fabric of her gown. "You may call me 'madam.'"

"Brigid," Sigrid admonished her friend with a wry look. The two women glanced between themselves.

"Are you from here?" Sigrid leaned forward over the table. He had pointed ears that marked him as the same as his two hostesses—an elf. Except, upon closer inspection, they weren't quite the same. Brigid's and Sigrid's ears cut sharply through their hair, but Baldr's ears were smaller. More humanlike.

"Hedeby," he said. His hands were folded together neatly on top of the table, his posture straight and chin up. "I was in the army. Moved here to be closer to my mother."

"A soldier?" Sigrid raised a brow. "You don't look like a soldier."

"I may not be sully and unwashed, but I assure you I can handle a sword."

Brigid gently stroked the end of her hair. It was pulled into two parts, each long with puffy sections separated by gold bands. She watched Sigrid with her lips pursed and crossed her arms over her chest. Sigrid ignored her.

"One of our girls, Cualli, recently had a rather unacceptable issue with one of her admirers. We managed to take care of him this time, but it would always be nice to have someone else in the home who can handle a sword," Brigid said.

Baldr tilted his head to one side, his eyes scanning over the outline of Sigrid's strong frame. "I can help with that," he replied skeptically.

Sigrid said, perhaps too quickly, "Then if you wish, you can hide here until you are sure the guards are tired of searching for you. There are plenty of other renegade elves in this city for them to stay occupied."

"But to be clear," Brigid asserted, "we would not work for you. You would work for us. Some men seem to think protecting and owning go hand in hand."

He lifted his hands in front of his chest. "No need to clarify. I have no intention of taking advantage of your hospitality for longer than you'll need me. I must admit, I am surprised to have found friends here at all. There is no reason for you to help me."

"I suppose," Brigid replied as her eyes cast over to her wild-haired friend. "Sigrid is generally good at reading people, so if she is comfortable, then I am willing to give you a chance. You may hide here so long as you keep men in line."

The first few days of Baldr's employment were uneventful. He kept himself hidden, save for the single time he needed make himself known to a particularly bold cull. As the days drew on, Baldr's sense of self-preservation seemed to wane.

"Let me go with you," Baldr said with a sweet grin, serving Sigrid a plate of eggs scrambled and fried with pieces of torn corn tortillas.

"What? No. The whole point of you staying here is to avoid the guards. You want to go with me across the city to watch me lift weights?" Sigrid did not hesitate to dig into the food. It was amazing how quickly she got used to his consistent cooking.

"I figured we could spar a little. You said you like to practice with swords."

Sigrid leaned back in her chair and placed her feet up on the chair next to her. "No. If you come with me, then you'll be on your own. What's the point of seeking shelter if you're going to be so reckless?"

He grinned. "I'll wear a hood. And I never said I'm never reckless. Besides, you can help me by keeping an eye out for guards. I'm going to go insane if you keep me in here any longer."

"Keep you here?" Sigrid scoffed and crossed one leg over the other. "You are no prisoner! If you want to risk a beating from the guards, you're more than welcome to come along. I think you're being unnecessarily reckless, though. I want that on the record." She flattened her hand over her dark hair that was pulled up high in a tight knot. Each strand was perfectly in place, though her attention to it caused a few to come loose. She wore a loose white shirt and leather breeches, and the ensemble was tied together with a pair of well-worn boots. It was a far cry from the image of an elegant painted woman she normally portrayed. The paint that would normally adorn her forehead, a signal of her availability for the day, was absent.

"Just a bit of fresh air for an afternoon. I'll be careful. I haven't gone anywhere in days, so they had to have moved on by now."

"I don't know ..." Her brows furrowed as she looked at him, and her chest tightened at the thought of something happening to him, despite the short time they'd had together.

"It can be a test. If nothing happens, then it might be okay for me to stop hiding out. Or at least return home."

Sigrid stuck a piece of fried tortilla and egg into her mouth, swallowed, and sighed in resignation. "Fine. If something happens, though ..."

Baldr grinned in his victory and hurried off to his little half room to change, leaving Sigrid to check herself in the reflection of their silver teapot.

The trek across the city to the elves' gymnasium was quiet, save for Baldr's constant questions.

"There wasn't a gymnasium in Hedeby. Well, there once was, but it was shut down when I was a kid."

"But I thought the Heddish pride themselves in sports?"

"They do. They just don't like us priding ourselves as well. It wasn't until I joined the army that I was able to access one again. Women were not allowed to use it, though. The Heddish army has few women. Some, but they are a rarity. Shield-maidens are aspirational and give them a good image, but few women ever make it to that point."

Sigrid nodded, glancing past her hooded companion toward a pair of guards trying to flirt with an elven woman with a lotus painted on her forehead. If they could see Baldr's face beneath his cowl, or if they noticed him at all, they made no move to abandon the painted woman in their presence. "We're lucky we have one, even luckier that it allows women."

"That's part of the charm of this city. It is one of the last places left where you can feel an elven presence. Hedeby is human through and through, even if it does have a fair number of elves. It's easy to forget a history that has been forced out of memory."

"It isn't out of memory here."

"Not yet," he replied mournfully.

Sigrid exhaled a sharp breath. "And not for a long time. Come on. Let's enjoy the day. There are never guards at the gymnasium, so you can take the hood off and join me."

That was enough to keep Baldr content to discuss more pleasant topics on the way. "It rains more in Hedeby," he noted, looking up at the sky. Though it was cooler than it had been in a few days, the sun shone brightly above them. In the distance was a crop of thick, dark clouds. "Been a bit dry the last few days. Looks like crops will get the rain they need."

Sigrid shrugged. "I know very little about farming. I know the farms around here supply much of the kingdom's wheat and corn, but outside of that, I am purely from the city. Why do you think I paint my face instead of finding a job as some milkmaid on a farm?"

"Not that there's anything wrong with being a milkmaid."

"Of course not. I just don't know how to do it."

Baldr laughed as they approached the large wall that surrounded the open-air gymnasium. "Neither do I, to be honest. I should learn to care for plants. Perhaps I can learn to cultivate a little basil."

Passing through the gate for the gymnasium, they made their way to a corner where Sigrid placed her bag against the wall. One half of the gymnasium had various rudimentary equipment, such as a series of boulders in various sizes meant to be lifted and carried to another spot. A group of solid wood bars was organized nearby, and each bar had a different weight of stone on either end. On the other side of the large space were sloppily stuffed dummies with a series of blunted swords sticking out of a barrel. At the perimeter of the gymnasium ran a large gravel track.

It was still early, so there were few others. An elven man repeatedly beat a dummy with a staff while another deadlifted one of the heavier barbells. Neither paid Sigrid and Baldr any mind past a polite smile and nod.

Sigrid took a seat at a bench and changed from her boots into a pair of soft leather sandals. "You said you had access to a gym in the army? You look like you still find the time." Her eyes scanned over his form, which was lithe but firm.

She diverted her eyes when she could feel herself staring for too long.

"I'm not afraid of some heavy lifting. Spending as much time on the go as I do is strenuous work."

She removed her shirt, revealing a tight band around her chest that kept her breasts in place as she ran. Baldr's eyes briefly fell on her chest before quickly darting to the side. Elves were generally more tolerant of skin than the Heddish humans, but Baldr had grown up in a city overrun by the Heddish's more puritanical conceptions of dress. Copper City's reputation was one of less strict morals, Sigrid thought, and perhaps he had been raised more modestly than she. Time had chipped away at how free the elves allowed themselves to be and what was appropriate, but she still felt comfortable in the leggings and bandeau. It was hard to be modest when one spent much of their life with little to cover their body. "Race me then."

"What?"

"Race me."

"I didn't wear the proper shoes."

"And? We can run barefoot."

"Quite a bit of rock around to just run barefoot."

Sigrid grinned. "Fine. Don't race me. You can spar with me, but I'll know you were too afraid to race me."

Baldr scoffed. "I am not too afraid. Fine. Keep your fancy running sandals."

He quickly pulled off his cloak and tossed it onto the bench. They stretched briefly before taking spots next to each other on the track.

"Get back to this spot first and you win," she said.

"What does the winner get?"

"I don't know. If you win, what do you want?"

He took a moment for thought, his hands on his hips. "Take me for a drink."

"That's it?"

"Yes. I want you to buy me a drink. What if you win?"

"Hmm. Two drinks. If you lose, you buy me two drinks."

"That hardly seems fair!"

She shrugged and took a running stance. He huffed and placed one foot in front of him.

"One. Two. Three!"

The two took off. She kept pace with him for a good while, but toward the end of the race, he managed to outpace her. "No!" she cried out through a fit of breathy laughter as he crossed back over the starting point a few steps ahead of her. "Ata save me, I thought I had you."

"I thought you were going to get ahead of me for a minute. Don't worry, Sigrid. We can't all be perfect."

She scoffed and stretched her arms over her head. "Oh, shut up." A grin spread across her brown lips. "I bet I am stronger."

"I bet not!" He flexed the muscles of his arms to her laughter.

Sigrid winked and rolled her wrists in circles, warming them up for the coming challenges.

"You are well built, my friend, but you have the sinewy muscles of someone who rarely lifts a heavy sword and more often outruns their opponents."

"I am always on the go. You saw me outrun those guards. You're right, though. Not since the army have I needed strength the way I have needed speed. Even then, I was often used as a courier to convey messages from one camp to another."

Sigrid positioned herself in front of a barbell, adjusted her footing, and hinged forward at the hip to take hold of the bar. With one breath held in her chest, she lifted the bar until she was standing straight, then set it back on the ground.

"I never enjoyed the repetition of lifting weights," Baldr said.

"It grounds me," she replied before inhaling another breath, holding it, and lifting the bar once again. Satisfied, she moved on to a heavier bar and repeated her steady, focused movements. "It forces me to be in the moment, in my body. In my line of work, it is easy to check out and it can be hard to check back in. This helps me remember that my body can do more."

His eyes never left her as she moved between equipment, from the bars to the large rocks she'd squat, lift, and throw over a stone wall. "I can understand that. I admire your self-awareness."

"My self-awareness?" She looked at him from over the short fence. "What does that mean?"

"Just that … I don't know. You know yourself enough to know what your mind needs. Not everyone can recognize their needs like that. It is easy to get caught up in what keeps others happy."

She shrugged, making her way toward the bench to take a seat next to him. Sweat glistened on her arms and chest, and strands of curly hair had begun to loosen themselves from the tight knot on her head and stick to her face.

He swallowed hard and averted his gaze toward the gymnasium entrance. The tinge of pink to his cheeks escaped Sigrid, whose attention was turned to adjusting her bandeau.

Baldr waited with Sigrid in the gymnasium for as long as she had the energy to train. They sparred, with Sigrid winning most of their matches. Baldr still managed to surprise her here and there, but it was clear who spent more time with a sword, even with his military training.

"I suppose I am out of practice," he admitted, plunging his blunted sword back into the barrel. "This part of the city is surprisingly lacking in guards compared to the rest of the city. I didn't expect them to be as ... numerous as they are back in Hedeby."

"It is a new development," she replied as she gathered her things. "At first nobody noticed, but over the last couple of years they've bumped up recruitment. Fewer standards, higher numbers, I suppose."

Baldr hummed and pulled his cloak back over his body, the hood obscuring his face as much as he could make it. "That's distressing."

"It is."

"But there aren't any here?"

She shrugged. "Just because we don't see them doesn't mean they aren't lurking about. At this point, I've gotten so used to seeing them it barely registers unless I can tell they're focusing on me. I can usually get out of whatever trouble they've brewed up with a smile and some flirting, but not everyone is so lucky."

The two walked through the gates of the gym, and Sigrid glanced around for guards. She didn't see any, which did not comfort her. "Perhaps they went on break," she said.

"Yes. Every single one."

"Weirder things have happened. Maybe they're off getting drunk."

"That sounds more likely."

Baldr glanced up, looking at his surroundings as they walked. The streets were hard and dusty; the buildings were a dark shade of terra-cotta and their doors had been painted brilliant colors. "It is so colorful here. I still can't get used to it," Baldr said.

Sigrid glanced around, trying to take in the scenery with the eyes of someone who hadn't been there quite as long. Sigrid had never been anywhere but the countryside surrounding the city, so the bright doors and colorful murals on the sides of buildings were the only thing she knew. "What does Hedeby look like?"

"Gray," he laughed. "The buildings are stone, the streets are stone. The architecture is far more ... Heddish. Like some of the buildings in the newer parts of town."

Sigrid frowned. "Ah, yes, they do tend to clash with what is already here. Fortunately, part of the charm of this city is what it looks like, so most humans try to mimic the architecture. Hedeby sounds depressing."

"The seafood is good," he said, shrugging. "I'm not saying Hedeby is always awful, but I do like the look of things here. It's more elven. More ... homey."

"I suppose it is rather homey," she admitted. "I guess I could be living somewhere uglier."

"Makes you appreciate it, huh?"

She smiled. "I'd like to see Hedeby one day, I think. I hear it is so much bigger than here."

Baldr frowned. "There are ... good things about it. Lots of great taverns, I suppose. The city park is beautiful."

"City park?"

He nodded. "Sort of near the center of the city is a large park. Trees, ponds, stuff like that. The city spends a lot of time and money on its upkeep. They care more about that park than the run-down homes of elves or even poor humans, but that park sure is beautiful."

Sigrid stopped, her eyes falling to one of the trees that lined the road. Copper City had been built to coexist with the land as much as it could. There were parks, but the whole of the city was full of trees and open areas where people could sit and enjoy the day. Many citizens had gardens, even those who lived in flats. Though their brothel lacked a yard, Brigid grew plants on the roof, many of which were used to feed them. Inside, Cualli kept plenty of plants, so many that some culls regarded the brothel as a bit of a jungle inside. Sigrid found it peaceful even if she didn't have much of a green thumb herself.

"You know," she said, "I'm feeling hungry. Let's stop at a food stand."

They were standing in front of what was probably Sigrid's favorite stand in the city. A window was built into the wall of the building, where patrons would line up to order. It was quick and stayed open late, which was helpful when she didn't feel like cooking after a cull left in the wee hours of the night.

As they waited in line, two large figures stepped in behind them, conversing in low voices. Baldr glanced over his shoulder, his face visibly losing color. Curious, Sigrid glanced at them, her heart nearly freezing at the sight of two guards.

"This is one thing Hedeby doesn't have," Baldr regarded, nervously looking at the menu written in chalk on the side of the building. "There are taverns, inns, even restaurants, but street vendors like this are nonexistent."

By the time he was done talking, Sigrid was already standing in front of the hostess behind the window. "Two of the smothered corn, please," she said, sliding a few coins across the small partition. Baldr watched from next to her, standing closer in an attempt to shield his face from the guards.

"Here," she said, handing him a bowl made of corn husks filled with corn, cheese, peppers, and lime. A small, disposable wooden spoon stuck out.

"Not that we don't eat corn in Hedeby, but it isn't usually dressed up like this."

"Ah, well, this is the Copper City way of eating it. We like a little spice in our lives, I guess." She winked. "Come on. Let's get back."

Before they could leave, one of the guards reached out a hand and settled it on Baldr's shoulder. "You're from Hedeby, friend?" the man asked.

Sigrid's stomach went cold. Baldr, to his credit, was able to flash a smile. "Yes I am, sir."

The guard nodded, elbowing his compatriot in the stomach. "Red here just came from Hedeby."

Baldr and Sigrid looked to the second guard. He was taller than the first, his vest pulled tight over a muscular chest. He looked ... *mean*. His eyes were settled on Baldr, searching, and his head seemed to cock in recognition. Sigrid quickly stepped forward and placed her hand on the guard's arm. "Oh, well, there are many perks to living in Copper City," she said with her best flirtatious smile.

The surly guard looked at her hand, forgetting momentarily about Baldr. "I think I've seen you around," he said.

"Have you? Red, was it?" Sigrid batted her eyelashes at him. "Perhaps in the Red District?"

"Ah," the two guards said in unison. "A painted woman."

Sigrid nodded. "Yes, that would be me. Perhaps you gentlemen could stop by when your shift is done." She did not say the name of the Pearl, and she hoped they were stupid enough not to ask.

"Perhaps we will," Red said.

"Next!" The four of them looked to the hostess behind the stand's wall. The woman regarded them with frustration and gestured to the line that was forming behind them.

"Ah, well, I think it is your turn," Sigrid said quickly, grabbing Baldr by the hand. "Have a good evening, gentlemen."

Practically yanking Baldr down the street, Sigrid led him away from the stall, out of sight.

"So ..." They stopped in front of the Pearl, and Sigrid fetched her key from the small pouch at her side. "When are you going to tell me why you were running from the guards?"

Baldr immediately grew distant. "I shouldn't. You said not to bring you any trouble. After those two guards ... I shouldn't have been so reckless by leaving today. I am sure the big one almost recognized me."

Turning the key, Sigrid looked at the half-elf. "Okay," she said tensely, opening the door and striding through.

Baldr followed with a sigh. "I'm not ... I'm not trying to hide anything."

"But you won't tell me why you were running. At first, I thought you were embarrassed, but now ..."

"It's nothing bad," he assured her, reaching out to touch her arm.

Sigrid felt a spark enter her skin. It made her stop and turn to him. "I'm not going to force you to tell me."

"I know, but ... now I feel bad."

"I can't help that."

Baldr groaned and pinched the bridge of his nose. "I can't say anything. Not yet."

She sighed and turned, dropping her key off in the bowl near the door. "All right."

CHAPTER THREE

Sigrid sat on the plushest sofa they had in their receiving room, her body stretched out and draped in fine fabric. With her head propped up on a crimson pillow, she dangled a bushel of grapes above her mouth and lowered it in. Popping one plump grape into her mouth, she glanced at the front door as it flung open.

"Einar," she said with more enthusiasm than she felt, sitting up in her cushions and placing the grapes on her fruit tray. "I was wondering when you would stop by. I have missed you!"

The man smiled awkwardly, ringing his hands. He was the son of some Heddish noble that enjoyed spending time in Copper City's Red District, spending his father's money on painted women and human courtesans alike.

"Sigrid," he said, his own smile spreading from one ear to the other. His cheeks burned bright red at seeing her dress. "I found myself in town again and wanted to see you."

"Of course you did," she purred, sliding from the couch and gliding across the floor. She placed an arm around him, her hand closing the door behind him. "Would you care to join me? I was just snacking on some fruit. I'll let you feed it to me."

"O-okay," he agreed, letting her lead him across the room.

Sigrid took a seat in his lap once he fell onto the cushions, and she reached again for the grapes. "So," she said, dragging one of the firm grapes across his chin, then up to slip it into his mouth. "You've come all this way from Hedeby just to see me. I am quite flattered."

"A-as you should be," he stuttered, his eyes drifting down to her breasts.

With him distracted, she cast a glance behind him, internally cringing at his attempt at displaying confidence. He was never very good at pretending to be arrogant, though he sure did try.

"Shall I fetch you some wine?"

He nodded, and she slipped gracefully out of his lap. Strutting across the floor, the motion of her hips exaggerated for his benefit, she gave him a single glance over her shoulder before disappearing down the hall.

Baldr sat in the kitchen, a book in his hand.

"Don't let the men see you," she said, pushing aside the curtain that hid their collection of wine from view.

"I'll be careful," he smiled, flipping the page without looking up at her.

From the cupboard she plucked three glasses and set one in front of Baldr, pouring into it the bloodred wine from the bottle she'd selected. "This one is good," she said, pushing it toward him. "Expensive."

"Don't waste it on me," he said, looking up, his eyes growing wide. He'd seen her earlier that day, before she'd readied for the night, but the sheer dress hiding little of her body was new.

She was powerful in the eyes of men. Her lips pulled apart into a sly grin, and she nudged forward the wineglass. "Shh," she said, lowering her voice to something just above a whisper. "Don't let Brigid know I'm sharing with you."

With that, she turned, feeling his eyes on her as she exited the room. Returning to the receiving room, she found Einar exploring the shelves of a bookcase against the back wall.

"Do you read much?" he asked her, not looking but hearing the fall of her steps as she entered.

"From time to time," she said, slipping the glass into his hand and filling it with wine. "Many of these are Brigid's, but many are mine as well. Some are gifts, some I purchased on my own."

"You have an extensive library."

"Thank you. I wouldn't mind having a true library one day."

Einar laughed, and it was all Sigrid could do to not cringe at the dismissal in his voice.

"But you're so good at what you do here. Why would you want to do anything else?"

Sigrid laughed, a high, tinkling laugh she reserved for her most annoying culls. Einar fit the bill, but he paid well, and she did not want to scare him away. "You're right, my love," she purred, guiding him back to the couch, where he plopped down without a word.

She retook her seat in his lap and brought her wineglass to her lips. Once, she hadn't been much of a fan of wine, instead preferring ale or beer, but now she found the higher alcohol content helped with culls like this, those who were not so intolerable that she tried to get the visit over with as quickly as possible, but insufferable enough to set her on edge if too sober.

It was a delicate game, knowing how much to drink. Things could get dangerous if she imbibed too much.

"And what have you brought for me today?" She grinned at him, her fingers drawing circles in the chest hair exposed by his tunic. "Hopefully something to show me how much you've missed me."

Einar grinned and reached into his jacket, pulling from it a velvet bag. Batting her eyelashes, Sigrid plucked it from his hand and opened it to peer inside. He'd always been generous with his contributions, so she had little reason to doubt it would be any less than normal.

But it was.

"My dear"—she smiled, pulling the bag tightly shut and slipping her arms around his neck—"you know the jarl increased penalties for operating. Surely you value my time more than this?"

The nobleman frowned. "Apologies, beautiful, but my father has been pulling the purse strings extra tight. I will bring more next time, I promise."

"Tsk, tsk." She sighed, brushing her fingers through his dirty-blond hair. "This will buy you an hour."

"An hour? You used to take that per evening."

"Like I said, penalties have gotten steeper, and we need to keep operating." She pouted at him, shifting so that she was straddling him. "Keeping a place like this open can be expensive. You understand, don't you, my love?" Her lips pressed against his cheek, then the tip of his nose, before they closed over his lips.

"As I said, I will bring more next time. Give me the evening, as we always do, and I'll make sure to bring you extra when I return."

Sigrid pulled away. "I do love spending our evenings together, and I would *love* to have you remain as you usually do, but I cannot lower my price for you, dear."

A dangerous storm brewed in his blue gaze, and his hands closed around her arms. His fingers dug into her flesh, and when she tried to pull away, they simply grew firmer.

Sigrid's stomach sunk.

"I don't understand why you're being so unreasonable," he said. "You know I'm good for the money."

"I'm not doubting that," she replied, her voice firmer and without the fabricated affection that usually filled it. "I am telling you how my business operates."

"Business?" He laughed, his voice booming and filling the room. "This isn't a real business. I could buy ten women for that price somewhere else in the district."

"Then do that," she replied firmly, trying again to pull away. His grip held tight. "Please, let go of me, Einar." Her eyes caught his, her jaw set hard. She hoped that she looked intimidating, that he could feel the muscles in her arms.

"Accept what I've given you and I will. I'm one of your best customers, I think I've earned this."

"You do not have a right to me," she hissed, attempting to yank herself free and nearly falling over when he abruptly released her. Her heart pounded in her chest, and she could feel the flesh throb where he'd grabbed her.

This wasn't the first time a cull had become upset, but it never got easier to handle. She wasn't as small and helpless as she'd been when she'd first started, when a man had first become violent. She'd learned. Sigrid had spent years strengthening her body so she wouldn't find herself helpless in these situations.

And yet, they always had the audacity.

"You're an elf," he spit, standing so fast he knocked her to the floor. He grabbed her by the arm and yanked her in the direction of the stairs that led to her room. "You deserve far less than what I'm offering. Take it and be happy."

"No," she replied loudly as he yanked her to her feet. He was strong, stronger than he looked, but she knew she had her own strength too.

Einar whipped around and procured a knife from somewhere in his jacket. He held it between them, his one hand still gripping her arm. "We're not arguing. I've spent enough money here to own the place. Let's go."

"I said *no*," she replied, though her voice faltered at the sight of the knife. It wasn't quite long enough to be a dagger, but she could tell it could just as easily slice through her if needed. "Einar, leave. Take your money. I will not tolerate this disrespect."

A deep voice cut between them, startling Sigrid and the man that gripped her.

"Let her go," Baldr said, his voice smooth but firm.

"Nobody asked for you," Einar hissed, turning so the knife was pointed in Baldr's direction.

The knife looked rather pathetic in comparison to the dagger held in Baldr's hand. She'd never seen him with a dagger, but this one looked deadly, the tip so sharp she was sure it could have split a hair in half.

"Let the lady go and be on your way. If you want a woman for the price you've offered, go somewhere else. Sigrid has made her price known."

Einar frowned but released Sigrid, nearly shoving her into the wall as he did so. "If I want a dirty elf's opinion, then I'll fucking ask for it. You going to use that on me? They'll lock you up so fast your head will spin. Then I'll get what I want for the price I want."

Baldr took a step forward, holding the dagger up with one hand and placing the other behind his back. "This isn't going to go well for you. Leave."

As Einar opened his mouth to speak, an infuriated Sigrid pushed herself from the wall and kicked at the back of Einar's knees. Surprised, he fell to the ground, and the knife skated across the floor. Baldr kicked it behind him and moved forward, grabbing Einar by the collar. With the blade firmly against the cull's throat, Baldr yanked him from the floor.

"Okay, okay," Einar said quietly, his hands up in surrender. "I'll go."

"Yes, you will," Baldr said firmly.

Einar was thrown from the brothel, hitting the ground outside with a definitive thump. Scurrying to his feet, the man turned and ran, but not without first shooting a look of hatred over his shoulder at the two standing in the doorway.

"Are you okay?" Baldr asked as he closed the door behind them.

"Yes, I'm fine." She sighed, rubbing at the spot on her arm where Einar had gripped her particularly tight. She wondered if it would bruise. "That caught me off guard. He's always been so polite."

"I'm sorry," Baldr said, brushing a bit of hair from her face.

"No, thank you. You did your job today. I thought I could handle him until he pulled out that damn knife."

"Hopefully he doesn't show his face again."

Sigrid sighed and collapsed on the sofa, her head hanging in frustration. "Damn. This isn't good. Einar was one of my biggest customers when he came to town. I never knew when he would be by, but he always came with more than enough for the evening. Sometimes we could afford an entire month of rent just off of what he brought."

Baldr took a seat next to her, his hand settling on her knee. "There will be others. I'm just glad it didn't escalate into anything worse."

"It might have if you hadn't been here."

"It's a good thing I'm here, isn't it?"

Sinking into the cushions, Sigrid closed her eyes and drew her hands over her face, smearing the makeup. "Fuck tonight. I'm not seeing anyone else."

"Well," Baldr said softly, setting something in her lap. "It wasn't such a loss."

Opening her eyes, she glanced down at what he'd given her. The bag! Einar's bag. "You grabbed it."

"It's the least he could do for putting his hands on you."

Sigrid tightened her fist around the small satchel, her heart still beating quickly from her cull's violence. "Thank you for being here."

"I'm sure you could have handled him on your own."

"Maybe. But that doesn't change the fact that you were there."

"Well … that's what I'm here for, isn't it? That's why you hired me."

"Looks like we make a good team."

CHAPTER FOUR

Sigrid pulled her finest dress from her armoire. Normally she reserved it for evenings with her highest-paying culls, but the temple was special. She slipped into the airy gown, the skirt of which was made of layers of thin white fabric. Two slits shot up the sides of her legs, all the way to her hips. Her fingers spread over the fabric of her white bodice. Feathers were embroidered into the fabric, dancing along her waist and around her hips in a gray thread. The dress was so light even a gentle breeze would rustle her skirts.

She felt enchanted every time she wore it.

Brigid was waiting in the kitchen. The shells of a couple of hard-boiled eggs were piled on her plate as she lazily flipped through the pages of a monthly journal.

"You look nice," Sigrid said, looking her friend over. Brigid's hair was pulled into many tight knots, and she'd dusted her cheekbones with a shimmering golden powder.

"Thanks," Brigid said, marking a page in the journal before setting it aside. "Are Cualli and Zuma coming?"

"No. Zuma drank too much last night, so Cualli has spent the morning babying her. It'll just be the two of us."

Brigid's lips curled at the corners, and she laughed as she rolled her eyes. "That's fine. We can stop for lunch on our way home. Where's Baldr?"

Sigrid shrugged. "Haven't seen him all morning. Probably sleeping in."

The walk to the temple wasn't long, but the two stopped at so many stalls it took them twice as long as it should have. The Temple of Ata wasn't large, but none of the temples were large anymore. Any that were large had long since been occupied by the Heddish, save for one in the southern part of the city where almost no Heddish ever went. It wasn't dangerous for the Heddish—it was just *too elven*.

The Temple of Ata had once served many of the same purposes as Sigrid's brothel. Instead of a cull's wealth buying a night, it bought a painted woman's magic. Couples came and, with a painted woman, manifested fertility. Tribal leaders visited to bring life to their fields. Now, the priestesses of the temple no longer painted their faces. They gave prayer and spells for fertility or power, but they did not exchange flesh for earthly magic. Though they were no longer painted women, the priestesses welcomed women like Sigrid and Brigid and gave them counsel and peace.

The splendor that the temples once had was now gone. Small offerings were left beneath the statues, and patrons paid tithes to keep the temples open. The paintings on the walls were old and faded, and the statue of Ata was nothing more than a facsimile of what she once had been. Trinkets of fertility hung on the walls, but they held no magic. Not like they once had.

Sigrid placed a few coins in the gold bowl at the center of the main room. The building was small, holding just a large center room and two to the side. A small clay idol of Ata sat on a woven mat. Incense filled the room as one of the priestesses lit a stick and placed it in a hanging bowl.

The room was far emptier than Sigrid could remember it being. "Priestess Qotzi," Sigrid said gently, "where ... where is everything?"

Sigrid looked above the small statue of Ata where a golden mirror had sat. The mirror had been old and ornate, with a frame of gold and precious gems that had given the room a regal feel. Now it was gone, leaving behind a bare wall that made Sigrid feel suffocated.

The priestess Qotzi looked at Sigrid and offered a sigh in response. "Royal decree. Some of our things were taken to pay a tax increase."

"What tax increase?"

"Elven temples have become expensive to keep open."

Sigrid looked to Brigid and, seeing the stricken look on her friend's face, took her hand. Qotzi went back to lighting incense, leaving Brigid and Sigrid to take a seat in front of the idol.

"Remember when we first started?" Sigrid said softly as she reached forward, placing a pot of rouge on the flower-covered offering table.

Brigid nodded, setting on the table a small bottle of the same gold she was wearing on her face. "I thought queens must live here."

"I thought I looked like a piece of art in that mirror."

"You are a work of art."

"A piece of work, certainly." Sigrid grinned, elbowing Brigid in the side.

The two fell quiet for some time, with both their eyes on the idol. Sigrid stared until her eyes began to burn, desperate to feel as she had when she'd first visited the temple. Had there been room for another priestess, perhaps Sigrid would have joined the temple instead.

She felt nothing. There was an open void in her chest where her excitement and her devotion had once been. She'd put so much effort into her appearance that morning, desperate to feel the connection to Ata she'd once felt. Instead, she found a hole. After the other night's encounter with her angry customer, she was desperate to feel a connection with her goddess. Glancing sidelong, she wondered if Brigid felt the same way.

If nothing else, Sigrid felt herself relax as time passed. Closing her eyes, she narrowed in on her senses; the lavender-scented incense, the chatter from the street, the soft taps of Qotzi's feet as she moved across the floor. Sigrid's body began to feel as if it were floating, and her breath grew slow and even. She felt nothing but the peace of being alone.

She wasn't sure how long they'd been sitting there. A woman, round and heavy with pregnancy, joined them at some point, but she did not acknowledge them. It wasn't until hunger began to gnaw at Sigrid's stomach that she finally stirred and reached out to tap Brigid's arm. "We should go."

Brigid nodded, a serene look on her features. "Yes. We should."

Baldr rapped gently at Sigrid's door. "I made strawberry scones," he said as he pushed open her door.

She was still lying in bed, her sheets crumpled up on the floor so that she was covered only by her nightgown. It was hot out, and try as she might to get comfortable in bed to read her book, she found herself constantly overheating. "Oh!" She started, sitting up in surprise. "Well, thank you."

"You are welcome. I come with an ulterior motive, however."

"Oh?" She swung her legs over the side of the bed and gestured for him to join her at the chair by her vanity. He handed a small plate with two warm scones to her and took his seat, draping one arm over the back.

"A letter came for me last night."

"I didn't even know anyone knew you were here."

"I know a few people." He swallowed, his brows knitting together. "You've been very kind to me these last couple of days, truly. I do not deserve the hospitality you have shown to me. I feel as if I can trust you, as you have trusted me with your home."

Bringing a scone to her mouth, she watched him as he spoke. "Why does it sound as if you're about to tell me someone has died?"

He laughed. "No, nothing like that. It's just ... I'm not just here to be closer to my mother."

Sigrid set the scone down and placed the little plate on her bedside table. "You're being weird."

"I am," he agreed with a sigh. "I wanted to talk to you." He paused, glancing toward the door, then back to her. "I can trust you, yes?"

"What?"

"Can I trust you?"

Sigrid's brows furrowed together, her lips tugging into a frown. "Yes? Have I done anything to make you think you can't?"

"No, you haven't. But this is …" He sighed, running a hand over his face. "Okay. I am going to tell you something, and I want you to be open-minded. I said I'm from Hedeby, which is true, but that isn't the whole story. I was a cook in the king's household, and I was drafted as a soldier into the king's army. A few years ago, when I first started working in the kitchens, I came upon a flyer posted in the marketplace."

"So you were a soldier before you were a cook."

Baldr blinked. "Sort of. Everything with the royal family is tied to their military prowess. I was a cook in the army, then I was stationed at the palace. The king likes knowing all his staff can slaughter an enemy should it come to it."

"I see."

Baldr continued, "The flyer … it was vague, but it implied the kingdom was … imbalanced. Around this time there had been a few peasant riots in the city, but the guards managed to squash them pretty quickly. They lasted only a few nights, but there was a … tension in the city."

"I remember," Sigrid replied. "I remember hearing about it. It was framed as a group of elves rising above their station. Whether it was heroic or not depended on who was telling the story."

Baldr nodded. "The violence was mainly contained to the poorest area of town, Lowside."

"That's a little on the nose."

He snorted. "The riots lasted a few nights. I was moved from the kitchens to guard noble families, but it hurt to be there. I was defending people who had never taken a moment to even be kind to me, who had so much power they didn't even realize it."

"What caused the riots?"

"A lot of things, I suppose. A guard had speared some young kid. The price of bread had gone up. There always seemed to be enough bread for the nobility but never enough for everyone else."

"That was the year the farmers outside of Copper City withheld their crops over some ... taxation issue, was it?"

"It was greed on the part of the king. I came to a meeting at a pub where we mostly just talked, but the more I went, the more they began to trust me. I was invited to more secret meetings. We talked about history and philosophy. They taught me how our whole lives have been shaped to the will of these humans who came after us! Wealthy humans invaded us and never left. It doesn't have to be like this."

Sigrid rubbed her fingers along the edge of her mattress. "I was working as a maid at the time for a noble family. General Heimer, I think his name was? He was always talking about selfish elves in the fields trying to claim wealth that didn't belong to them."

"The king worked out some sort of deal with the merchants, and everything went back to the way it had been. It was as if nothing had happened! So we went to work."

"Who is we?" Sigrid leaned forward, drawing her knees up to her chest and wrapping her toned arms around her knees.

He didn't answer right away. She could see the gears working behind his eyes and the conflict he felt. She reached out and touched his arm, and only then did he speak.

"The Collective. That's what they call themselves. What *we* call ourselves, I suppose. It had been building for years in Hedeby, creating a network of common people. We worked to put as many grains of sand in the king's wheel as possible, disrupting where we could when we could. We are led primarily by a group of Elders, and recently they decided those of us in the city had to leave. They decided there were enough of us to ... to cause real trouble for the king."

Sigrid stared at him with her mouth shut tight, as if her lips had been glued together. No words came even as she tried to force them from her mouth. After a few moments of silence, she popped another scone into her mouth and chewed.

Baldr continued, "A few months ago the king decided to issue an order forcing all elves to live in one part of the city. Ultimately it impacted few, as many of the city's elves preferred to live in Lowside. We had our own community there, and except for extra attention from the guards, we made do without humans. This was such an unnecessary move, but it was deliberate."

"I hadn't heard about that."

"It is difficult to find rooms to live in Hedeby. I was lucky in that regard. I was a soldier, even if I was a lowly one. I did not have to pay for my bed. Most rent a room, or they are a family and can afford a flat of their own. Rent became more and more expensive every year."

"Things are the same here," Sigrid remarked.

"It was beginning to cause a lot of unrest in the city. Instead of trying to fix the problem, the king fed the flames by saying it was our fault. There are too many elves, he said, and we take space and jobs from the Heddish who are trying as hard as we are to survive. The strife that has existed for hundreds of years felt fresh and new every single day, as if a wound was opened every night. The Collective had enough. We couldn't sit back and let our people be bullied anymore. We put out the word for all those in our network to prepare to leave. We have allies in the Kingdom in the Mountain."

Sigrid's eyes grew wide. "How? They have barely had contact with that kingdom in a long time. Elves from the Kingdom in the Mountain rarely cross the border. How did you make alliances there?"

"Our Elders. Sigrid, things are coming. I can smell it in the air. The king has something planned, and we don't know quite what it is yet, but we know it will be devastating. We had a man intercepting messages, but he's ... gone quiet. Whatever the king is planning doesn't bode well for our people. I'm here with a few others to recruit and call together every member of the Collective in the city."

"Wait"—Sigrid raised a hand, her palm facing Baldr—"I've never heard of this organization here. I'm no stranger to action, especially this sort of action, and I've never heard of them. Sounds like a group we could have used." She looked past him, her lips pressing into a thin line as she recalled the upheaval the Red District had experienced when Copper City's jarl tried to close the brothels.

"Their presence isn't as large here as it is back in Hedeby, but we've had success over the last year. We work as quietly as possible, gathering information and taking risks only when the reward is worth it. When I met you the other day, I was delivering correspondences."

"The package you were carrying?"

"Yes. It was"—he swallowed, looking uncertain—"information on the city guard and any messages they were able to intercept from Hedeby. We think there will be a crackdown on elven activity in Copper City, the way there was in Hedeby."

Sigrid rested her chin on top of her knees. Her eyes were cast to the side, staring out the window as he spoke. It was difficult information to process, but perhaps not the most surprising thing she'd ever heard. Her grandmother had always spoken of a time before the Heddish had arrived. The elves had magic on their side, but the Heddish had more advanced weapons, and ultimately her people had been too trusting of these new people from across the sea. Elves who weren't conquered at the point of a sword were forced to assimilate until only scraps of elven life remained.

"So you're a rebel."

"I suppose you could call me that."

"Why are you telling me all of this?"

He paused. His eyes cast to the floor as he contemplated his answer. When he spoke, he caught her eyes with a steady gaze. "You ... you have experience. You're no stranger to action. I feel like ... like I'm getting to know you, Sigrid."

"I suppose," she said.

He shrugged. "You're intelligent. I've heard you talking with some of the men who come here. They jabber on with all the fancy education they've been given, and yet you still talk circles around them. You're good at reflecting their politics when they bring them up, but I know you don't buy them. I know you find this life unfair."

"What about this life?" Sigrid recoiled, her arms crossing over her chest. "The lives of painted women are varied. We do not all hate our jobs."

"That's not what I meant," he clarified with wide eyes. "I think you have a lot of skills we could use. I think you resent the Heddish as much as I do. I saw you the other night, the look of contempt on your face after we kicked that man out. I know you must hate how those men think of themselves as being above you."

"Of course I think life is unfair. I wouldn't have worked so hard to get out of my parents' home if I was content sleeping in a one-room flat. Aren't you half-human anyway?"

His cheeks darkened. "Half or not, I am still an elf. Don't deflect. I see you light a candle to Ata every night and burn incense during every encounter for protection. You leave milk and honey out on your balcony every night. You don't even pretend to take on the Heddish faith. You worship our gods."

Sigrid stood from her bed and ambled across the room to her vanity. Like Brigid's, it was covered in paints and brushes, and a small lamp sat next to the large mirror. A small flame burned in it and was kept alight through a bit of magic learned in her childhood. She placed a hand on the tall, thick red candle next to her paints. "You've paid quite a bit of attention to me."

Baldr cleared his throat. "Everything I've said is true. I think you want to do something, more than you've done yet. I sent a message to my leader about you. If you're willing to learn, she'd like to have you. It won't be easy, and you may have to fight to earn her trust, but I think we could use you."

"I don't know … What you're saying sounds nice, but I'm not trying to get killed in a rebellion. You want to overthrow the monarchy. That won't be easy."

"Of course not. We know it won't happen overnight. We also recognize small victories when they happen, but things are boiling over. The Heddish know only a thirst for power and wealth."

"Are elves any better?"

Baldr exhaled, one of his hands clenching. "Things haven't always been this way. Nobody is trying to flip the system upside down and create a mirror with elves at the top. We want a world that takes care of everyone."

Sigrid took the chair in front of her vanity and busied herself with organizing the various brushes and paints that littered the surface. "What sort of things happen in this … organization of yours?"

"Well," he began, crossing one leg over the other and watching her from across the room, "we educate. We gather when we can and talk about what is happening across the kingdom. We watch people change and become more willing to listen. We pass around books and teach our history to those who have forgotten. We also actively work for a more equitable kingdom—*no* kingdom. We had no kings before the humans came, and we do not need them now. Things weren't perfect before the Heddish came, but they were our problems to solve. The Heddish brought *their* problems. They took a world, a people, who lived differently than them and forced us to assimilate at the tip of a sword. We've made strides in progress since then, and we pay respect to those who labored before us by continuing."

"You said things are getting worse."

"You know they are. You can feel it too. We all can. You said yourself the other night that penalties and fees were beginning to rack up—things like that don't happen alone."

Inhaling deep into her chest, Sigrid stood once again and faced the raven-haired man. "This is a lot to ask of someone you haven't known very long."

"I am not asking you to do anything. I am giving you options."

Sigrid frowned and turned to face her new friend. "What would I even do in an organization like this?"

"That's up to you and our leaders to decide. You've done things before, have you not? Organized?"

"It isn't the same. I've fought for women like me. Painted women. It's the only battle I've known how to fight."

"It's the same fight, Sigrid. Imagine what we could learn from you. The intel you could gather."

Sigrid frowned. "I have other skills too. I can fight, if we needed to."

"I know. As I said, it wouldn't be up to me."

Sigrid crossed her arms. "What do you do? You said you were a soldier. Soldier to rebel is quite the jump."

Baldr sucked his teeth. "I got caught with literature they weren't fond of, so they cut me loose. It's for the best. I'm lucky they didn't take my head for treason. As for what I do now, mostly I stay to the shadows. I'm far better at sneaking around and going unnoticed than I am at brandishing swords in the open. I can, of course, but that isn't my strength. I was stupid to get caught before, but it taught me to be more careful."

"Well," Sigrid replied after a pause, "I'll ... consider things. This is a lot of new information. I need to process it."

Baldr stood and nodded. "Do what is right for you. You have options, though. Things can change."

As he stood to leave the room, a sudden thought occurred to Sigrid. "You said you were here to be closer to your mother," she said as his hand rested on the door handle.

He turned to look at her. "Ah, yes, well, that is still true. But she's a story for another time."

CHAPTER FIVE

Angry voices wafted through the open windows of the brothel as Brigid hurried through each room to slam the shutters closed. Sigrid watched her silently and could still hear the heated shouts of the crowd that had begun to form outside.

"What's even happening?" Zuma asked, returning to the common room after shuffling a cull out the back door.

Sigrid turned her tired brown eyes to the waif of a woman, but it was Brigid that spoke.

"The jarl put out an order from the king. All the temples—the elven temples—are to be shuttered until further notice. Tithes should be put toward Heddish shrines."

"What?" Sigrid sat up from her seat on the sofa, her heart sinking into her stomach. "When did you hear this?"

"An hour ago," Brigid said as she busied herself with the windows.

She went to check the front door, pulling and tugging on the handle to ensure it was properly locked. Incense filled the room so fully that Sigrid was forced to put it out lest they all suffocate from lack of airflow.

Zuma sunk into one of the cushions, her small body nearly swallowed up by fabric. "Cualli and I left Hedeby to escape this. This isn't fair."

Sigrid shot the younger woman a look of sympathy.

Brigid pressed her ear up against the door to listen to the crowd forming outside. Normally their location was a boon. They were close enough to humans to attract wealthy Heddish men with a fetish for elven women but close enough to their elven community to maintain their connections. This positioned them near the most bustling parts of the city. There were bars and restaurants near grand theaters to keep them entertained and for them to take their highest-paying culls for a night out. They did not have to suffer the hateful glares of Heddish wives in the human-dominated districts of the city, and they did not have to risk running into family while with a cull. It was, generally, a rather perfect part of town for Sigrid.

She did not feel so lucky suddenly. Zuma's dark skin drained of blood, leaving her ashen. Her hands were clasped tight against her stomach.

Sigrid released Brigid's hand and stood. "We should join them," she said finally.

"Are you insane?" Zuma gasped.

"At the very least we should go out and see if we can find Cualli." Sigrid looked toward the shuttered windows.

Brigid shrugged. "I'm sure she's fine. She's with her latest patron for the evening. He likes her enough to take her to an apartment he rents just to see her. If she's smart, she'll stay there."

Zuma pursed her lips. "Maybe Sigrid's right. We should go find her."

"No," Brigid doubled down. "She'll be safer there than she would be rushing through the streets to get back to us. Cualli is the most street-smart of all of us."

Sigrid, not listening, disappeared up the stairs only to return a few minutes later changed into pants with the flower washed from her forehead. Sitting next to Brigid again, she bent to pull her leather boots over her feet and lace them up to the knee.

"Excuse me," Brigid said crossly. "You're not going anywhere."

"Why not?"

"Because it is dangerous, and we need you to stay here. Nobody else knows how to use a sword."

Tightness constricted Sigrid's chest. "They're taking parts of us, Brigid. How can we just stay inside? Shouldn't we give them all our anger? Isn't that what they deserve?"

Brigid looked at Sigrid as if she'd sprouted three extra heads. "Of course it's what they deserve. I'm angry too. Those guards will not hesitate to hurt us too, though. You can be reckless, but this time I'm not letting you."

"I'm going, even if you aren't," Sigrid said as she laced up the final boot and stood to draw her cloak over her shoulder. "I'll see if I can find Baldr and stick with him."

"Of course," Brigid sighed, bowing her head and placing it in her hands. "Fine. Zuma and I will stay here in case Cualli comes back. Go find Baldr, burn the city down, whatever. Just make sure you come back."

Sigrid leaned down and pressed a kiss to Brigid's cheek. "I'll be fine. I just ... I can't sit back anymore. We should fight for Ata, for what she means to all of us. And not just her, but all the others. We were here first. Why should we give up our temples to fund their shrines? We were quiet when they raised the penalties on brothels, but are we going to stay silent when they take religion from our people?" She didn't mention the guilt that propelled her. Guilt for feeling nothing in the temple. Guilt for being unsure. She didn't mention the desperation to feel that connection again, or the hope that perhaps this would bring it back.

The flower on Brigid's forehead was a pastel pink that complimented her dark skin, and on her cheeks was a brilliant shimmer that made it look as if she were glowing from within. Her beautiful features were marred only by the worried look that overtook them. Brigid pushed her many long, thin braids over her shoulder and looked up at her longtime friend. "This is just ... Never mind. Just come back, okay?"

Outside a large crowd had gathered. Shouting could be heard from every direction, and the air was thick with the heat of their bodies. Sigrid pushed through toward the head of the crowd where she could see a woman standing on top of a crate. Everyone turned to face the woman as she called out to them, but Sigrid was not close enough to hear her words. Whatever she said, those closest to her raised their fists and voices in agreement.

Notably, there did not seem to be any humans in the crowd. Everyone she saw as she pushed through the masses had pointed ears.

As she grew closer to the shouting woman, she began to hear the words she called out into the crowd. "They have our city," the woman cried out over the chorus of voices. "They took our language, our customs, and now they take from us our gods! No more!"

Goose bumps spread across Sigrid's flesh. Though it wasn't cold, she drew her cloak tighter. The woman continued her speech as the crowd continued to grow. Their voices grew quiet so that all that could be heard were her words.

A hand reached out from the crowd and grabbed Sigrid by the shoulder. Startled, she whipped around with a fist raised, ready to plant it in the face of whoever had grabbed her, only to find Baldr with his hands in the air.

"Whoa, whoa," he said. "I was just headed back to the Pearl to check on you. What are you doing out here?"

"You were right," she said, lowering her fist and leaning in so nobody else could hear them. "All of this? I couldn't sit back and not … be here. I had to show up. For Ata."

Baldr nodded soberly and snaked an arm around her in an embrace. "I'm glad. Come on. I'm with a group, and we are safer in numbers."

She followed him through the throng, his hand clasping hers tightly so they wouldn't be separated. The woman on the podium continued as the crowd listened intently, but as they drew closer, she ended her speech and turned. Lifting a finger, she pointed in the direction of the Shrine of Wotan. Baldr pulled Sigrid closer as the crowd lurched forward in the direction of the shrine, and they were forced to move forward.

"Looks like we might be stuck," Baldr said, looking around. They marched toward the shrine with the crowd, passing by the shuttered windows of Heddish homes. Some threw objects at the Heddish houses, others threw red paint at their doors.

"Baldr, look," Sigrid hissed, pointing down one of the cobblestone streets to a mass of armored guards that were approaching the crowd. Down alleys and streets, she could see guards and soldiers beginning to gather in rows with their shields up in front of them.

"Shit."

A man came to the front of the gathered guards. His armor was shining, and the fabric of his cape was unblemished. He wore the signet of a commander on his chest. Raising a hand, he spoke to the crowd before him with a booming voice. "Go back to your homes! This will achieve nothing but disrupting your community!"

People yelled obscenities in return. The man looked about him smugly. The crowd's anger did not faze him at all. If anything, it seemed to strengthen him.

"This is a warning," he cried out into the air. "Return to where you belong! I understand your anger, but this is not the way!"

Sigrid felt someone shove her, and she nearly lost her balance. Baldr's steady hand was the only thing keeping her from falling into the next person. There was another shove, and the crowd lurched forward. Above them, rocks began to fly.

"Baldr!" she called out, pointing to a group not far behind them that charged forward with knives and hatchets raised.

The guards lifted their wooden shields to protect themselves from the crowd's assault of stones and debris and drew their weapons. Someone in the crowd screamed out, and the crowd lurched again, this time in the direction of the guards. Men with clubs and makeshift weapons burst through the crowd and charged at the soldiers. At first, the guards used only their shields to knock away protesters, but as more stones and objects were thrown, a piercing scream filled the air.

Sigrid's blood went cold.

"Shit," Baldr cursed, dragging Sigrid away from the guards and up the opposite street. "Shit, shit, shit."

"What's happening?" Sigrid said under her breath as they ducked into an alley.

Baldr pressed her against the wall and kept his body close to shield her from a crowd of people that ran past.

"We need to get out of here," he said.

"Well, let's get back to the brothel."

"No, we can't go that way. Come on. Follow me."

He pulled her out of the alley and down the road. Behind them, the crowd clashed with the guards. No longer were the people only armed with bats and wood, at some point people with swords and makeshift shields had taken to the front of the crowd. Though their weapons and armor were nothing compared to the city guard's, they were far more numerous. The sound of metal against metal filled the air, and the coppery smell of blood met Sigrid's nose.

"Baldr!" someone called out.

Baldr turned and ducked into an apartment with Sigrid in tow. The voice that had called out surprised them. Sigrid stared.

"Sigrid," Cualli said with a relieved expression. Her raven-black hair was pulled back in a tight bun, and she lacked the painted flower on her forehead. Sigrid had never seen her so dressed down before.

"What are you doing here?"

"Baldr introduced me to ... some friends."

Things began to fall into place as a look of dawning comprehension fell over Sigrid's face. "So ... your new patron. There is no patron."

Cualli shook her head. Freckles spread across her nose and bunched together as she scrunched up her face. "Ah, no. No patron. Just, you know, revolution."

Baldr, having no patience for the revelation, cut in. "Where are the others?"

"A few of them are attempting to use the chaos to ... destroy the Shrine of Wotan."

"What?" Sigrid gaped.

Cualli nodded.

"That wasn't the plan." Baldr frowned. "The plan was only to agitate, not to start a riot. We aren't ready for that kind of confrontation yet."

"Well, hate to break it to you, but we're there already. The guards came out swinging once the crowd grew too large, and they are attacking people in different parts of the city. The Elders believe the only option we have is to fight back."

Sigrid leaned against the door. Outside she could still hear the crowd screaming at the guards. "I should have stayed with the others," she said under her breath. "What if something happens to them while I'm gone?" Inwardly, she cursed her rash decision-making.

Baldr glanced at her. He tugged her to his side and wrapped his arms around her, catching her by surprise. She could hear his heart in his chest and relaxed against him.

"We'll check on them," he said. "The people are angry. This riot will last through the night, so we can't go out now. Cualli, I'm going to leave Sigrid with you and see if I can find our commander."

"What?" Sigrid pulled away from him, her hands firmly grabbing his shoulders so he couldn't wriggle out of her grasp. "Uh, no, you're not leaving me behind. We're safer in numbers, remember?"

"I'm needed," he huffed.

"Yes, here. If you're going anywhere, I'm coming with you. You wanted me to get involved, so here I am."

Baldr didn't respond. He went to the window and pulled aside the curtain to look out on the street. This one was lucky, it did not attract quite so much action, but there were still people fleeing through the streets. When he turned, his eyes were hard, and they settled on Sigrid. "Are you sure you want to be out there?"

"Tell me what I need to do."

Before he could answer, someone burst into the room. They were tall and had a scarf wrapped around their face. Sigrid stood up with her fists raised, but Baldr stuck out a hand to keep her from lunging forward toward the stranger.

"Baldr," the person huffed as they tried to catch their breath. "Everyone is to gather at the shrine. There are injured we need to get out."

"How many?"

"Six. We can't take them back to headquarters or we'll lead the guards there. We need to find someone sympathetic who will let us sneak our injured into their home. The doctor will meet us, but he cannot put himself at risk by going to the headquarters."

"Shit." Baldr frowned, rubbing his hands down his face. "Okay. Think. People are congregated at the shrine, which is closest to the Red District and Maize Square. Who do we have in that part of town, Tepiltzin?"

The man shook his head. "We have nobody in the Red District, but there are too many children in Maize Square. Too many families."

With that, Baldr slowly turned to Sigrid with a stricken look on his face. "I ... I shouldn't ask you."

"What?" Sigrid fidgeted with a strand of her hair.

"The Pearl. We need the Pearl. I know it is a lot to ask of you, to ask of the others, but we need somewhere safe to go."

Sigrid fell quiet as all eyes in the room fell on her. Cualli slipped to her side, took Sigrid's hand in her larger one, and squeezed.

"We can do this," Cualli said, her heavily lined eyes boring into Sigrid's. "We're needed. But the house is run by you and Brigid. Only you can make this decision right now."

A million different scenarios played through Sigrid's mind. She could see them dragging injured into the Pearl, their bruised and battered bodies bleeding on the floor. She could see guards kicking in the front door and arresting them all. Still, despite it all, despite the danger ... she could see the terror and desperation on their faces.

"Okay. Let's go."

The masked man guided them through alleys and small streets until they could hear the cries of rioters near the shrine. Poking her head around the side of a building, Sigrid could see elves attempting to bust through the front door. Outside, screaming guards banged their swords and axes against shields to attempt to scare off the mob, but they simply continued their demands. Behind the crowd was a group of guards, but not nearly enough to clear the area. Sigrid guessed others must have been spread to other parts of the city, likely defending the wealthy homes of hiding Heddish. There was a group to the side where people were crowding around some person lying on the ground.

Baldr motioned for her to wait and disappeared into the crowd, popping up near the group of injured and those tending to them. Words were exchanged before they began to lift the injured, some onto shoulders and others into the arms of unharmed elves.

There was a loud boom before Sigrid's nostrils filled with smoke. She coughed, covering her mouth and nose with her cloak. Another explosion went off, filling the entire vicinity with smoke. The crowd began to push, and screams filled the air.

Frantically looking around, she could see guards throwing small, round projectiles into the crowd. Smoke grenades. The guards began to push forward with their shields in the air and lances drawn, while others behind them began to throw round, flaming jars into the crowd. Through the smoke, she watched one hit a man in the chest. Immediately he fell to the ground, his flesh charred by the explosion.

Horrified, Sigrid continued to search for Baldr, but a grenade landed a few feet from her. It exploded, catching a merchant's empty stall on fire. Diving away from the explosion, Sigrid gasped for air and tried to rub the smoke from her eyes. The crowd grew more and more panicked, some shoving and pushing to escape, others grabbing injured and pulling them out of the street. People cursed at the guards as they left, but the guards did not care. Sigrid watched as some smiled gleefully as their grenades made contact with the street and occasional person. There was blood on the cobblestone, its coppery scent mingling with the smell of fire and smoke. The stall that had caught fire began to spread to the building behind it.

"Sigrid!" Baldr burst through the smoke with people in tow. There were far more than she'd agreed to take in before, but there was no time to think. They needed to get out of there.

She wordlessly motioned for them to follow and took off down an alley. They steadily put distance between themselves and the fiery riot behind them. Now and then they came across a street they had no choice but to cross, though it seemed the guards had grown distracted by the fire their comrades had set. People were fleeing through the city, and each home they passed had closed doors and shuttered windows.

Finally, the back door to the brothel was in sight. Ducking under hanging laundry, she ushered those who were following her through the stone alleyway and into the building.

Hearing the noise, Brigid rushed into the kitchen just as the injured were being brought in. "What the hell?" she exclaimed. Without thought, she procured clean cloths from the cabinets and handed them to those not injured.

"We needed to get them away," Sigrid replied with labored breaths.

"Did anyone follow you?"

"I don't believe so. The riot was getting out of hand, and the guards started a fire while attacking us. They'll be distracted for a while. I brought them through as many back ways as I could. We need to help them."

Brigid stared, horrified. "Sigrid, this isn't safe! You can't …" She faltered as she looked at all the people. "We'll discuss this later. Zuma is in the other room, have her fetch my medicine bag."

Sigrid nodded. Zuma was seated in the common room, her face still ashen and worried. "Cualli? Did you see her?"

"She's fine," Sigrid replied. "We need you right now. We have injured. Go to Brigid's room and grab her medical kit, then meet us back in the kitchen."

Without waiting for Zuma's response, she turned on her heel and returned to the kitchen. The most injured, the man who had been hit by the jar grenade earlier, was placed on the table while others were arranged on the floor. Sigrid pointed still others into the common room.

"There's more room and couches in there," she declared, going through all the cabinets for every clean cloth she could find.

Baldr and Brigid stood over the injured man as Zuma brought the medical kit into the room. Brigid may not have been a formally trained healer, but in all her years as a painted woman, she'd taken it upon herself to learn as much as possible about medicine. All those nights staying up with a medical book gifted to her by a wealthy patron were finally paying off.

Sigrid could barely breathe. She rushed from place to place at Brigid's orders, wanting to be useful but knowing nothing that could help. Eventually, as the Collective's doctor arrived with a few masked rebels, Baldr pulled Sigrid from the room. He guided her away, ignoring her protests, and shoved her through the door of her bedroom. There was already a bucket of water for her to wash the blood from her hands. When did he have time to draw water?

"We should go back out," she said, staring at the bucket.

"No. It won't do any good. You need to stay here. The situation is too chaotic, it cannot be controlled. We lost control of the situation."

Sigrid frowned. "This isn't a game."

"Of course it isn't. But we still rely on strategy, and our strategy failed."

She turned to him and exhaled, adrenaline pumping through her body. She wanted to lash out, to push him aside and do what she wanted. Instead, she took a deep breath and held it in her chest. "What is going to happen now?"

He did not answer right away. Eyes cast to the ground, he exhaled through his nose and flexed his fingers. "I don't know."

CHAPTER SIX

Despite the unrest that had occurred, the people of Copper City came together and began to cleanup during the day. They scrubbed graffiti from walls and swept debris from the road. Though there was a somber cloud hanging over them all, those who gathered to help put the city back together were determined to keep a happy face. Zuma left early in the morning, as soon as the sun rose into the sky, but Sigrid found herself stuck in bed.

The previous night's events were still clear in her mind. Most of the injured they'd brought in had, thankfully, not needed serious medical attention. Brigid and Zuma attended to what injuries they could—cuts, scrapes, a couple of burns. Anyone who needed more attention than that was carted away to a secure location with the doctor.

By the time Sigrid was able to get to her bed, she thought she might faint. She begged her mind for sleep, got up, and smoked the last of the dream herb she kept to help on restless nights. At first, it did nothing other than slow down her thoughts, which in and of itself was a small victory as far as she was concerned. Soon, despite the terror she'd experienced that evening, she drifted away into a dreamless sleep.

When she awoke, the sun was still up but heading for the horizon. Nobody had disturbed her, or if they did, she had been too deep in her slumber to notice. The main room had been cleared of any people when she made her way down the stairs, though it needed to be cleaned from the number of people that had filtered through the night before. Couches and cushions were out of place, the rug had been removed from the middle of the floor. She wondered if Brigid had moved it at some point, or if blood had spilled on it and she'd decided to throw it out. Brigid had always loved that rug.

In the kitchen, Brigid sat with a cup of coffee in her hands. It didn't look like she'd had any sleep at all. Baldr was across the table from her, his brows knitted together as he rested his chin in his hands.

"Ah," he said, looking up as Sigrid entered the room. "Glad you got some sleep."

"Doesn't look like either of you did."

"I slept a bit." Brigid shrugged. "Not much. I wish I'd been able to."

Sigrid took a seat at the table and reached out to rub Brigid's shoulder. "I'm sorry I burst in like that. I would have warned you if we'd had time."

"Baldr and I already discussed it," Brigid replied with a tired sigh. "I'm not angry. You did the right thing. There were no perfect answers."

Baldr frowned. "You did plenty. None of us was ready for what happened last night. We should have been, but we weren't."

Sigrid cast her gaze to Baldr. "What do we do now?"

Baldr sipped from his cup of coffee before responding. "The Collective is regrouping to figure out what to do next. A few of our members haven't been seen since last night."

"Guess we should get ready."

Baldr shook his head. "No. Stay and rest. Not many were absent last night, but those who were have stepped up to take leadership this evening, in case things get bad. You don't need to be in the streets tonight." He looked over her with a touch of fear in his eyes, but he could not meet her gaze.

Sigrid leaned forward until her forehead touched the table. Every muscle in her body was tense, the remnants of last night's adrenaline exhausted her. Images of the chaos were burned into her mind. Would they ever go away? Would they haunt her dreams?

Her stomach knotted. Despite how truly awful the night had been, she couldn't imagine abandoning the movement now. She could tell Baldr she didn't want to do it anymore and leave him to handle the city's troubles, but what good would that do? Would they get the temples reopened? Would she just be resigning herself to a world where she could only worship in private? The Heddish were taking everything from them. They always had been.

"You should stay here," Baldr said. "Perhaps we can use the Pearl again—"

"No," Brigid spoke up. "You can't keep using the Pearl if things go bad. Switch it up."

"Brigid," Sigrid said, her voice muffled by the table, "you just said we did the right thing."

"And you did. But if we get too much attention, it'll bring the guard down on us. Our culls will dry up. We'll be out of business by the end of the month if that happens. No, you cannot bring anyone else here, not until we are more prepared. Better trained. Last night was a mess."

Sitting up, her forehead red from pressing against the table, Sigrid exhaled an exhausted sigh. "It wouldn't have been chaos if they hadn't closed the temples."

"I am as upset about that as you are, but we can't put ourselves in danger like that."

"Why?" Sigrid crossed her arms. "Why shouldn't we? This isn't the first time we've put ourselves in a bad position. You remember the first time they raised penalties, don't you?"

Brigid frowned. "Don't. I was as involved in that as you were."

"Don't you remember the meetings we held? Right at this table? In the receiving room? All the painted women from across the Red District met up *here* to plan our next move."

"Yes, and our next move failed."

Baldr looked between them with confusion written onto his handsome face. "What happened?"

Sigrid glanced at him. "It would have been before you came. About five years ago. The jarl raised penalties on operating brothels, so much so that many couldn't keep up. If a brothel can't stay open, the women have to find another way to make ends meet. Some took their losses and moved on to make garments or clean wealthy homes, but none of those pay like working in a brothel. We met, we drafted demands, and we presented them to the jarl. All he did was have us violently kicked out of the palace."

Baldr folded his arms on the table and leaned forward. "I didn't know you'd done anything like that."

Sigrid and Brigid nodded in tandem. Brigid said, "We thought we could make a change if only we worked together. There were so many of us that we thought they would surely make some concessions, even if they just lowered the penalties a bit. Any change would have been a victory.

"But they didn't listen to us, and as a result, many brothels shut down. We were lucky. Our brothel was mixed with human courtesans and painted women, and our madam was a bastard daughter of some wealthy nobleman. She kept us afloat. Others were not so lucky."

Sigrid leaned back in her chair, her chest squeezing at the memory.

"And that's exactly why we can't take any more risks with the Pearl," Brigid said, her voice stern. "If you want to gather with the others, you are free to do that. Hell, I'll join you. But we cannot bring more people here."

In defeat, Sigrid nodded. She could feel the grip of the guards as they dragged her screaming from the great hall of the palace. She could see the unaffected jarl as he waved his hand and had them removed. The angry screams of her sisters rang through her ears. She could recall the blood splattering across the floor as one of the guards knocked a painted woman to the ground, slurs spilling from his mouth like water from a spicket. "Okay. No bringing people here."

"You should stay here," Baldr said again, a look of guilt drawn onto his features. "I'm sorry. I shouldn't have involved you like I did last night. I see now that it was a mistake."

"What? No. You weren't listening."

"Please, Sigrid." Baldr sighed. "Two people died last night, that we know of. We don't know how many were injured. It is bad enough we put your livelihood in harm's way—"

"Are you going out?" Sigrid interrupted, crossing her arms and shooting him a stubborn look.

"Well, I have to," he said.

"You don't get to tell me if I can go out or not."

Brigid reached out and touched Sigrid's arm. "He's not telling you what to do, but this could get dangerous again, Sigrid. You know how to use a sword, but you've never had to use it against someone, not really. Knocking out culls with their pants off who get a bit too handsy isn't the same thing as fighting fully trained guards."

Sigrid huffed and straightened in her wooden seat, placing her hands gently on the table in front of her. She looked past Baldr, out the windows to the alley behind their home. Something inside of her urged her to get angry, to yell, but this was not an unfamiliar feeling. The tension that built up inside her so quickly might have overtaken her when she was younger, but she'd learned to keep her outbursts under the surface. They always threatened to break free, especially when she found herself overwhelmed. For now, she did not boil over like the teakettle she felt like. She inhaled a deep breath and held it for a count of eight before exhaling. "What, if not attending, should I be doing?"

Baldr reached his hands out to settle on top of hers. She felt a burst of electricity shoot through her body, and for the moment, that teakettle was removed from its flame.

"Come with me to the safe house. There is an emergency meeting soon. I was going to wake you soon to bring you."

"Why didn't you just say that?" she snapped. Perhaps the teakettle wasn't entirely removed from the heat. She inhaled a deep breath again. "I mean, I'd love to come. Let me get dressed."

The safe house was packed. She'd never seen this many members of the Collective together at once. Frankly, she'd never seen too many in general. It wasn't until that moment she realized just how massive the Collective was. It wasn't a few dissidents. Intellectually she'd always known it was far larger than she could imagine, but seeing so many gathered shocked her. There were even a few human faces in the crowd, which surprised her even more than the numbers.

An older woman stood on a box at the back of the largest room. All the furniture had been moved to other rooms to make space for everyone, and yet still people poured out into the halls. Baldr kept his hand on the bottom of Sigrid's back, guiding her through the crowd as Brigid, Cualli, and Zuma followed close behind. She could feel the heat of his hand through her shirt. His touch helped her remain grounded and calm as they waded through the crowd and kept her blood from boiling over and her heart from racing out of her chest.

"Everyone, quiet!" the woman called out to them. The crowd continued to talk, half those gathered not having heard her. "I said quiet," she cried out again. This time, the room fell silent.

The four of them came to a stop just in front of her.

"Last night was the result of years of buildup. This unrest will continue. There is always a risk for this sort of violence when the enemy does not see us as people."

A few in the crowd cried out in agreement. Sigrid swallowed hard and inhaled a deep breath, holding it in her chest for as long as she could stand it.

"This escalation will continue. We should not feel defeated by this but instead prepare for the opportunity to finally make a change. They would not respond with this sort of violence if they did not find our people a threat. We should expect the king to further crack down on elves, especially if this continues, which I expect it shall. That is why we must send for help. We've been busy in the countryside, rallying support, but we cannot do this alone. We cannot face the army of a king without help from others who hold power. We must send for help from the Kingdom in the Mountain, Uruachi."

The room erupted in a roar of questions. "Why would they help us now?" one person exclaimed. "They've never sent aid before! They've forsaken us!"

The woman held her hand up for everyone to quiet. "I believe if there were ever a time they would help, it is now. They've hidden away in their mountain, but we are still their people, even if the Heddish stole this land. Whatever they say, we must send for aid now, before things get worse. And they *will* get worse. I ... have seen it."

Whispers spread through the room. Sigrid's eyes widened.

"I was visited in a dream," the white-haired woman continued. "A raven warned me that if we do not act soon, we will give up our rights, our history. The raven showed me a future where our temples are wiped away, our history rewritten. The Kingdom in the Mountain shut itself away when the Heddish conquered everything to the south of the Blue Mountains. They knew everything would be lost. But no longer; the raven showed me that they are ready to retake the land. They are ready to reclaim what was theirs, and it is our duty to bring them into the fold. If we do not act now, we might lose our chance, and we run the risk of alerting the king if we wait overlong. I will be sending one that I trust to bring their aid. For now, I ask that you remain safe if you take to the streets again tonight. Do not take unnecessary risks. Going forward, we will meet in small groups. We cannot run the risk of giving away our membership. Continue to check in with your brigade leaders for updates. Keep tabs on each other so we know if the guard attempts to disappear any of us."

Sigrid shivered at the idea. Would the guard do that? Simply make it as if they had disappeared into nothing? Of course they would, she thought. If they had no issue taking an elven life, why would they blink at disappearing a rebel? Her heart beat so rapidly in her chest she was sure it would burst out.

Baldr placed his hand on her shoulder and squeezed. "Come with me," he whispered into her ear as the woman continued speaking to the crowd, answering what questions she could as they were shouted at her.

He pulled her through the crowd and slipped through the kitchens to the back stairs. Drawing her into the dark, narrow stairwell, he dropped his hand from her shoulder to take her hand. "She's going to send me," he said.

Sigrid gasped. When he'd pulled her aside, she expected a few comforting words, perhaps a hug. Instead, she felt as if she were going to throw up. "What? No. We need you here."

"I have to," he said, his warm fingers brushing over her bicep. His touch was gentle, reassuring, but he struggled to meet her gaze. "I am the only one she'll trust to go."

"Then take me," she blurted before her mind had had a moment to think of the consequences. "Take me with you. I can do it. Whatever you need of me, I can do it."

"What? Sigrid, no, you are needed here."

"No, I'm not," she replied, reaching out to touch him but stopping herself. "Baldr, take me with you. Please. I am fast, and I can speak to people. I may not know exactly what we will face, or how long the journey will be, but ... let me go with you." Finally, her hands sought his, and she held them firm.

Sigrid caught Baldr's eyes, and she stared deep into them as his hands gripped hers in return.

"Okay," he replied.

Bound together in a silent stare, the two didn't notice the presence at the end of the hall. It was only when the woman was standing next to them that they finally looked, their hands still entangled.

"Mother," Baldr said, his grip tightening.

Sigrid's eyes widened. "Mother?"

The woman was as imposing up close as she had been standing above everyone in that room. Her hair was a salt-and-pepper mixture pulled into a loose bun, and her brown eyes simmered in the dim light. Sigrid felt naked beneath them, and the pit of her stomach was cold, as if ice had been packed into it.

"Who is this?" the woman asked, her intense gaze skimming over Sigrid's form.

"This is the woman I told you about. The woman who gave me refuge. Sigrid, meet my mother, Anam."

Anam stood about as tall as Sigrid, and her skin was the same tawny brown as Baldr's. She was slight of figure, but she stood with such assurance that Sigrid was sure there was a hidden strength to her. The lines around her eyes told the story of a long life, but it wasn't just her age that gave her the distinction of Elder. This was a powerful woman, and she made Sigrid want to shrink away.

"You said you found out about the Collective because of a flyer." Sigrid looked back at Baldr, her lips flattening into a thin line.

"That wasn't a lie, but it wasn't the full story either. That is a story for another time. My mother had her own life and troubles while I was away in the army. Our ancestors guided us down these paths separately, but with the same destination."

Anam nodded. "They did. Baldr was … out of my reach for quite some time. Now, we are here."

Sigrid looked between the two, the ice in her stomach beginning to fill the rest of her body. "It's an honor to meet you, ma'am," Sigrid said, pulling her hands from Baldr's and giving a shaky bow. "He told me he moved to be closer to his mother, but I had no idea his mother was so … important."

"Aren't all mothers?" Anam said, the corners of her lips twitching into the briefest of smiles. It didn't put Sigrid at ease. "Baldr is good at keeping important information close to his chest. You gave him shelter, and I am grateful to you for that. Baldr is not usually so reckless."

"I wasn't being reckless, Mother."

Anam pursed her lips. "As you say. Do you plan on joining us then, Sigrid?"

Sigrid nodded.

"Of course," Baldr said, raising his voice and giving his mother a steady look. "Actually, there was something I wanted to speak to you about."

The thought of telling Brigid that she would be leaving left Sigrid nauseous and jittery. Only two days had passed since the emergency meeting, but every moment Sigrid didn't tell Brigid her plans felt far too long.

The two of them had been together so long that she didn't know how not to be around Brigid. They had met as their womanhood began to blossom while working as maids in the home of a wealthy man. They had been together ever since. Together, they had been recruited by the same madam, who they worked for over several years, and they'd even shared a room when they first began.

Sigrid could still see it in her head, clear as a painting. That brothel hadn't been very big, so they slept together in the same four-poster bed that creaked when they sat on it. They stayed up late at night when they were done working, lying together in that creaky old bed with their hands intertwined. It was during those years that Sigrid fell in love with Brigid, even if that love would never be returned. At least, it would never be returned romantically. Sigrid may not have found a lover, but she loved Brigid more as a friend than she could have imagined. They'd created a small family together, saved enough to start the Pearl together, and now she was risking so much by leaving.

She had to, though. She knew she had to go. Rapping gently on Brigid's door, Sigrid held her breath until the shorter woman appeared. "Hey," Sigrid said awkwardly, the smell of Brigid's incense wafting through the doorway.

"Hey," Brigid said with a bright smile, turning back to her room and taking a spot in the cushioned chair in one corner. It was gold and red and looked almost like a throne. Sigrid had once seen Brigid perched there with a man on his knees before her. For now, Brigid was sitting in front of a journal with a pretty human woman printed on the front wearing a simple blue gown. Commoner-inspired fashion was popular of late.

"Did Baldr leave?" Brigid asked.

"Ah, yes," Sigrid replied, taking a seat on Brigid's bed. She had a sudden image of the two of them a decade prior, laughing while curled up beneath the blankets of their old bed. This one was far sturdier, but part of her missed that ancient bed. "It's been a wild few days, hasn't it?"

Brigid sighed, leaning back in the thronelike chair. "It has. Things seem to be cooling off ... for now. I met a woman through the Collective who is willing to teach me about herbs and healing so I can be more helpful next time things go off. Hopefully that won't be for a while."

"Yes, hopefully," Sigrid replied, though in truth she wasn't entirely listening. Her eyes were set on the dark woman in front of her, focusing between Brigid's to give the appearance of listening. "I ... have something I'm going to do for the Collective too. I was actually hoping to talk to you about it."

"That's good."

"Yes," came Sigrid's slow reply. "After the meeting the other day, Baldr told me Anam is sending him to the Kingdom in the Mountain as an emissary. I ... asked to go with him."

Brigid stared, unmoving, for what felt to Sigrid like the longest few seconds of her life. When a soft smile spread across Brigid's face, Sigrid was caught off guard. Had the situation been reversed, how might she have acted? She asked herself.

"That's great," Brigid said. "I mean, I'd prefer that you didn't have to go so far, but I think that sounds like the perfect job for you. Baldr's skinny ass needs your protection anyway."

Laughter broke free of Sigrid's lips. "Is that it? You're not going to yell at me?"

"Why waste the breath?" Brigid leaned forward, her inky eyes finding Sigrid's. "We'll manage fine without you if that's what you're worried about. I handle the finances anyway. Being down your wages will hurt a little, I won't lie, but it won't be forever. Besides, you clearly want to go. If you didn't, we'd be having a different conversation."

"So … you don't think it's a terrible idea."

"I mean, it probably is, but all of this is probably a bad idea. We watched part of the city go up in flames for two days. Things are going to get just as dangerous here as they are outside the city, so if anything, the safest place for you is probably in another kingdom anyway."

Sigrid felt her eyes begin to well up with tears. "Fuck you," she said, laughing and wiping away a tear that managed to escape. "How dare you make this so easy for me!"

Brigid laughed and leaned forward, her lips tenderly meeting her friend's cheek. "Fuck you too."

CHAPTER SEVEN

Physically, it was easy to leave the city. No guards paid them any mind, and the trek from street to street out of the city took an hour at best. When they reached the city gates, Sigrid almost couldn't ride through them. It took a few moments of convincing herself she was doing the best thing she could by leaving with Baldr. Staring up at the gates, she almost turned her horse around, her heart sinking into her stomach. Try as she might, she couldn't make herself spur the horse forward.

"Are you okay?" Baldr asked, his horse trotting up next to hers.

"I'll be fine," she said, not looking at him, her eyes focusing instead on the gateway into the countryside.

His hand reached out and settled on her shoulder, squeezing tenderly. "Let's go."

There was no way to guarantee a courier could deliver the message safely. No, it had to be them, and Sigrid wanted this. Copper City would be there when she returned.

Baldr didn't push her to talk as they rode from the city gates through the fields surrounding the city. They passed farm after farm, tall wheat and corn fields springing up the further from the city they got. She hadn't been more than a few miles from the city her entire life, and they quickly passed the furthest point she'd been. Five miles turned into ten, ten turned into twenty, and by the time the light began to dim, they had put almost thirty miles behind them. Sigrid had never ridden so far in her life.

Baldr decided on a spot near a stream to spend the night and helped Sigrid from her horse. She was sore and tired. Sensing her exhaustion, he wordlessly built a fire and allowed her to take a seat beneath a tree. The horses were tethered to a tree near the water, close enough for them to drink.

"What are their names?" she asked, realizing she hadn't inquired.

"What?" Baldr glanced at her as he rustled through a bag at one of the horse's sides.

"The horses. What are their names?"

"Oh. Uh ..." He pointed to the one in front of him, a large tawny creature. "Skinfaxi. And ..." He pointed to the other, a lovely mare with gray hair. "Hrimfaxi."

"Are they Heddish horses?"

He nodded. "They're from a lower nobleman who supports our cause. He can't participate in any real way, but he can provide us horses."

With that, a silence fell between them again.

Sigrid pulled a leaf from her hair and let it go into the wind. It danced in circles as a gust took it. She watched Baldr as he built a small fire. "Do you need help?" she asked awkwardly, leaning forward to watch him strike flint against steel.

"No," he replied with a shrug. "I travel often. We have provisions, so I don't need to forage tonight, which means you can enjoy a break."

"I feel silly just sitting here, being of no help."

"You're coming along, aren't you? That is helpful enough. It is not safe to travel alone unless absolutely necessary."

"The further from the city we get, the more I realize how little travel I've done before. Why allow me to come?"

"Well, mostly because you were willing," he replied with a laugh. From his pack he pulled a loaf of bread and some dried meats. Placing them on a clean bit of fabric, he spread the food between them and took a seat. "We have the safest route mapped. We probably won't even run into soldiers. This should be a safe mission."

"Why would they bother us?"

"Fun? Suspicion? A number of reasons. This close to the city, we're fine. Beyond that, we could be a target, which is why we're not taking a special route. Too many elves live without much oversight from the king. Sometimes soldiers are dispatched just to remind everyone they do not rule themselves."

Sigrid frowned and brought a bit of cheese to her lips. After so much riding, she was famished but hadn't realized quite how hungry she was until the food was in her sight.

The two grew quiet as they ate, content to sit and listen to the stream. Trees arched over the water, creating a natural tunnel for it to pass through. It was lovely. Sigrid felt suddenly that, despite her insecurities, she was quite glad to be out of the city she'd spent her whole life in.

Feeling a chill, Sigrid scooted a few inches closer to her companion. He tensed for a quick moment before his muscles relaxed, and he reached over her to grab a blanket and spread it over both their legs. She felt the heat of his body as he reached across her. Her cheeks grew warm and her breath caught in her throat.

"Thank you," she murmured, turning her gaze toward the fire.

They sat quietly for a few moments before he cleared his throat and leaned back. "You know, I was a little surprised you wanted to come with me at all."

"Yeah? I suppose I was a little surprised too."

"You decided to run off with some man you've only known for a short while to participate in some underground political movement." Baldr placed a comforting hand on her knee. "Think of all the adventure we could have now. You haven't made a mistake coming with me. I would have been sad to say goodbye anyway."

"Oh?" She winked and elbowed him in the side. "No, you're right." She didn't tell him how strangely comfortable she felt at his side. It had been too long since she'd sat next to a man and felt comfortable. Normally the best she could hope for was a man who bathed that day and chewed some mint before making his way to her bed. She appreciated a cull who tried, as opposed to the ones who felt entitled to her enjoyment. It was rare that a cull felt like a friend instead of a source of coin. "Besides, I get to see new things! Who knows what the future will bring us? War could keep me from new things before I know it."

Baldr sighed. "That is a very real threat. Kings do not give up power willingly. We are lucky so far."

Sigrid leaned her back against the rough bark of the tree. She turned and placed her head on his shoulder, suddenly very tired. It struck her how foolish this entire journey likely was.

"They must really trust you," she said sleepily.

His arm wrapped around her shoulders and held her in place.

"What?"

"To let you bring me. They must trust your judgment."

"You're the one who housed me and gave me refuge to avoid the guards. I was the one who had been foolish that day."

"They still don't know me, not as they know you."

"So?"

"That seems important!" She lifted herself to look down at him, her hair hanging over her shoulders. Her eyes grazed over his lips, noting every curve and line, before meeting his gaze.

"You know injustice when you see it. You know when someone has been wronged. You're far smarter than you give yourself credit for."

She inhaled a deep breath. There was a shock of energy between them that kept her close, like one magnet drawn to another. "You don't know how smart I am."

"You're right," he teased, reaching up to brush a strand of hair behind her ear. "But I think I'm getting an idea."

Sigrid cleared her throat and lay back against the tree as the heat rose in her chest. They busied themselves in quiet for some time, Baldr content to sit and stare at the water nearby. It was nice with him when it was quiet. She felt at peace, and there was no pressure for her to carry a conversation. She was often exhausted by the conversations she had to carry, so having a few moments of quiet at the side of someone she enjoyed being around was a pleasure she'd rarely appreciated. Even Brigid could be unbearably chatty at times, but Baldr seemed to know when to let her have her peace.

As the sun began to set over the horizon, Baldr stood and stretched, guiding his body through a series of stretches and poses. She watched him, her eyes absorbing every line of his body.

"You're very flexible."

He laughed, bending forward so his head hung between his legs. "Helps me sleep. My mother taught me as a child, and I suppose I got into the habit." He took a seat, his legs bent so the bottoms of his feet pressed together, and stretched forward.

"Your mother is an intimidating woman."

"Always has been," he said, groaning a bit as he nearly folded himself in half.

She chewed her bottom lip. "I was very surprised when I met her. She seemed to know far more about me than I knew of her."

"A bit," he admitted, straightening up. "She doesn't know you're a painted woman."

"What does she think I am?"

"I haven't said what you are to her, just that you helped me."

Sigrid's brows furrowed. "Why doesn't she know what I am?"

Baldr paused as he rolled his head in a circle, his eyes turning up to look at her. "I thought it best to leave that a mystery for now. She didn't ask of your profession, and I did not offer it. I didn't think it was my place to do so."

"Ah. I don't mind if you tell people. I am not hiding what I am."

"I know. I'm not hiding what you are either. I just ... know my mother."

"Does she ... not like painted women? Is that what you're afraid of?"

An uncomfortable silence stretched between them.

"She ... has opinions. Opinions painted by the Heddish that she hasn't broken free of yet. I wanted her to see you in action first, so she could form an opinion free of stigma."

Sigrid crossed her arms as irritation pooled in her chest. "I see."

"I just didn't want her to mistrust you immediately. She let me choose someone to bring with me, and when you asked, I wanted to have your help. It wasn't a difficult sell, since you'd saved me from those guards, but it would have been far more difficult if she'd known. She would think ..." He trailed off, a pained look taking over his sharp features.

"She would think what?"

"You have many dealings with the Heddish. Wealthy Heddish too. Such close contact would make her mistrustful of you, and you haven't earned that mistrust." He sat up on his knees and crawled toward her, his hand reaching out to settle on her knee. "I'm sorry. I know this is not fun to hear."

"Well, she wouldn't be the first woman to have *opinions* on painted women and courtesans."

Sigrid didn't respond, instead she shook off his hand and stood. She didn't look at him when she walked to her bag and dug through her belongings. Finding the small tin case she'd been looking for, she returned to her spot and flicked it open, revealing a row of five rolled joints. She knew she'd have to be sparing with them on such a long trip, but she needed something to relieve the anxiety and frustration brewing in her body.

Lighting one of the little rolled joints with a match, she stared away from Baldr as she inhaled. Then she inhaled again, and again, until she could feel her body begin to relax. Baldr remained quiet the entire time, waiting for her to speak.

"I get it," she said finally. "I don't like it, but I get it. We're an object of curiosity for most, and one of contempt for others. Living in the Red District for so many years now, I've been in a bit of a bubble of acceptance. It is just ... disheartening to hear this from someone who is supposed to lead our people. Shouldn't she be more open-minded?"

He nodded. "Yes. She should be. For the record, I don't share those opinions. I hope I have shown that."

Sigrid cast him a half smile and a nod. He'd never said anything disparaging about her profession nor treated her or any of the women in the Pearl with disrespect. He'd never offered to buy her services. He wasn't his mother.

"Tell me about her," she said, offering him the joint.

He eyed it for a moment, unsure, before taking it and bringing it to his lips. Inhaling a small amount, he coughed before handing it back. "Hmm. She ... she's always been a strong-willed woman. She's from Hedeby, like me, obviously. Married my father rather young and had me. I think for a few years she internalized much of the negative things he said about our people. He didn't respect elves in general, and he didn't respect her."

"I know the type."

"In a lot of ways my father was a good man. He provided for me. Made sure I had food and clothing on my back. I have pleasant memories of him that are hard to reconcile with the man that kicked my mother out of the house when I was ten."

Sigrid's eyes grew wide. "That's awful."

He shrugged. "She had an affair with an elven man. Maybe if the man had been human, my father would have just been angry and accepted it, but her lover was an elf, and that enraged him. Probably made him feel like less than a man or something. Inadequate. How could she want an elf more than him? So he kicked her out, and she had nowhere to go but with the man she'd had an affair with. I saw her very little after that, mostly because my father made sure that I didn't. I didn't know that at the time and wouldn't for many years. It wasn't until I was in my twenties that I was able to reconnect with her, and even then, it was by happenstance."

"What happened?"

He held his hand out for the joint, which she handed over without question. He inhaled, held his breath, and stared at a spot just above her head as his mind churned over his answer. "That ... that's a story for another time, I think. Suffice to say, I found her again when I was stationed in the king's kitchens." His voice faded and his eyes closed as he held the burning joint between his fingers.

Sigrid nodded, though he couldn't see her. She thought of her own parents back home and a knife churned in her gut. She opened her mouth to speak, to confide in him her own family mysteries, but couldn't find the right words. Instead, she leaned forward and plucked the joint from his fingers, meeting his gaze when he opened his eyes.

"Come on. Let's get some sleep," she said.

Two days flew by without incident. They passed a few bands of soldiers, but the men paid them no mind. "We'll need to stop at a village tomorrow to restock a few things. We're rather low on bread," Baldr said as he pulled the rope to hoist their remaining supplies into the trees as Sigrid rested next to the fire.

The peaceful evening was quickly interrupted as a high-pitched whistle cut through the air. Sigrid sprung into a sitting position, her mind still half in the trance that had nearly carried her off to sleep. Baldr darted to her side. He put a finger in front of his mouth, and a second later they could hear men yelling. They couldn't make out the words, but the voices were agitated and the urgency of their words was clear, even if their meanings were obscured.

Just then, a man burst through the trees. He was heavily hooded, his half-rotten cloak obscuring leather armor. He looked at the two with confusion and surprise before springing forward and sitting down next to Sigrid. She gawked, but Baldr drew the dagger at his side.

"Whoa, whoa," the stranger said, lifting his hands in surrender. "I'm not here to hurt you."

"Who are you?" Baldr hissed as the sound of running men grew louder.

"A friend, I promise, if you can pretend that I am part of this merry little camp."

"What—" Baldr didn't have a chance to finish his question before two men burst through the trees.

Soldiers. Army. Their swords were sheathed—for now.

"Oy," the taller of the two grunted, pointing at the three seated around the fire. "You seen a woman come through here?"

Baldr and Sigrid gave him puzzled looks, and the stranger appeared as confused as they were.

"No," the stranger replied. "Been a quiet night."

The shorter soldier, his beard braided in two, huffed. "Dogs caught a whiff through this way." He peered at them, his eyes narrowing. "She's a woman, Gunther."

The taller soldier scoffed. "Too dark. Princess is fair, like the queen. Fuck. Gorm is going to be in a foul mood."

The stranger next to Sigrid tensed, but his features were calm. He flashed a smile, and Sigrid caught a better look at him from beneath his hood. He was handsome, his eyes were a brilliant blue even in the firelight. Curly bangs fell in front of his eyes, and his hair was the color of the sun.

"Well, we'll keep an eye out," he said.

The soldiers turned to leave before the shorter of the two paused. He glanced over his shoulder at them. "What business do you have traveling now? You're a bit off the road."

Sigrid felt her heart sink. What would they say? They had no explanation for being there, and these guards didn't look like the sort to just leave them be without a proper explanation.

"My wife and I are traveling to see our parents. This gentleman is our hired hand. You know how the roads can get." Baldr offered the soldiers a smile.

Sigrid shot a smile at the guards as well, following Baldr's lead. "We just married," she said, swallowing hard and meeting the taller soldier's gaze. She reached out and took Baldr's hand in hers, giving him a look that she hoped was one of adoration.

The soldier's eyes turned on Sigrid, boring into her flesh in a way that made her feel as if she needed to hide. "Elves do make pretty wives," he said, then turned and pushed the shorter man by the shoulder. They disappeared back into the woods, the light of their torch disappearing into the distance.

It was a good moment before any of them dared to speak. When they were certain the soldiers had gone, and once the shouting had grown faint, Sigrid and Baldr turned their gazes to the stranger. He flashed them a brilliant smile and lowered his hood. His golden hair was pulled into a haphazard bun, and loose strands fell to curl around his angelic face. Sigrid was a little caught off guard—he was rather attractive for the sort of man to stumble across their camp in the middle of the night. Though his clothing was rustic, he had a noble air about him that was impossible to ignore.

"Agnar," he said. "My name is Agnar."

"Great." Baldr frowned. "What's happening?"

Agnar glanced around once again as if checking to make sure they were truly alone. "Not important. Think I can stick around a little while longer? I'd hate to run into those soldiers again. Probably wouldn't be so polite the second time around."

Baldr gave him a flat look. "We aren't in the business of picking up strangers. You'd probably rob us in our sleep anyway."

"Whoa, whoa," Agnar said, lifting his hands with his palms out. "I promise I'm not here to rob you. I just need to lie low for a bit, you know?"

"Why are you running from the soldiers?"

"Well, I'm not," the man replied. "But I know where someone is that they're looking for."

Sigrid shifted in her seat. "They mentioned the princess. Why would they be looking for the princess out here, this far from Hedeby?"

Agnar cleared his throat. "Well, she's ... not at home. And they may be a little concerned about where she is."

Baldr's dagger was in his hand in a moment, the tip pointed directly at Agnar's face. "You're not involving us in any weird royal plots. You're Heddish. Whatever you've got going on, we want no part of it."

"Sure, sure, sure. I don't want to involve you! Just let me enjoy your company for the evening, and I'll be out of your hair in the morning. Here," he said, reaching into a pocket and pulling out a few gold coins. "For your trouble. I will not bring you harm. I promise."

Baldr looked at the coins with a frown, but Sigrid could tell he wanted to take them. The money would help them restock any supplies they needed on their way to Uruachi. Sigrid sighed and plucked the coins from the stranger's hands.

"Fine," she said. "You can stay. But over there, away from us."

"Of course." He looked at Baldr and flashed a wide grin. "I won't let anything happen to your bride, friend."

Baldr and Sigrid exchanged long looks. Baldr's eyes said he'd do what she wanted. Sigrid looked back at the stranger, trying to determine whether he was a threat. In the end, there was something about him that felt comfortable. Trustworthy. Against her better senses, she nodded. "You can stay."

Agnar flashed a brilliantly white grin. "Wonderful! You are as kind as you are beautiful, madame."

Baldr audibly groaned.

"Don't worry! I won't lay a finger on your wife, sir."

Sigrid giggled but thought it prudent to continue the charade of their marriage. Baldr, not arguing with the verdict but not happy with it, excused himself to lay their bedrolls beneath a large tree. Together. Well, they were pretending to be married, so it only made sense. Sigrid's stomach tingled. Turning to the strange guest, she peered at him with more suspicion than she felt. He didn't seem dangerous. Did he really know where the princess was? She was surprised the entire countryside wasn't full of soldiers. Perhaps the king didn't want word to get out. It certainly wouldn't look good for his daughter to have gone missing.

"What can you tell me?" she asked.

"Pardon?" the man asked, raising a blond brow.

"We covered for you. Surely that entitles us to a bit of information," she replied.

"Do you really want to know anything? You and your husband are innocent. I would hate to give you information that might bring you harm."

"Could your presence bring us harm?"

The man grew silent, casting his eyes to the flames. "It could. I'm sorry," he replied, turning an apologetic gaze back to Sigrid. "I saw your fire in the distance. I panicked. I'm just trying ... to do the right thing. That's all I can tell you. I won't let harm come to you. I just need to hide for the night."

She could hear Baldr rustling around behind them. "It's fine. I believe you. Where are you headed?"

"Njarovik."

Sigrid blinked. "We're headed there."

"Ah," the man replied. "How curious."

At that moment, Baldr kneeled next to Sigrid and settled a hand on her shoulder. "We should go to bed," he said quietly. "We have a long journey tomorrow."

"Yes, it is a day's ride away," Agnar said, moving to lie down next to the fire. "A good place to resupply. I'm afraid I had to abandon my belongings running from those thugs."

Sigrid laughed, then stood and moved across the campsite with Baldr. He'd situated their things beneath the gnarled branches of an ancient tree, which loomed overhead and provided shelter from above. She wanted to ask their new acquaintance a million questions, but they were questions she knew she didn't need the answers to. They had their mission, she reminded herself. This was not a vacation where she had the freedom to sit and chat with every intriguing fellow they came across. Whatever he was doing, she knew he had to handle it himself. It wasn't her business.

"Good night, my lady," Agnar said from next to the fire, waving at her. "And you, sir. Thank you for being kind."

Sigrid beamed, but Baldr soon obscured her view as he lifted the blanket to slide beneath. She joined him, her face growing hot. She couldn't remember the last time she had slid into bed with a man and felt such a reaction from herself. Swallowing hard, she turned away from him and covered her mouth with her hand. It was blazing hot beneath the blanket, though the air around them was crisp. Thoughts of the seemingly friendly stranger in their camp were quickly overcome with a near panic about his closeness. Baldr lay on his back, his hands beneath his head, and she wondered if he was as aware of her as she was of him. Did every hair on his body also stand? Did goose bumps erupt across his arms when he accidentally touched her back?

It was far easier to sleep than she could have guessed. When the first light of dawn crept across her face, she was curled up at Baldr's side. Her head rested on his chest, and his arm was around her body. Glancing up, she noted the length of his eyelashes as they rested against his sharp cheeks. Her fingers itched to trace the outline of his lips, but instead, she kept them where they were, her entire body going rigid.

Baldr's eyes shot open. "Sigrid?" He looked down at her, his brows furrowed together in confusion.

Her cheeks warmed. "I'm fine," she reassured him, sitting up now that they were both awake. Her eyes cast across the camp at the man next to the fire. The flames were nothing but embers now, and he was curled up beneath a shabby blanket. It was one of their blankets, a particularly worn one she'd brought from the Pearl. Had he taken it in the night?

"I couldn't let him freeze," came Baldr's quiet voice. "I hope you don't mind."

"What? Oh, no, of course not. I'm just upset I didn't think to offer him one."

The two stood and began to fold their bedding and strap their supplies back on the horses. As they moved, Agnar finally began to stir. Sitting up, he regarded them with curiosity before his memory seemed to set in.

"Ah, good morning," he said, giving them a wide smile. "I hope you two lovebirds slept well."

Sigrid chuckled, untying the rope that had been thrown over a tree branch to keep their food off the ground. Lowering it, she reached into the bag and tossed Agnar an apple.

"Do you think it is safe for you to travel now?" she asked.

Agnar nodded and hungrily bit into the apple, his stomach growling so loud she could hear it. She wondered when the last time was that he'd had a meal.

"Are you still heading to Njarovik?" she inquired, helping fasten their supplies to the horses as Baldr fed them.

"I am," Agnar replied, standing and dusting off his clothing.

He was as lovely in the sunlight as he was in the dark, Sigrid thought. Her eyes traveled to her faux husband, whose features were so different from Agnar's. They were both tall men, but Agnar's hair curled in ringlets around his face. He was spun from light, where Baldr was of the earth. Baldr's softness was not so easily seen on the outside, unlike their newfound friend, who seemed to be made of sunshine. She wondered if Agnar was as harmless as he appeared.

Baldr licked his lips. "Why don't you come with us, then? We have two horses. You can ride with one of us."

The blond man's eyes opened wide. "I couldn't impose on you."

"It is no imposition," Baldr replied sternly, his eyes raising from the horses only long enough to catch Sigrid's gaze. "We'll part ways there, but it isn't far. If we run across soldiers, you'll still look like you're with us."

"Then you can head to see your family in peace." Agnar nodded.

"What?" Sigrid blinked. "Oh! Yes."

Baldr shot her a look, and she responded with an apologetic smile. "Will you be staying in Njarovik?"

"No," Agnar shook his head and pulled the string from his hair, allowing the curls to tumble around his neck. "I'm heading further north."

Sigrid and Baldr glanced at each other.

"Then we will see you off. Do you plan on staying in Njarovik long?" Baldr asked.

"No. A night, at most. Long enough to buy some supplies and sleep. I have quite a journey ahead of me, and I can't waste time. I've already been diverted long enough."

Baldr nodded, and Sigrid could see his mind working beneath his eyes. She wondered if they'd have to wait for the stranger to leave. Could they take another path? It was best if nobody could tell which direction they were headed. Although this man seemed to have his own problems to worry about, she thought, and she doubted that he cared much for their journey at all. They were nothing more than a couple on the road, following the river to the north as many travelers might.

Njarovik was as gray and angular as the newer, Heddish-dominated portion of Copper City, Sigrid thought as they made their way into town. It was clearly a Heddish settlement. The walls around the town were tall and spiked, and the buildings steepled into tall points. Where elven homes were made of clay, these buildings were made of stone wrenched from the earth. Sigrid found them daunting and intimidating. The whole place clashed with the bright green of the trees that surrounded it. The Heddish had been seafaring people once. She wondered if they used so many shades of gray and blue because it reminded them of the ocean they'd left behind.

Agnar rode with Baldr. Sigrid had offered to let him ride with her, but Baldr had insisted. The two rode ahead, Baldr quiet nearly the entire ride. Agnar made a few attempts at conversation but stopped an hour or so in when it was clear he was riding with Baldr to be kept away from Sigrid. Part of her was frustrated, and she wondered if Baldr didn't trust her to keep the information quiet. Whatever Baldr was thinking, he kept it firmly locked away, his face a stoic mask that she thought made him look like someone else.

As they made their way into the village, Agnar kept his hood up. Gone was the good-natured, talkative man they'd met in the forest—now he was quiet. There were some guards scattered about, but mostly the town seemed safe. Whatever Agnar was hiding, whatever business he was involved in, he had put a lot of trust in them. He did not make eye contact with anyone. He must have wanted to fade into the background, his head was down and his shoulders were hunched.

Sigrid hopped off her horse and asked a woman selling flowers for directions. The woman regarded her for a moment, curious, but was polite as she pointed to a large building at the center of town. The inn was busy when they arrived, the first floor teemed with locals beginning the evening in their cups.

"Here," Agnar said, sliding a few gold coins into Sigrid's hand. "Can you ask for a room for me? I'd rather be not be—"

"I get it," Sigrid interrupted, offering a smile she hoped was calming. "I'll get one for you."

The innkeeper was an elven woman, tall and plump with child. "You're in luck," she said to Sigrid as she led the three up the stairs to the second floor. "Last two rooms for the evening."

The rooms were small. Sigrid and Baldr's room was a bit larger than Agnar's, and they discovered they were lucky enough to have a fireplace. Agnar's room was almost a closet and had only a small bed next to a tiny window overlooking the town. Agnar didn't seem to care and quickly disappeared into the room. Assuming he needed time alone, Sigrid and Baldr took to the room they'd been given.

One bed, of course, as expected. They'd kept to their story, telling the innkeeper they were newlyweds traveling to visit family. Their night beneath the tree was still fresh on her mind, and her body sizzled where he'd had his arm around her.

"I can sleep on the floor," Baldr said as he closed the door behind him.

"It's okay." She smiled, feeling her cheeks grow red. She admonished herself for feeling so silly and turned away from him. "It'll be more comfortable in the bed. Warmer. I won't bite, I promise." Even as she said it, she wished she could take the flirtatious words back.

Baldr chuckled. "Don't make it seem so tempting." He winked at her and sank into the rickety bed. The sound of creaking sent lustful images of her crawling on him as the bed groaned beneath them. Her eyes chanced a look at him before she forced herself to look out the window, hoping to appear contemplative instead of embarrassed.

She tried to think of the last time she'd felt her body respond to someone's mere presence like this. Her culls rarely did anything for her. So seldom were they her type in any capacity. She was good at pretending, good at making men think she wanted them. Now that she did find herself wanting and desiring someone, her stomach ached from stress. They were on an important mission. Surely that was it, she told herself. She was in close quarters with a good-looking man and would be for some time. Of course she would feel something. She wasn't dead, she reminded herself. She was still young, when most women were in their prime, so that part of her was bound to respond to the beauty of a good man.

But she no longer knew what to do with her feelings.

"You look glum." Baldr's voice cut through her thoughts. "Are you all right?"

Sigrid looked at him and offered a sheepish grin. "I'm fine. Just thinking. Should we go check on our new friend?"

"He'll be fine."

"Still, wouldn't want to let him feel forgotten."

Baldr's lips curved into a frown. "We shouldn't have more to do with him now that we're here. He said he was going to leave on his own, and we should let him. He's into something, and we can't afford to be caught in anyone's web. We have a message to deliver."

He was right. She drew the curtain over the window, leaving just a sliver of light. "I know. We have to be careful."

"I'm not trying to ..." He paused, mulling over his words. "I'm not trying to tell you what to do."

She clicked her tongue, her hand settling on her hip. "I'm not going to go telling him anything. But aren't you curious about what he's into? What he's running from? If the royal family is having problems, that would be vital information to convey to your superiors."

"Our superiors," he corrected. "You joined the Collective. You're on a mission. You're one of us."

Sigrid licked her lips and turned for the door. "Come on."

CHAPTER EIGHT

"I need a bath," Agnar whined as he opened the door with Sigrid's hand still midknock.

"There's probably a town bath," Sigrid suggested, taking a step back.

He was wearing the same ruddy clothing he'd been wearing before. Though he seemed to have a good amount of coin on him, his clothing would suggest he was barely above a beggar. Dirt smudged his cheek, but somehow he was radiant despite the grime. At the suggestion of a bathhouse, his eyes widened in glee, sparkling despite the dim light. Quickly, however, their light dimmed.

"No. I shouldn't go anywhere public. I'll ask the innkeeper if she can spare a bucket of water." He lifted his hood and slid past her.

Sigrid closed his door behind him and turned to Baldr, who was leaning against the stair's banister.

"I'm not opposed to visiting the bathhouse," he said casually, picking at his fingernails. "If that's where you want to go."

Three days was too long without a bath. "If we can spare the time, I'd love to."

He pushed himself forward and clapped his hands together. "Then to the bathhouse we go!"

They passed Agnar as they left, and the strange man gave them a polite nod as he hurried up the stairs, careful that his face was always beneath that hood.

They were in luck. There was indeed a bathhouse. It was far smaller than the one in Copper City, and they separated her away from Baldr into a women-only pool. There were a few other women present. One, a plump redhead, noticed Sigrid upon entering. Sigrid could feel the woman's eyes on her as she took a seat in the warm bath, a breath of relief escaping her lips.

"You're new," the stranger said. The women around her looked toward Sigrid. A couple of the women, including the one who spoke, were elves. A few of the others were human.

"Just visiting," Sigrid replied. "I'm here with my husband."

"Oh, well, I'm sure if you're traveling, then this is a much-needed break from him!"

Sigrid laughed as she undid her hair. It fell around her shoulders, and the ends floated on the water. She dipped quickly beneath the water, coming up a moment later. "I enjoy his presence," she said simply, pulling her hair over one shoulder.

Another woman spoke. "Where are you from?"

"Copper City!"

"Ooh," the redhead said with a grin. "Very exciting. Well, welcome. I hope everyone has been pleasant."

"Much more than I anticipated," Sigrid admitted.

"How do you mean?" the redhead asked, her flaming brow raising.

"Well ..." Sigrid chewed her lip. "I've never spent much time outside Copper City. This is my first time. I suppose I didn't expect people to be so ... polite." She glanced at the elves, then the humans. "Well, not this far away I suppose!" She didn't want to say that she hadn't expected people so far from the city to mix so freely.

The redhead laughed. "My husband is the mayor of this good town. The elves farm the countryside, so we keep good relations. I suppose you were expecting this entire town to be full of ignorant heathens, hmm?"

Sigrid flushed red. "No! No, I didn't mean it like that."

"It's okay," the woman responded with a grin. "I know what you meant. I'm from Hedeby."

Sigrid swallowed. "Ah. I've never been to Hedeby either. I shouldn't make assumptions about places I've never been."

One of the human women snorted. "It's fine, lass. We're all naked together. Ain't no judgments here."

Sigrid nodded sheepishly. The women began to giggle among themselves, leaving Sigrid to swim to the corner and wash in peace. There was a pit of embarrassment in her stomach, and she realized suddenly how far she was from home.

The bath was pleasant enough, though the women mainly gossiped about happenings in the town. There were more soldiers than normal, Sigrid learned. The village was mostly quiet, save for the tavern located on the main road, which was the only place anyone outside the village seemed to visit. The villagers were no strangers to newcomers, but it seemed such a number of soldiers was unusual.

Refreshed and renewed, Sigrid found Baldr waiting for her outside the bathhouse.

"You have a lovely smile," he said as she approached.

Sigrid's cheeks warmed. "I feel good. A good bath will do that."

"Come, I was thinking we could pick up a few supplies while we're out."

They moseyed together through the village's small square where all the merchants seemed to be located. They filled their bags with bread and dried meats, as well as a few bits of dried fruit Sigrid insisted on.

"It'll be a treat after a long day," she said, holding up her small bag of fruit.

He smiled and took the satchel, placing it with the other food in his bag. "There's one more thing I thought we should get, just in case."

"What?"

He cleared his throat, looking unsure, but ushered her toward one of the stalls. Jewelry had been laid out, the nicest of which was displayed in a glass case.

"Good afternoon to you, lad," the merchant said. "Looking for something in particular?"

"Yes," Baldr said. "I was looking to get my wife here a wedding band."

"A wedding band after the wedding? Very unusual," the merchant said, his eyebrow lifted. "I have a good selection of wedding bands over here."

"We're having a bigger ceremony when we get to our families," Sigrid lied, her eyes on Baldr as he searched through the rings. "I keep telling him we don't need to do this now, that we can wait until we arrive."

"Now is good," Baldr said, picking up a simple gold band. "I would hate for someone to mistake us for an unmarried couple."

He turned and lifted her hand, sliding the ring onto her finger.

The merchant beamed. "It looks lovely, missus."

Sigrid shot Baldr a puzzled look as he paid for the ring.

"Why a ring?" she whispered as they moved away from the merchant.

"To make the lie more convincing," he said.

Sigrid stopped and opened her mouth to speak, when suddenly someone knocked into her from behind. "Oof," she grunted. Baldr's hand reached out to steady her.

"You should watch where you're going," the man said.

He was a soldier and an important one, if his immaculate suit was any indication. Standing tall, the man had a grizzled beard and heavy lines around his eyes. The signet of a commander gleamed on his chest.

"Sorry," she replied, her chest squeezing when she saw the signet. "A stall caught my eye. I should be more careful."

"Yes, you should," the commander said dryly. "I shouldn't expect much from country elves." His voice dripped with disdain as he looked at them.

Sigrid swallowed, but her cheeks burned. The disgust in his voice curdled in her stomach and she wanted to break his nose.

The commander laughed. "Didn't like that one, did you?" He crossed his arms.

"It was rather rude," she replied.

Baldr cleared his throat. "We'll just get out of your way, sir. Sorry to be a bother."

The commander turned his eyes on Baldr as if seeing him for the first time. Another soldier arrived next to the commander, his brows furrowing as he looked upon the scene. "Commander Gorm, is everything all right?"

"These two are in my way," the commander said. "Such a pity."

"You heard him," the soldier said, shoving Baldr. "Get moving."

A couple more soldiers surrounded them, attracted by the commotion. Their faces were equally disturbing to Sigrid; their eyes alighted with amusement and scorn all at once. It was disconcerting.

"Hey," Sigrid huffed. "We haven't done anything. You don't need to get physical."

"Yeah?" The soldier raised a brow and took a step closer to her. "And what will you do about it?"

She swallowed. She couldn't start trouble, not now, not so early into their journey. Her fist itched to make contact with the soldier's jaw, but instead she simply stood there, her face drawn in anger.

"Look at her ears," Commander Gorm laughed. "Turning red. Looks like a knife pulled out of a fire."

"Very original," Sigrid retorted. "A knife joke about my ears? Never been done before."

Gorm's smile quickly faded. He raised a hand and quickly brought it down, smacking Sigrid across the face so hard her head snapped to one side. Her flesh stung where he'd made contact.

Baldr stepped in front of her, his arms outstretched. "We said we'd leave. We're going."

Gorm laughed and motioned for his soldier to grab Baldr. He was quick, taking Baldr by the arms while Gorm settled his hands on his hips. "I do love it when elves try to speak above their station. It makes it so much more satisfying to put them in their place."

Baldr spit at Gorm's feet. Without another word, Gorm took Baldr by the shoulder and brought his fist into Baldr's stomach. Hard. Baldr doubled forward in pain, coughing, but Gorm hit him again. And again.

"Stop it!" Sigrid cried out, trying to grab Gorm's arm, but she was shoved to the ground by the commander.

Letting Baldr drop to his knees, the commander and his soldier laughed. Baldr struggled to suck in air as they hooted, each laugh echoing like razorblades on Sigrid's ears.

Baldr pushed himself to his feet and stood tall, his chin out and his lips drawn into a straight line. "I'm not afraid of you," Baldr said, his voice pained but otherwise firm. "Beat us all you like, we know we didn't do anything."

Gorm's face shifted from one of amusement to one of pure spite. "You're rather insolent, even for a savage," he growled, reaching out to grab Baldr by the collar.

Just as the man's hand stretched between them, Baldr smacked it away. Immediately, each soldier surrounding them—now there were at least five, Sigrid counted—drew their swords.

Sigrid's body went cold. "No," she pleaded, trying to step forward, but finding herself unable to as strong hands gripped her shoulders. She pulled, desperate, but with every tug of hers, the hands of the soldiers holding her grew tighter.

"Stupid boy," Gorm growled, closing the distance between him and Baldr.

His gloved hand raised again to grab Baldr by the throat. The half-elf grabbed Gorm by the wrist, trying to break free of his grasp, until he was thrown to the ground.

"I could have you beaten," Gorm said, his voice dangerous and quiet. "I could have you flogged in front of the entire town square. Who do you think you are?"

Baldr coughed and gasped for air, his hair dislodging from the bun he kept it in.

The soldiers surrounding them pointed their swords at Baldr, each waiting for Gorm to give the command. Time seemed to draw out as Sigrid waited for them to drive their swords into her friend. Maybe they'd be lucky, she thought. Maybe the soldiers would simply beat them and be on their way. The journey might be a bit more painful, but at least they'd both be alive. At least she'd be able to return home with him instead of delivering a corpse. Oh, his mother. She'd blame Sigrid, and Sigrid wouldn't even be able to disagree. They were supposed to stay out of trouble. They had one mission. One job.

Gorm cracked his neck. "Let's go. Fetch the horses. There's nothing of importance in this town."

The soldiers holding Sigrid shoved her to the ground and followed their leader out of the square.

"Baldr," Sigrid gasped, diving for him and grabbing him by the face. "Baldr, are you okay?"

"I'll be fine," he grunted, his eyes still bloodshot and watering. "Just another power-mad asshole. It's fine."

"No, it isn't fine, that could have been—"

"Sigrid," he said firmly, grabbing her by the shoulders. "I said I'm fine. We've attracted enough attention. Let's get out of here."

CHAPTER NINE

Sigrid pushed open the door to their room and helped Baldr, who still had his hands over his stomach, stagger inside. He collapsed with a groan.

"Do you need anything?" she asked, wanting to fuss over him but not knowing where to start.

"I'll be fine," he said, breathing hard. "This isn't the first punch I've taken."

"I know," she sighed, kneeling next to the bed and taking his hand. "I'm sorry. This is my fault."

"I don't think either of us could have really avoided it. Men like that use every excuse to seek trouble."

"Still. I should have diffused the situation. I should have done something. What good am I if so soon into our journey we're already finding ourselves on the wrong side of Heddish soldiers?"

He coughed and winced. "Sigrid, it's fine. They left us alone in the end. If the worst encounter we have with soldiers is that one, then we're doing good. We just need to be more careful."

She nodded, though the guilt in her chest did not dissipate. After a few moments, Baldr sat up and gave her a soft smile. "Let's get a few drinks in the tavern tonight, forget about these bruises."

"Is it wise?" she asked, perking up at the suggestion.

"After today, we've earned it. Let's go have a drink. My treat."

She eyed him from her seat. "Fine," she gave in, moving to the mirror and leaning forward to rouge her lips. It was the only cosmetic she'd brought with her, and if she was going to spend the night partying, she at least wanted to feel a little better.

Her dress was practical. Looking at herself in the mirror, she couldn't help but notice how different she looked. There were many things about her job she could live without, and there were certainly days where she was exhausted by the effort she was forced to put into her appearance, but deep down she enjoyed the ritual of dressing up. She missed sweeping kohl along her eyes and painting the flower on her forehead. She enjoyed the way her dresses flattered her form. Even if her company was not always pleasant, at least she found solace in the practiced motion of getting dressed. Now she felt like a shadow of herself. The dress she wore was a plain blue, and she had on her traveling shoes. She hardly looked like the painted woman she usually saw.

Oh well. Deep down she knew she'd have to return to work eventually. Perhaps there was much to enjoy in being a traveling wife.

Together, Sigrid and Baldr walked down the stairs to the tavern below and took seats near a window. It was early enough that there were still tables yet to be claimed, and the bard had yet to arrive. They'd heard him practicing earlier as they'd left. Amid such stressful travel, some music was a welcome reprieve.

"Evening," the server said to them, lifting her skirt as she bustled over to their table. "Saw you come in earlier. Traveling through, aye?"

"Yes," Sigrid said with a smile. She noticed the server's curved human ears. "My husband and I thought we'd have a drink and listen to the bard."

"Well, he'll be out soon enough, I'm sure. What'll you have?"

"Mead," Sigrid answered.

"I'll take an ale." Baldr nodded.

The bartender nodded in return and hurried off to gather their drinks. They sat quietly for a few minutes, both content to listen to the noises of the tavern and watch as others began to file in. There were tables against the walls and arranged throughout the expanse of the room. Large wooden beams were decorated with paintings and the taxidermic heads of wild animals.

The bard eventually arrived and took his spot in the corner of the room large. Lyre in hand, he began with a jaunty tune about a man getting so drunk he married a tavern wench. Sigrid and Baldr talked between taking deep pulls of their drinks. Sigrid's muscles began to relax, and her shoulders drooped. She hadn't realized how tense she'd become. As time passed, Sigrid felt her stomach warm. "You know what," she said as the bard convened a song and went to the bar for a break. "We should get some whiskey. This was your idea, right? So let's do it justice."

"Oh!" Baldr laughed and finished off his drink. He took her empty mug from her hands and stood. "If my wife bids it," he said louder than he needed to, "then I must acquiesce!"

Sigrid watched him with an embarrassed grin on her face.

"You're new," came a voice from the other side of the table. Looking over, she spotted a young elf woman with milky skin and flaming-red hair. "We get travelers, but rarely ones so pretty."

Sigrid laughed. "Just passing through with my husband." Something in her core heated every time she said that. It was far too easy to lie about her relationship with Baldr.

"Ah, well, perhaps my husband and I can join you?" She pointed toward the bar where a tall, bearded human was busy trying to catch the bartender's attention. "I'm not sure how much more I can handle the same crowd I see from morning to night!"

Sigrid shrugged and gestured to the seat next to her. "You'll have to tell me your name first."

"Teicah," she said as she took her seat next to Sigrid. She was shorter than Sigrid and far thinner, but her smile was wide and her eyes blazed. "How long have you been in town? Not long if this is the first I'm seeing of you."

"No, we just arrived yesterday. We are resting today and leaving again in the morning."

Teicah's eyes turned again toward the bar. "Asmund!" She waved, signaling for her husband's attention. "Where are you coming from?"

"Copper City," Sigrid answered. Just enough truth to not invite attention.

"I've never been there," Teicah said wistfully as her husband took a seat next to her. "I hear it's lovely, though. Every door a different color, tall buildings, parties. Is it really as raucous as they say?"

Sigrid laughed and dipped the entire contents of her drink into her mouth. "We have fun," she said, wincing at the strength of the drink. "I suppose we wouldn't have a reputation if it wasn't at least partially true. It is never so alive as it is during the spring equinox."

Baldr returned shortly, setting down a glass in front of Sigrid as he took his seat next to her.

"So I've heard," the husband chuckled. "A friend of mine accompanied some lord he was working for, and I couldn't believe some of the stories he told. Is it true men and women fornicate in the streets freely?"

Baldr almost spit out his drink. "I'm sure it's happened," he said through harsh coughs. Composing himself, he cleared his throat once more. "I've lived there for the last year, and it is definitely more alive than Hedeby, but I wouldn't go so far as to say there are orgies in the streets."

"Bah," Asmund waved a dismissive hand. "It was more fun when I thought there were tits galore."

"Hey!" Sigrid waved her finger. "Nobody said there weren't tits galore! The Red District on the night of the equinox is a sight to behold."

"Ooh," Teicah teased, now halfway through her drink. "Your husband lets you visit the Red District?"

Sigrid blinked and caught Baldr's gaze. Had she said too much? Were the drinks making her lips too loose?

"Ah, well," Baldr said. "We were married around the equinox. We spent a good amount of time celebrating."

Good one. Sigrid let out a breath of relief. She couldn't tell if she was overthinking it. Perhaps she was under-thinking it.

Asmund elbowed Baldr as if they had been good friends for a lifetime. "I see! So tell me, Baldr, how did a man like you find such a lovely elven wife?"

A man like you? Sigrid looked Baldr over. Humans and elves had some differences—elves were often taller, often darker, but it was the ears that separated them. Long and pointed, they stuck out, even beneath Sigrid's mane of hair. But for Baldr, they did not. Far shorter and with a far less pronounced point, they were distinct but easily hidden beneath his hair. Their guests had not seen the gentle point beneath his locks. They believed him to be human.

"Just lucky, I suppose." Baldr shrugged before tipping a second drink into his mouth. "Speak for yourself, though. Your wife is as lovely as a sunrise. Did you steal her from a more handsome man in combat?"

Asmund roared with laughter, his voice so loud it nearly drowned out the bard. Teicah grinned and downed the rest of her drink. "He'd like to think! I was working as a cooking maid to a nearby lord when we met. Ten years later we have two children, who are currently sleeping soundly while we drink our troubles away. Do you two have children?"

"No," Sigrid said as she shook her head. "Not yet. Perhaps eventually." She looked at Baldr, who seemed to be silently choking on his drink.

"Oh, well, you're in no hurry. The next time you wake up from a nap, decide whether you liked it or not. If you did, wait to have children. Ah, love them." Teicah leaned back in her seat and draped an arm over the back of her chair.

Baldr took the bottle of whiskey and poured it into her mug. "Sounds like you could do with something stronger." He turned to her husband and held the bottle up. Asmund nodded vigorously and held out his empty mug.

Sigrid and Baldr soon found the lies too easy to come up with. Every time Asmund or Teicah asked about their relationship, the two of them took turns coming up with various tales. The drunker they became, the easier it was to pretend they were married. Before Sigrid knew it, she'd crossed the table to sit in her "husband's" lap. Her arm looped around his neck to hold her steady as she laughed.

"Dance with me," she said to him, sliding out of his lap and taking his hand. It was so easy to be close to him, and she couldn't tell if it was the alcohol or not. The world outside the tavern faded away. The mission, Agnar in his room, the journey ahead—it all felt so very far away.

The bard was singing something quick and fun, and others had begun to dance across the floor. Baldr gave in to her request without protest. He stood from the chair and allowed her to drag him closer to the music. With a cheer, she brought herself close to his chest, so close she could smell the whiskey on his breath. Or was that hers? He wrapped one arm around her waist and took her hand into his. Despite the amount of drink sloshing around his stomach, he was very light on his feet.

Sigrid was suddenly very aware of her senses. His body was hot against hers and her skin burned where he touched her. Her stomach swelled with giddiness as if she were a young girl enamored with her first attraction.

Suddenly she was in the air, Baldr's hands were tight around her waist as he lifted her. She squealed and tossed her head back in laughter. As her feet hit the floor, their bodies swirled through the crowd. She could hear his laughter in her ear, the sound warm and breathless. As the song came to an end, she collapsed into his arms, sweating and desperate for air.

Those without a partner disappeared from the floor, leaving a few couples to drunkenly hold each other in their arms. Sigrid wrapped her arms around Baldr's neck. They were doing an awfully good job of pretending to be a couple in love, she thought. Her cheek pressed against his shoulder as they swayed to the melancholy tune. This song was about a man leaving his wife for the sea, then coming back with riches only to find her gone without a trace. He searched high and low for his beloved wife, realizing he had wrongly chosen his mission to find riches over a great woman.

As the song began to end, Sigrid lifted her head. Her cheek grazed against his, and in her stupor, she allowed herself to nuzzle against him. His arms tightened around her. She marveled at how strong he felt. She'd spent quite a bit of time in men's arms, but this felt like a dream.

"We should go to bed," he murmured. "We still have to travel tomorrow, and I'd hate to set us behind."

She frowned and tipped her head back to look him in the eyes. "Fine," she huffed, and allowed him to pull her through the dwindling crowd toward the stairs. Their new friends had disappeared, and she wondered if they'd said goodbye, but she couldn't remember. She whistled with each step up the stairs she took, a lazy smile plastered on her face. As he guided her down the hall, she felt her body collide with the dresser on her way into the room.

Sigrid laughed so hard no sound came out of her mouth. The empty bottle of whiskey fell from her hand and hit the wooden floor with a loud clank. When had she grabbed it on their way out? Her arms wrapped around Baldr to steady herself as he lifted her from the floor.

"Let's get you to bed," Baldr said with a grunt as she tripped over the whiskey bottle and nearly brought them both tumbling.

He gently guided her into the bed.

"This was a good idea," she giggled.

She lost her balance and grabbed onto him, pulling him down onto the bed with her. As if to stop the ceiling from spinning, she reached out and grabbed his hand. He did not protest. Sigrid rolled over onto her side and propped herself up on an elbow to peer down at her companion.

Her eyes fluttered over the curve of his lips and the sharp angles of his jaw. His dark hair was splayed out around his head like a black halo. He'd always been beautiful to her, but at that moment she thought he was so handsome he could only be carved from stone.

"You're beautiful," he said softly. "I often want to say that, but I'm always afraid you'll find it inappropriate."

"I never tire of hearing about my beauty," she joked, taking a few strands of his hair into her hand to twirl about her fingers.

"I'm certain you hear it often."

"Yes, but it means more when it comes from someone I enjoy being around."

"Ah, you enjoy being around me?"

"I do," she admitted.

He grinned, his fingers reaching up to brush along the side of her face. Shivers passed through her body, and her eyes fluttered closed.

"You are a woman of many talents, it seems. Conversation. Dancing. Swordsmanship."

"Ah, you have not yet experienced *all* my talents," she purred, nuzzling her face against the palm he held to her cheek.

"I am not worthy of those talents."

"You are far more worthy than any man I've met so far," she replied softly, meeting his gaze. Slowly, she lowered herself until she was nearly touching him. His breath was warm against her face, and all her body wanted to do was claim his lips.

He groaned, swallowing hard, and slid his palm to the back of her head. Gripping it softly, he tugged, bringing a gasp from her lips.

"You could have made many moves by now," she said breathlessly. "Why haven't you?"

"I respect our mission," he replied as he slid his other arm around her body. Suddenly, she was against his chest and he twisted, his knee between her legs. Resting her against the bed, he released her hair. "I don't want to compromise anything. It would be rather unfortunate if a romantic tryst hurt our goals."

"Oh, you're so paranoid," she whined, snaking her arms around his neck.

"I am not," he replied in a hushed tone. "You're drunk. I'm going to get you water, and then we will go to bed."

Sigrid pouted, sliding her leg across his hip. "You can get me water later."

"Sigrid," he said firmly, grabbing her by the knee and bringing her leg back to the bed. "You're drunk. You are a very, *very* tempting woman, but you are also drunk."

Sigrid exhaled a defeated sigh. "You're so smart," she whined. "How can you be so smart? Do you know how many men would risk their livelihoods for a drunken night of fun?"

"Well, it is tempting," he purred as he brushed curls from her face. "But we must show at least a little restraint."

Sigrid shifted her eyes away from him. "It is very late."

He hesitated above her. His eyes met hers with such an intensity that she wondered if he was even drunk at all. Perhaps he could hold his alcohol better than she. Whatever he was feeling, he pulled away from her and began to gather blankets to lay across the floor.

"You can sleep here," she offered. "No funny business, I promise."

He looked at her for a moment with something akin to longing in his eyes. "I think it best if I sleep here. Good night. Rest up, we have a long journey before we see another town."

CHAPTER TEN

They were so focused on leaving before the sun was up that Sigrid did not think to check on Agnar. Whatever business he was on, she wished him well, but she had her own journey to handle.

They traveled for some time before the heat of the day began to beat down on them, forcing them to rest in a clearing of trees.

She blinked at the brightness of the sun and glanced around their resting spot only to find Baldr had vanished. His horse was still present, but he was nowhere to be seen. For a moment panic swelled in her chest. She forced her heart to slow, hoping that he was just out of sight.

Clouds had begun to form in the sky. They were large, white, and fluffy. Occasionally one would roll in front of the sun to give her a reprieve from the heat.

Stretching her arms as high above her as she could physically manage, she sat up and cast her gaze into the wooded area not far off. Something large and black was moving through the trees. A bear? It was the right size, but she'd never heard of bears inhabiting this region. Perhaps they were closer to the mountains than they realized? Not that bears were something she had any expertise in, she thought.

The thing continued to move. Soon, it came out into the open field. It was a bear after all, she decided. A small black bear most likely. She didn't think it would bother her, but she stood and made her way to her horse to retrieve her sword anyway. When she looked back toward the animal, it was gone.

Sigrid grew increasingly nervous as her eyes scanned the bright field it had entered. The grass was tall, but not so tall that the animal would have been able to hide. It must have run back into the forest.

"What is it?"

Sigrid jumped at the deep voice that came from behind, and she spun to find Baldr standing with a bag.

"I think I saw a bear," she said, looking back over her shoulder. Nothing was there.

Baldr lifted the bag and shook it. "Was hoping to find rabbit, found mushrooms instead."

"The fun kind, I hope."

"Afraid not," he chuckled as he stored the bag away in his saddlebag. "But they'll go well with dinner tonight. We should get going before we lose too much more light."

Without another thought for the bear, Sigrid hopped back on her horse and joined Baldr for the remainder of their day's journey.

The day remained hot, and by the time they found a spot to camp for the night, the two of them were tired and in need of a good bath. The road had intersected with the river again, allowing them to find a spot off the path near a clearing of trees. The wheat fields had finally come to an end. A near perfectly straight line of trees separated the farmland from the woodland that had yet to be cleared for agriculture.

Baldr left Sigrid to busy herself with the fire in hopes of foraging berries. The thought of having berries as a dessert made her mouth water and stomach rumble in anticipation.

Suddenly she heard a light rustling noise from some nearby bushes. "Baldr?" Sigrid called out. He hadn't gone far, but she assumed he'd be gone for a while longer. "Successful already?"

There was no response. Assuming it was a rabbit or perhaps a squirrel, she returned her attention to the fire. The horses were still, resting beneath a tree, and gave no indication that anything was amiss.

Sigrid held her hand out over the fire, inhaling a deep breath. She did not know much magic—most elves did not—but in her teens she'd taught herself to light a small fire. Lighting candles was the extent of her ability, but she figured tinder couldn't be any harder. Closing her eyes, she focused on visualizing a flame. Her breath grew deep and measured as she blocked out all distractions. A heat formed at the center of her palm. Opening her eyes, she looked down at the small flame that had formed in the nest of tinder.

Again, she heard the rustling noise. A cold feeling radiated from her stomach. Carefully, she stood and removed her sword from her side. Since seeing the bear earlier that day, she'd decided it was safer to have it as close as possible.

It was as if the sound had been sucked right out of the air. No bugs or birds were chirping. There was no soft whistle of wind through the trees. Everything was perfectly still. The world had begun holding its breath. The horses stood eerily still, save for their eyes, which darted around rapidly.

Sigrid whirled around just as she heard something crunch a dry twig beneath its foot, and she managed to jump out of the way just as a large black creature charged from the bushes. It was the size of a bear, hunched over on four legs with scaly black ridges that began on the beast's head and followed along its spine. Sigrid could see the thing had no fur and instead was covered in black scales, but the face was similar to that of a dog. Talons dug deep into the earth as it steadied itself to attack again.

"Baldr!" Sigrid cried out. She brought her blade up so that it shone in the light of the fire between her and the beast.

The creature crouched low and snarled before launching forward at her as the horses neighed loudly and attempted to tear free from their restraints.

This time she was prepared and swung the sword at the creature. It flashed its teeth, revealing sharp rows with two long fangs at the center. A low growl escaped the thing's throat, reminding her of the sound of metal against stone. Every hair on her body stood on end.

The creature's breath was hot on Sigrid's face. One hand held the hilt of her sword, while the bladed end was in her other palm, cutting into her flesh. She cried out, kicking the creature off her. It readied itself again, growling, its eerie yellow eyes settling on her.

Blood dripped down her arm, but she barely noticed the pain as she grasped her sword again. The beast lunged, snapping, and she jumped out of the way. For a split moment the creature turned, and she brought her sword down on its back. It screamed so terribly that Sigrid wanted to break into a sob.

"Go away," she called out to it. "Go! Get!" She swung her sword at it again, hoping perhaps she could scare it away.

But the creature did not relent. Though it was injured, it made another attempt to bite into Sigrid's flesh. With a cry, she slashed the sword upward, the tip piercing through the soft part beneath the creature's jaw.

"Holy shit," Baldr's voice cut through as he came running, his sword raised.

Sigrid pushed herself from the ground with shaky hands. "What the hell is that?" she said under her breath, looking down on the dead monster with wide eyes. "Where the *hell* have you been?" Anger coursed through her veins, fueled by the adrenaline that still kept her on edge.

"I'm sorry!" He looked at her with wide eyes. "I went to set a trap so maybe we'd have fresh meat in the morning!"

Breathing rapid, shallow breaths, Sigrid looked at him with daggers in her eyes. The rational part of her brain knew he'd been off doing something useful, but as the red-hot pain began to set in, all she could see was her fury. "Fuck, Baldr." She brought her injured hand to her chest as droplets of blood hit the grass beneath.

"You're hurt," he gasped, dropping his sword to reach for her hand. His flesh against hers was warm and seemed to temper some of the fire inside her.

"It's shallow," she said, opening her palm for him to inspect.

"I'll clean it. Hold on."

The adrenaline began to fade, leaving Sigrid shaking as Baldr quickly retrieved his small medical kit from his horse. The creature, still spooked from the earlier fight, neighed and pulled at its lead rope. At least they hadn't escaped, Sigrid thought.

When he was finally able to retrieve the kit, he silently cleaned the wound. It wasn't so deep either of them thought it needed stitches, but neither of them was willing to admit they had no real way of knowing. Brigid might have known, perhaps. Sigrid's stomach flipped at the thought of her friend, her guilt at having left once again flaring in her mind.

Baldr turned to look at the creature, its doglike face illuminated by the fire. Sigrid looked toward the sky. When had the sun set?

"Are those ... scales? A dog with scales?" Baldr knelt next to the creature.

"I don't know."

He placed his hand on it. "Cold to the touch," he murmured. "It has fangs. If I didn't know better, I'd say this is a chupacabra."

"I'm sorry, did you say ... chupacabra?"

"I did."

"Those are fairy tales for farmers' children so they don't leave animals unattended. This must be ... something else."

Baldr frowned. "What else? How many dog-faced creatures can you think of that have scales?"

Sigrid frowned. "Should we ... tell someone about this? If it is a chupacabra, surely someone would want to know that fantastical creatures are stalking main roads."

"We should tell the Elders." For a few moments, he fell quiet again. "It looks thin. You can see its ribs."

"Maybe that's just how they look?"

"Maybe." He frowned. "But it could explain why it attacked. Legends say these animals go for livestock, not people."

"That ... could be right."

"Unusual that it would be spotted during the day. They're supposed to be nocturnal."

Sigrid ran her finger along the hilt of her sword. "Could explain why he waited to attack." Looking at her hands, she frowned at the blood that coated them and had begun to dry. "I think I should go to the river to bathe. I don't want to stink of blood all night."

Baldr nodded. "I'll go with you. If there are more of these animals, I don't want you to be caught alone. We should be more vigilant about staying together. We got too comfortable."

CHAPTER ELEVEN

"Wait, look," Baldr said, pulling his horse over to a tree. In the tree were what looked like dolls made of sticks and moss. The two of them searched their surroundings and found more of the little dolls in the trees, as well as circular arrangements of sticks hanging from branches. Woven within the intricate patterns was green thread with beads and colored glass strung in it. The immediate word that came to Sigrid's mind was *rustic*, but upon closer inspection, they were far too detailed for that. They were works of art spread out among the trees, and as far as she could tell, they seemed to be leading in one direction.

"Your contact," she said, taking one of the dolls from a hollowed-out tree and holding it in her hands. Something about it seemed to vibrate. "They said we'd know we were close because of ... decorations, right?" She placed the doll back where she'd found it, certain in her gut that if she didn't, she would regret it.

"Yes. This is a good sign. Let's keep going."

The dolls and statues grew more plentiful as they found their way back to the main road. Where the Heddish road had been paved in the dirt, they found the road now cobbled. Sigrid drew her horse up next to Baldr as they crossed onto the road, the hooves of their horses so much louder on the stone. As they marched along, they came to a large stone arch that crossed over the path. Vines grew over the structure, and she could make out carvings of people underneath. Had they more time, she would have stopped to inspect the carvings, which at a quick glance seemed to be scenes of a story. After some time, they came to another arch, then another, and finally a fourth. The final one was wider, with stairs built to lead to a platform at the top of the structure. Beneath were stationed two guards.

The guards' armor was notably different from the Heddish guards. Their armor was lighter, more easily allowing them to move and climb over the mountain rocks. It was a cool day, so beneath the armor they wore fur, and they wore leather helms that did not restrict their movement.

Baldr and Sigrid slowed their horses as they approached, and the two guard elves held up one hand each in greeting.

"Hello," one of them said. "Names?"

"Baldr," he said, surprising Sigrid by giving his real name. "And Sigrid. We are friends of Inda Foxblood, Elder Foxblood's granddaughter."

The guards nodded, glancing at each other with a hint of curiosity on their faces. "Foxblood, eh? Didn't know they had many dealings with Heddish elves."

Heddish elves? Sigrid held her tongue.

Baldr frowned. "Are we allowed to pass?"

The guards stared at him blankly.

"Huh? Oh, of course," the first guard said. "But before you go, can I ask you a question?"

"What?" Sigrid asked, looking down at the guard that spoke.

The guard looked between them. "Do Heddish elves always have such weird names?"

It was close to nightfall by the time they arrived at the city gates, but even at a distance, Sigrid could see the city was larger than any she could have imagined. Even at first glance, it made Copper City look like a small town. All her life, Sigrid had been told the Kingdom in the Mountains was full of poor elves who barely survived in the cold lands of the north. Though she'd rarely met anyone from Uruachi, the prevailing narrative painted that they were in desperate need of aid but too stubborn to receive help from the noble Heddish. The noblemen who took her to plays and showed her off in secret parlors loved to remind her how people fled the Kingdom in the Mountain for more civilized cities like Hedeby. "I hope Copper City doesn't become *too* civilized," one cull had joked with his drunk friends.

What they found was quite the opposite. Intellectually, Sigrid had known there was more to Uruachi than what they were taught. The common message was that elves would escape the kingdom for Hedeby, but Sigrid had met very few elves from the kingdom in the first place.

Copper City was beautiful. With its colorful buildings and green spaces, Sigrid could not have painted a more beautiful city if she'd been asked. But stepping through Uruachi's front gate left Sigrid feeling as if Copper City were just a reproduction. The elven elements were certainly here. The colorful doors and the inclusion of nature into every bit of the city made her feel oddly at home. Although Copper City was, well, far more copper in color from the mud used to build most of the structures. Uruachi was the color of the mountain itself: dark gray, green, and brown. The buildings had colorful murals painted on the sides of them that reminded Sigrid of the central hub of Copper City. The river they'd followed all the way from home cut through one part of the Uruachi. Streets were built around it, bridges over it, and a blue-painted wall separated the river from the surrounding city.

The gate they'd entered through sat to the side of the river, and the street was railed off with waist-high stone that allowed someone standing to look down at the crashing rocks below. Sigrid hopped off her horse and walked to the edge of the road to look at the river, marveling at it. The air was crisp and cold as the sun began to set, and her breath was visible in the air as she exhaled. She was grateful for the furs they'd been given by the Collective for the journey.

She stood gaping at their surroundings and the sheer number of people and buildings.

"We're supposed to meet her … here," he said, pointing at a marked spot on his map of the city.

"Did you have that the whole time?"

"Yes."

Sigrid laughed, taking the map from him. Even just looking at it on paper, she could tell the city was far larger than Copper City. Streets, which crisscrossed up and down the mountainside, were interspersed with green open spaces. Miniforests had been scattered throughout as if they couldn't bear to be rid of all the natural splendor of the mountain. Buildings were built into the mountain's side almost to its peak, which was topped with an eagle statue so large she wondered how it did not topple onto the city below.

The marked space on the map was toward the north end of the city. The two of them took their horses by the reins and lead them on the journey up the side of the mountain. Though the light was beginning to dim in the sky above, there were lamps along the road that burned an unnatural shade of white to illuminate the street. There didn't seem to be anything powering them, leaving Sigrid to wonder if they were kept alight the same way she kept her candle from burning out back home. That spell was difficult enough as it was, she couldn't imagine how they possibly kept so many lamps lit.

Magical resources were limited, since so few had ever learned. Her mother had been taught to keep a fire burning and passed that tiny bit of knowledge on to Sigrid, but Sigrid couldn't think of anyone who knew more than that. Sure, there were supposed witches that sold charms and spells, but if their magic worked at all, it certainly wasn't instant. Sigrid had always been too skeptical to try, though Cualli swore by a psychic on the Eastside.

As they crept up the mountain, Sigrid peeped through the open doors of any tavern or shop they happened to pass. Most of the shops seemed to be built into multistory buildings, perhaps where the owners or workers lived. The buildings were carved out of stone and were so well designed she couldn't see the lines of stone, a stark contrast to the copper mud and red wood that made most of Copper City's buildings. Beautiful murals were painted on open spaces, and people spilled out of some of the bars. Merry laughter filled her ears. Nobody looked their way, but Sigrid took in every detail she could: the fur-lined cloaks, the feathers that were braided into the hair of many. She found her eyes drawn to the hooded cloak one woman wore, the fabric white and vibrant, giving the stranger the look of a regal snow queen. Sigrid wanted to stop and dip into one of the many clothing stalls they passed, but Baldr looked so determined she did not dare ask him to stray from their mission. Instead, she looked wistfully into a shop window at a fur gown she desperately wanted to try on.

The higher they climbed, the more difficult Sigrid found every step. Stopping, she climbed back on her horse. "It's so hard to breathe."

"Mountain air is thinner," Baldr said. "There are mountains near Hedeby. Have you ever seen one?"

"No. These are my first."

Baldr laughed, patting Sigrid's thigh before hopping back on his horse. The animals whinnied in frustration but moved at their leaders' behest.

"There, there," Baldr murmured to his horse. "We'll get you fed and rested soon. Don't worry."

The sun had set and Baldr was forced to ask for directions multiple times, but eventually, they came to a three-story building. The front door was painted a bright crimson and some sort of birds cast in gold sat at the center. Around the side of the building, she could see another, smaller building, surrounded by a wooden fence. The stables, she assumed.

Sliding off the horses, the two stood awkwardly at the door, glancing at each other.

"I'll ... knock," Baldr decided, stepping forward to rap his knuckles against the painted wood.

The woman that answered was tall and rather imposing. Her hair was cut short at her strong jaw while the back was twisted into two long black braids that fell over her shoulders. "Can I help you?" Her voice was thick and deep, wrapping around Sigrid like a mother's hug.

"I'm Baldr," he said, extending to her a sealed envelope. "You're supposed to be expecting me?"

Sigrid stood behind him, awkwardly holding the reins of both horses. He was the emissary, not her.

The woman took the envelope and opened it, scanning through the contents before turning her deep-set eyes back to Baldr. "Ah, I wasn't sure when I'd next hear from the Collective." Inda turned and spoke in a low voice to someone behind her. A man who looked strikingly like Inda passed by the woman, moving to stand in front of Sigrid.

"Ah, hello," Sigrid said.

The man didn't say anything. He simply took the reins from her hand and led the horses around the side of the building toward what Sigrid had correctly guessed were the stables.

Inda waved the two of them in. The home inside was brightly lit with the same white flames she saw on the street, though these flames sat in sconces along the walls.

Crystals dangled from circular stick designs somewhat similar to the ones they'd found in the forest, though these were more finely crafted. As they ascended a flight of stairs, Sigrid caught a glimpse of herself in a decorative mirror and gasped. Her hair was pulled back and messy, and she looked as if she'd lost a little weight. The woman in front of her was markedly different than the one who had left Copper City two weeks before. She felt a sinking feeling in the pit of her stomach as she thought about the oils and cosmetics she'd left at home. They were such insignificant things, but they'd been so much a part of her daily life that seeing herself without them for so long made her heart drop.

Inda pushed open a door and extended a hand for the two of them to enter. It was a bedroom.

"You two look like you've been on the road for a minute," she said, giving them a smile that softened her hard features. Bowing her head slightly, she gestured toward a bucket full of soap and a clean cloth. "Clean up and meet me downstairs when you're ready. And what was your name, darling?"

"Oh," Sigrid said, looking up at the woman. "Sigrid. Sorry."

"No need for apologies, my dear." The woman chuckled before turning out of the room.

Neither of them spoke until they could no longer hear Inda's steps, but Sigrid immediately dropped her bag and made a dash for the washing pale. "Okay, water, where to find water?" she said to herself, leaving Baldr with an amused expression. Sigrid explored the bedroom, which was quite a bit larger than hers at home, though this one seemed to section off into a privy. There were pipes inside that dispensed water. Sigrid thought Inda must be wealthy if she had private bathrooms in her house. Back home, she and Brigid had found a home with enough plumbing to bring water into the kitchen, but they had to rely on washtubs and the city baths.

Quickly, Sigrid bathed, wanting to stop and enjoy the hot water but knowing it wasn't the time. Wrapping a towel around her body, she reentered the bedroom. Baldr wasn't in the room. "Must have gone without me," she said to herself, a bit frustrated but equally as happy to have had the opportunity to bathe.

Retrieving her only other clean set of clothing from her bag, she dressed and braided as much of her hair as she could before tying it on top of her head to keep it out of the way. Stepping into the hallway, she glanced around. The hallway was narrow, and there were two other doors on that floor before a slim set of stairs led to the next story. Quickly, she hurried down the stairs.

Hearing voices from a room toward the entrance of the house, Sigrid stepped into the room. Instead of couches or chairs, cushions adorned the tiled floor in large heaps.

Inda lounged on one pile, while Baldr sat awkwardly on another.

"Ah, you're ready," Inda said pleasantly. "Baldr was just telling me about your journey. He says you encountered some sort of strange beast you couldn't quite identify."

"Yeah, something like that," Sigrid replied, taking a seat next to Baldr despite the third unused pile of cushions.

Inda lifted a glass of some amber liquid to her lips and drank from it. Her eyes were dark and lined with kohl, and her lips were painted a brilliant shade of crimson. Again, Sigrid had that sudden ache for the luxuries she'd left behind.

Inhaling a sharp breath, Inda said, "Well. Anyway. I'm sure you two are very eager to pass your message along to the Elders. Tomorrow I will meet with them and set up an emergency meeting for you. We are aware of the troubles in Hedeby, and we've watched for some time with great concern. It will be an uphill battle to get all the Elders on the side of backing a war."

Sigrid swallowed. War. That's what they wanted, right? Revolution meant war. Hearing it out of the mouth of a stranger made her feel cold.

"The sooner we can meet with them, the better." Baldr looked to Sigrid, reaching out a hand to settle on her knee. He squeezed. "You can come if you want, or you can explore the city."

"What? I didn't come all this way just to be a tourist."

Inda laughed. "Spirited. I will do my best to get a meeting as quickly as possible. I know this is a timely matter, and I will do everything I can to help you."

CHAPTER TWELVE

The main hall of the mountain palace soared above them as they entered. The view from the outside had been beautiful enough but Sigrid's breath caught in her throat when they stepped into the stone fortress. Walls of rock jutted high, pillars held up the ceiling. Somehow, the ceiling had been painted with a beautiful mural in a circular dome. On one side it told the beginning of elven mythology, the beginning of the world, and each scene had a familiarity to it. There was Hutzil, easily picked out by the massive, colorful feathers worn around his head. He held the world in his hands, and from it, a river flowed across the wall. There was the mother goddess Chalchi giving birth on the bank of a river, the elven people springing forth from where she bled into the soil. Some scenes were not familiar to her, like one that seemed to depict the elven people building great structures.

Halfway down the mural, she spotted a figure she would have recognized no matter the incarnation. Ata stood with two men at her feet, their lips pressed against her toes. The land around her was barren. The men worshiped at her feet, hoping to be lucky enough to lie with her and bring fertility to the soil. The top half of Ata's face was painted red, and she had a golden rose between her brows.

Sigrid could have stood there forever, staring upward with her mouth open, her eyes absorbing every fine detail of the mural, if Baldr had not gently touched her arm and guided her further into the palace. She shot her eyes back for one last glimpse of the most regal painting of her patroness she'd ever seen. It wasn't fair, she thought, for their temples at home to make do with crude carvings. Perhaps once they'd had great art too.

People busied about them. Like in the rest of the city, people seemed to work together to accomplish the day's needs. Soldiers milled about, but unlike the Heddish armies she had become so used to, these soldiers and guards did not all carry weapons. Sure, there were a few at the gates to the city and in various places along the path to the palace, but the ones inside mostly assisted others in their tasks.

"We'll meet with the High Elders here in a bit," Baldr said so that only Sigrid could hear. "Inda should be around here somewhere."

A stir caught their attention. Turning, Sigrid watched as guards marched into the palace. A person was being held between them, shackled with their hands behind their back. Whoever this person was, they were distinctly not an elf. Their hair reached their shoulders in a blond mass like the mane of a lion, but she could see the curve of their ears as they were hurried through the crowd. The guards passed, and Sigrid locked eyes with the captive, whose eyes were large and blue. The prisoner's lips were full and bloodied, and there was a scuff on their cheek.

"Agnar!"

"What?" Baldr peered through the crowd.

The procession was out of view before Sigrid had a chance to process what she'd just seen. Agnar's face was not one she had expected to see again. Ever. She'd certainly never expected to see him in Uruachi.

"Come on," Baldr said, taking Sigrid's hand and pulling her through the crowd after the procession. "Don't get distracted."

"How can you not get distracted? We ran into a strange man on the road and just so happen to see him carted in as a prisoner in a foreign nation!"

Baldr didn't respond.

They followed the guards into a large stone room where three High Elders sat at the top of a dais. Two were not as old as Sigrid had expected, but each of them had white or gray hair that fell in two braids over their shoulders. In the center sat the oldest of the three, her wizened face all lines of many years passed. Her deep-set gaze was cast forward over the prisoner.

"You say you're the child of the Heddish king," she said, her voice almost a croak. The two Elders on either side remained quiet as they waited for Agnar's answer.

"His son," the man confirmed.

"A bastard?" the male elder inquired. "I recall only hearing of one child."

"No, I'm not a bastard. I've known for some time that I am his son, but unfortunately I was never able to tell him," Agnar responded.

Sigrid's mind chugged along as she tried to process Agnar's answer, but it eventually clicked into place. It wasn't that he knew where the princess was. He was the princess. How had she not seen it? Suddenly it was so glaringly obvious that she was embarrassed not to have figured it out.

The three Elders each nodded in understanding. Inda had described them the night before. There were two women, Elders Xochitl and Tozi, and a man by the name of Elder Tonuac.

"Tell us your name, boy," Elder Tonuac said.

Agnar lifted his chin and squared his shoulders, though his lips twitched at being called a boy. "Agnar. I am here with a warning."

"Why should we trust you?" Tozi leaned forward in her chair. She was quite a bit younger than Elder Xochitl, but the lines of age were still clear on her face.

"I cannot answer that for you, but know I would not be here if it were not important. I would be on a ship to anywhere else if it were up to me, but I came because I will not let any more people die unnecessary deaths at the hands of a tyrant."

"Xochitl," Tozi said to the ancient woman next to her.

"Shh," Elder Xochitl said with a wave of her hand, casting a flat look at Elder Tozi. "What danger is there?"

Agnar took a step forward. "My father likes to believe he comes from a long line of conquerors, and that they were set on their path to take what is theirs. I do not need to tell you your own history, how they came and stole your cities and burned your fields until you were forced back into your mountain capital. Now, those elves that remain in Hedeby come under continued fire. The king will not stop with outlawing your religion in the south or keeping your language dead. He is setting his sights north on the Kingdom in the Mountains—on Uruachi—and gathers his armies to invade. There is a rebellion brewing in Hedeby and Copper City, and once they have put down the rebels, they will come for you. The Heddish believe this is their land, and they will not stop until every inch of this land belongs to them. You have been safe for this long because the mountains offer protection, but my father has determined that sorcery will be the key to your destruction. I am begging you to listen to me."

The three Elders leaned in close to each other. After a few excruciatingly long moments, they turned back to Agnar with dark looks on their faces. "You bring very serious news," said Tonuac. He stood and strode down the stairs of the dais to stand in front of Agnar, extending his hand to the human. "We will have more to speak of, but for now you are welcome here. We will give you shelter and safe harbor. Whatever information you can provide, we will listen to."

Baldr's eyes grew wide. He leaned in and whispered in Sigrid's ear, "This changes things."

"Hopefully they will realize it is better to take action now instead of waiting for an army to arrive on their doorstep. Let's see if we can speak with Agnar when this is done." Sigrid tightened her jaw.

Soldiers escorted Agnar back through the crowd, the three Elders following behind. As the prince passed, his eyes caught Sigrid's. Excitement pooled in her chest as his gaze lingered. Soon he was shuffled out the door, leaving her gaze to remain in the direction he'd left until she felt Baldr's hand settle on the small of her back.

"Sorry," he murmured as she jumped.

"It's okay." Sigrid smiled, turning toward the doors with the others as the crowd began to disperse. There was nothing more for them to learn right now.

"Come. We need to see if Inda can still get us an audience."

CHAPTER THIRTEEN

The three High Elders sat at the center of a curved table, with what Sigrid learned was the Elders Council around them. Unlike what the name suggested, they were not all made up of "elders" in the main sense of the word. The Council was made up of elected officials from the city and surrounding towns, and some were as young as Sigrid, while others were old enough to be her great-grandmother. They each sat with a white cloak pulled over their shoulders, save for the three High Elders, whose cloaks were gold and feathered.

Sigrid stood behind Baldr as Inda spoke on their behalf. "We are prosperous," Inda said, squaring her shoulders and clasping her hands at the small of her back. "I believe now is the time for us to aid those who were left behind when we were driven from the south. With me are two revolutionaries sent by a close friend of mine. When I was in Hedeby, I met a woman named Anam, who has now become the leader of a large network of people determined to take power back for the common man. They've lived a life beneath the heel of a king for too long. Baldr, Sigrid, step forward."

Oh boy. Sigrid took a deep breath and strode forward, doing her best to look imposing. She held her chin high and pulled her shoulders back, but in truth, she felt small in front of the eyes of so many important people. The weight of her decision to come felt heavy, and she felt a quick pang of uncertainty in her chest. The monster on the road seemed distant and easily manageable compared to being in front of so many judging eyes.

"Thank you," Baldr said, moving forward as if he had no fear. His voice was strong and clear. Sigrid didn't think her voice would be so assured. "I am Baldr of Hedeby. What Inda says is true. What began years ago, when I was just a child, as a grassroots resistance to the crown and Heddish rule eventually began to grow. Over the years, repression has spread throughout Hedeby. I was forced into the army for simply breaking a curfew, but I was not alone. The drafting of young men as punishment for minuscule infractions runs rampant.

"In the city of Hedeby, our capital, restriction of elvish customs has been steadily on the rise. Though they do not enslave us with chains, they take our history and rewrite it. They take our religion and either bastardize it or force us to believe in Heddish ways. For a while, the further away from the capital one was, the safer they were from the king's proclamations. As long as farms were tended to and food found its way to wealthy tables, the Heddish allowed their influence to spread slowly, like a virus. Now the king has decided we've had too many freedoms, too much choice. What few elven temples there were in the city of Hedeby closed when I was a child, and now that proclamation has spread to the entirety of the nation."

Baldr inhaled, looking between those who were listening. When nobody spoke or attempted to interrupt, he continued, "When I was growing up, elves were restricted to one portion of the city. This was not a rule for all cities and towns, but Heddish human and elf lives are often segregated. Though we were there long before the humans, we are looked down upon, seen as lesser. Even those of us with human heritage are not human enough. Despite all of this, there remained at least one place that retained its heritage, its history: Copper City, which lies slightly more than halfway between here and the capital of Hedeby. My companion here"—he motioned to Sigrid, who clenched her jaw and offered a polite nod—"is from this city. Humans and elves of all walks tend to be more integrated, but the city itself is a bastion of what our land used to be, a relic that must be protected. The king has set his sights on cracking down, closing our temples, and sending Heddish guards to police our streets. They've killed and maimed with impunity. They are not satisfied with taking away our history and our culture, they want to make examples of us. They've killed for stolen loaves of bread, for loitering, for whatever they deem reason enough. They give us schools where we learn of the Heddish conquest and tell us we should be grateful that we're taught to read at all. They call it kindness, generosity, to have our ancestry rewritten.

"I understand this is quite a bit to take in. Over two hundred years have passed since they first arrived, and I am sure it is easy to feel as if we are separate people. But we have come here to ask for your support because we know that we are not separate. We know we come from the same place, and the elves of Hedeby yearn for a time where decisions are not made by conquerors but by those who live and work and make the whole society run. We have already begun to make strides. Unrest has been brewing in Copper City for some time, and it has finally broken free. Just a few weeks past, before we made the journey here, the people of Copper City had had enough. After temples were closed and there was murder in our streets, the people rose up and pushed back against the city guard. The people succeeded in pushing the guard back. It was a small victory, but one that could be felt by the people. We know it is only a matter of time before the king sends his army, who I know to be far more capable than the pathetic city guard, and that is what truly strikes fear into me. I am asking for your help for when that day comes—because it *will* come."

The large room grew eerily quiet, save for the soft gurgling noise of the large fountain behind the Elders.

Elder Tozi leaned forward in her seat. "And you?" she said, looking at Sigrid. "He speaks quite a bit, but you stand tall and proud. You do not strike me as the meek sort. Who are you?"

Sigrid exhaled a sharp breath out of her nose and took a step forward to stand next to Baldr. "Sigrid of Copper City."

"That much I know. How are things from your perspective?"

A million answers swam in Sigrid's mind, and she had a hard time focusing on just one. Her voice caught in her throat, suddenly unable to break free. She fidgeted with the hilt of her sword, thumbing along the iron, and stared forward at the expectant eyes. Pulling from that bit of her she only brought out for work, she stepped forward and held her head high and confident.

"It is as Baldr said." She lifted her chin, the words now flowing from her lips unimpeded. One hand rested on her hip, her elbow out, the other gripped tight the hilt of her sword. "I love my city. I love my people. Not every Heddish person I've met is some elf-hating bigot, but the Heddish leadership sees us as second class. They've grown violent, oppressive. The elves of Copper City are brilliant, like a fire, but the Heddish are nothing more than boots stomping us out. I do not want what we have to be lost. We need help."

The Elders Council broke out into soft murmurs at her words. They turned to each other, discussing what Baldr and Sigrid had said as if the two of them weren't even in the room. After several long minutes, Elder Xochitl stood and raised her hand. "It took quite a bit of courage for the two of you to journey this far. Asking for help is no easy task, but we all find ourselves needing it from time to time. Tell me, both of you, what sort of aid is it you want? Military? Supplies?"

"Supplies and soldiers, first and foremost, but from there whatever can be spared, whatever can help us push the Heddish out of Copper City," Baldr said.

"And Copper City wishes to, what? Become independent? Join Uruachi? Will they ask us to march further south to the capital?"

"With respect," Baldr cleared his throat, "the Collective has tested the waters, has gotten a sense for how people would respond to the Kingdom in the Mountain taking leadership. But that's the thing: you are not a kingdom. You are a nation, a unified people, but our people have been separated for some time. Copper City wants independence. We want to trade openly and freely with Uruachi. There are many towns and villages between Copper City and Uruachi, and territory can be divided. The people will come together to decide what is best. Right now, we need your help to push the Heddish out of Copper

City. Once we achieve independence, we can work together as two elven nations."

More murmuring among the Council broke out. The three Elders at the center spoke in hushed tones between them. Tozi seemed calm, but Xochitl had a look of pure uncertainty on her face. This time they were quieted by Elder Tozi, who stood with both hands raised. "This is an important matter, and I am afraid we will not have an answer for you tonight. Please, we invite you to remain in Uruachi as long as you'd like. Inda, you are hosting them, correct?"

"Yes, ma'am," Inda replied, stepping forward from the shadows.

Tozi said, "Do you need anything, Baldr and Sigrid? Anything to make yourselves comfortable while you are here?"

Inda spoke up. "I can handle whatever it is they need. I look forward to showing them our city, as it is only natural they get to know who we are if they want our help. I've been needing an excuse to visit my favorite shop anyway."

Tozi sighed, exasperated. "Of course, I wouldn't expect any less from you, my dear. We will discuss this among ourselves over the next few days, as we have much that has been brought to our attention. You might have seen us introduce the young Prince Agnar."

"We did," Sigrid replied, glancing sidelong at Baldr.

"Then you know you are not the only one who brings warning of this Heddish king and his aspirations. Give us time, and we will provide you an answer before you return home. You have my word."

While Baldr and Inda spoke with a few Council members, Sigrid stood before a large tapestry. In it, a woman sat on her knees with three golden bowls in front of her. Each bowl seemed to be filled with different ingredients, and colored thread rose from each one as if the bowls were emitting colorful, shimmering smoke. The woman was smiling as she worked, and the colorful smoke rose above her head and formed a circle, where a hunter pointed his arrow at a stag.

"This is Mixcoa, our spirit of the hunt."

Sigrid turned to look at the woman who spoke. Elder Tozi seemed taller up close. The intricate braids on the side of her head fell over her shoulder, a mix of stark-white and peppered gray. The lines on her face weren't deep, but her eyes made her seem older than her appearance alone.

"Spirit?" Sigrid raised a brow, looking back at the tapestry. "For us, she is a goddess. In Copper City, we call her Mixcoa, but I hear in Hedeby they call her Mixa."

"Ah, gods." Tozi nodded. "I've heard of our spirits referred to in such a way by Heddish elves."

Sigrid struggled for a moment. "The Heddish have their gods, and we have ours. I suppose ... they aren't gods for you, are they?"

"No ... not really. We don't have gods. We have spirits."

Sigrid's eyes followed the lines of smoke that ascended into the circle. "I suppose that's one more thing they changed about us."

"Perhaps." Tozi shrugged, turning to fully face Sigrid. "That is how one conquers a people. You don't simply take their land, you change their identity. Calling gods spirits seems small, but it alters how you see them, does it not?"

"Maybe," Sigrid replied, her brows furrowing together. "I suppose I don't think of them as spirits. The concept isn't ... that different, I guess. It makes sense how they would influence such change."

Tozi took Sigrid by the arm and guided her down one of the large hallways, past several more tapestries, each with their own scenes. "Spirits are the souls of the land. They provide us with magic, and in return, we offer them sacrifices. Magic always requires something to give."

To that Sigrid gave a hearty nod. "I was taught that by my mother. Magic is not common in Hedeby, not even in Copper City. It exists, of course, just ... in small batches. Keeping a candle lit. Finding a lost item. Charms for small bouts of luck. But we have nothing like what I've seen here."

Tozi sighed wistfully and gave Sigrid a sad look. "Such a pity. Elves have been in touch with magic since we were created by the spirits. Magic should come innately to us."

"I can only do little amounts. I've always wanted to learn more, but ... there just isn't any way to learn. Anyone with access to those ways is likely Heddish or rich. Or both, usually."

"Humans have their own magic, of course. I don't know if it is different than ours, but they certainly seem to treat it differently. I have heard from Inda that there are a few humans who practice, but otherwise, it is a rather ... closed subject, isn't it?"

The tap of their feet through the hall grew louder as they made their way down yet another hall of tapestries, and the loud cacophony of voices faded into a dull whisper. "I've heard there are those who are rather proficient," Tozi said. "It is too bad you must leave when we have your answers. You could learn here, you know."

Sigrid thought about this carefully, her eyes falling on another tapestry. This one showed a man with horns growing from his head holding a bundle of burning herbs above him. She wondered, briefly, which spirit this was. She could think of no god with horns to compare it to. "That is ... such a tempting idea. Learning magic would be a dream. There is so much I wish I could do, but truth be told, I have a family waiting for me back home. People who rely on me. This journey ... must come to an end. I have to return home."

Tozi nodded. "Understandable. Well, we should return. Looks as if we took a little detour. You and I will surely find more time to discuss this, however. I have a feeling about you, Sigrid."

"A feeling?"

Tozi simply shrugged and guided her back to the now dwindling room of Council members. "I have good intuition when it comes to others. I can tell you have the makings of a great woman. Even if you aren't able to become a great practitioner of magic, I know there is a grand future for you. A hard one, maybe. But grand."

"There you are," Baldr said, turning to greet the two of them. He was speaking with Elders Tonuac and Xochitl. "I was telling the Elders about the attack we experienced in the woods. The creature."

"This is very concerning," Tonuac said, nodding, his heavy brows nearly concealing his eyes. "What you call a chupacabra, we call the ahuizotl. It is a spirit beast, but it rarely attacks people, and has not been spotted in decades."

"Wait." Sigrid held up a hand. "There're more of them?"

Tonuac nodded. "They are rare creatures, but if what Baldr says is true, something has brought them out of hiding. They are intelligent creatures. They frequent bodies of water where animals stop to drink and capture their prey there. Were you near water, by chance?"

Sigrid nodded. "By a river."

"Not an unusual place for them to hunt. It was once thought they lured people to drown, though that is an old superstition created by those who do not understand them."

Sigrid frowned. "Well, that unusual creature tried to kill me. It was wild, like it was starving. There were cattle nearby, though, so that doesn't make any sense. Why attack us?"

Tonuac fell quiet in thought, his bony hand holding tight to a staff that all but kept him upright. "As I said, these are spirit creatures. We would do well to consult with priests. Perhaps they might know why this creature acted in such a way. It is too bad you could not bring the body."

"Yes," Sigrid replied flatly. "Such a shame."

Baldr placed a hand on Sigrid's arm. "Elders, I do believe we've had quite a long day. If you don't mind, I think Sigrid and I will head out for the evening. Get some fresh air. We will hear from you soon, yes?"

"Oh, yes, yes." Tonuac nodded. "We will not keep you waiting any longer than we must. Good evening."

Baldr steered Sigrid away from them, and the further away they got, the more she felt the muscles in her body relax. "That was more stressful than I realized it would be," she said to him as they passed through the doors into the fresh, crisp evening air.

Baldr smiled at her, slipping an arm around her shoulder. "Yes, and we've been traveling for a long time. I doubt we'll hear from them tomorrow, so we should spend the day getting some much-needed rest. Inda wants to take us for food. They eat lots of fish from the river, and I hear it is good raw."

Sigrid made a face. "Raw fish? That sounds ... unappetizing. But I trust Inda, I suppose."

Baldr pulled her close and squeezed her shoulder. "You did well in there, by the way."

"Did I? I felt like a fool. I've never done anything like that before."

"Not many have. I'm proud of you, Sigrid. You've come a long way."

Heat rushed to her face and suddenly she was very aware of the warmth of his body, even through the fur-lined clothing she wore. The urge to kiss him was strong, but she resisted. Now was not the time, she told herself. Not. The. Time.

"Hey!"

Sigrid and Baldr looked around toward the voice, soon spotting an unexpected visitor.

"Prince Agnar," she chirped.

"Ah, well, you don't have to call me Prince Agnar. But yes. That's me." He gave her an awkward smile. He looked tired, she noted. There were purple bags beneath his eyes and his golden hair lacked its previous luster.

"So you knew the location of, well, yourself," said Sigrid.

Agnar laughed. "Ah, yes. Seems fate has intervened. It took everything in me not to do a double take when I saw you in the crowd."

Baldr was deathly quiet and motionless. She'd never seen him shut down so quickly in front of anyone. "Are you staying here, at the palace?" Sigrid offered him a wide smile to offset Baldr's cold stare.

Agnar nodded. "They've been kind enough to put me in a guest suite, though I've been instructed to remain within the palace unless I have an escort. I should be grateful they aren't as inhospitable to outsiders as my father."

"Then we'll come calling tomorrow. Tonight, I think I'd like to get some early rest," said Sigrid.

"Completely understandable." Agnar laughed, bowing slightly at her words. "If I had to run into strangers in the wood, it seems I ran into the right pair."

A smile gave way on Sigrid's lips. "Oh, we'll have questions for you. Good night, Agnar."

Agnar bowed gracefully and turned to disappear into the mountain. A few feet away, someone began to follow him. The escort, Sigrid assumed, based on the hatchet at their side.

"What's with you?" Sigrid frowned, climbing onto the back of her horse that was tethered outside. Inda's horse was gone, so thankfully they remembered the rather easy trek back to her home.

"What?" Baldr huffed.

"With him. I've never seen you so cold to anyone."

"I wasn't cold! I'm just ... wary."

"Baldr, you were frigid." She frowned, watching him climb on the back of his horse and head down the road. She signaled her horse to follow. "I don't think he's a threat."

"We don't know."

"I suppose we'll find out."

CHAPTER FOURTEEN

Baldr's mood had been sour all morning. He remained in his room until the time came for them to leave, and the three made the short trek to the mountain palace to greet Agnar. Meeting them in the main hall, Agnar smiled brightly, though Baldr could not be bothered to smile in return.

"Where should we go?" Agnar asked.

Inda shrugged. "The Commons is always an easy place to go."

"The Commons?" Sigrid and Agnar asked at the same time, their eyes meeting. He shot her a quick smirk.

"Food hall, basically," Inda replied. "We have a few around the city, but the Commons is the largest."

"Oh!" Sigrid looked down the road at the expanse of the city. "We have a couple of places like that in Copper City. We had more, but they've ... mostly been shut down in the last few years. One or two are still around, thankfully."

"Well, ours aren't going anywhere, and I'm starving," Inda replied, leading the three of them on foot through the winding streets. Seeing the city in the daytime was a new experience. It was full of bright colors, and even the cobblestones in some streets were painted and cheerful.

The building they arrived at was far larger than Sigrid had expected. Where the cafeterias back in Copper City were far smaller, more akin to restaurants, this was a massive building. Easily three stories tall, there were various kitchens where people could line up for whatever was on the menu that day. There was far more variety than anything in Copper City. Long tables filled the center of the room, and Sigrid watched people climb the spiraling stairs to sit in the upper levels.

Agnar gaped at the sight. "So, what, this is like a communal ... kitchen?"

Inda shrugged. "Sort of. It exists to ensure everyone is fed, no matter who you are. Do you not have these in Hedeby?"

"No," Baldr replied before Agnar could speak. "Not like this. A few restaurants, taverns, places like that, but no places where you can get a free meal. If you cannot afford food in Hedeby, you do not eat."

Agnar shifted, his head lowering and eyes casting toward the ground. Sigrid watched him. "I'm starving," she said. "Let's find what we want and meet somewhere?"

"I'm a fan of the third floor," Inda replied. "You can get a table overlooking the city."

"Third floor then. To the food!"

Inda, knowing exactly what she wanted, strode off to one of the kitchens near the back of the building. Sigrid, Agnar, and Baldr wandered from kitchen to kitchen, eying the menus written in chalk on the stone wall. Though Baldr and Sigrid found food that piqued their interest, Agnar found himself unsure. He followed close to Sigrid as she briefly separated from Baldr, taking a spot in line for a hearty bean stew served with a fried, crispy flatbread. He hovered behind her with his hands tucked into his cloak, his hair falling forward to half mask his face.

"So ..." Sigrid cleared her throat. She'd never been around royalty. "You came all this way alone?"

Agnar nodded, his blue eyes peeking out from beneath his golden hair. "Save for the night with the two of you, yes. I gathered maps, a horse, provisions, and waited for an opportunity. Truth be told, I couldn't have prepared in every single way. If I'd taken someone, though, I'm not sure I would have made it this far."

The line moved a few steps.

"I imagine it took quite a bit to make it all the way here. This is a long way from home. You could have gone anywhere."

"I suppose," he shrugged, straightening up a little. "At first I thought about catching a ship and sailing wherever I could find solid land far, far away. But ..."

"But what?"

Agnar shook his head, his brows knitting together. A jolly-looking man handed them both rounded wooden trays, each with a bowl of stew and the crispy bread. Sigrid got the distinct impression he didn't want to speak so publicly, and she couldn't blame him.

Upstairs, they found Inda and Baldr seated at a table near a window. Inda was right—it was a rather nice view of the city. In truth, most angles were rather beautiful to Sigrid, as the city lay on the slope of the mountain. The view was breathtaking, especially from so high up. It almost made the thin air more bearable.

"What did you find?" Sigrid asked as she sat next to Baldr.

"Turkey!" He gestured to his plate as if presenting a dish of gold. "Stuffed bread, turkey, rice. Honestly, this alone makes me not want to go home."

Inda laughed. "Our food is certainly one of our best qualities. You should see the Commons when there's a festival! Worthwhile if you don't mind waiting an hour to eat."

Sigrid didn't hesitate to dig into her food. The stew was savory, and the bread made for a nice scoop. She danced in her seat as she chewed. "Finally, something good about this journey."

"Hey now," Baldr teased. "We've had a good time together."

"I suppose we have." She sighed, turning from him to feign ambivalence. Peeking at him with one eye, her lips curled into a smile.

Inda waggled her fingers at them as her other hand lifted her wooden cup to her lips. "Quite the journey you two are on. It must be exciting."

Agnar glanced between the two. "I may be a little late in realizing this, but you're not married, are you?"

Baldr and Sigrid glanced at each other before a grin spread across Sigrid's lips. "Yes ... Married."

Inda peered between the two. "Is that how you traveled? Disguised as a married couple? Oh, how scandalous."

Sigrid laughed, seeing out of the corner of her eye the darkening of Baldr's cheeks. Everyone but Baldr smirked. "It seemed like the most believable lie. Women don't travel alone very often."

"Why is that?" Inda popped a piece of chicken in her mouth.

"Heddish men are pigs, and they've worked very hard at spreading their rather unfavorable views of women to our men."

Agnar shifted in his seat. "Heddish women run the household," he said. "Some are allowed to become warriors."

Baldr tore apart a piece of bread. "And some are spoiled housewives."

The noise of the building faded away as tension rippled between Agnar and Baldr. Sigrid settled her hand on the small of Baldr's back as if to tell him it was okay.

"They see their women as second-class citizens, regardless of status," Baldr said as he tore into a piece of meat.

Agnar exhaled a sigh. "It's gotten better."

Baldr's eyes narrowed. "Perhaps for the wealthy."

With that, Agnar raised his hands in defeat. "I am not here to fight you, Baldr. I can understand if you don't trust me, but I am not your enemy. I'm here. How many other humans can say that?"

Baldr's eyes did not move from Agnar's face for a long moment. "You're right," Baldr said simply, using his bread to pick up a piece of turkey. "I am in no mood to spoil my dinner anyway."

It was silent for some time, but Inda eventually cut through the awkward fog like a hot knife. "I heard you were attacked by something on the road."

"Yeah, an animal," Sigrid said, laughing into her cup. "Did you come across anything strange on your journey here, Agnar?"

He shook his head. "No, not really. I was pretty good at staying out of trouble, and nobody really noticed me. Just another rover." He sighed. "Everything feels surreal. Maybe that's just because I've never spent this long away from home before."

Sigrid nodded, flashing him a smile and reaching across the table to pat his hand. "I can understand. I've never been this far from home either."

"At least you are among others like you. I doubt there are more than a handful of humans in this entire city."

"Yes, it must be quite awful to be in the minority," Baldr replied, his voice dripping with his distaste.

Inda clicked her tongue. "Baldr, be nice. Agnar has come a long way, and from what I can tell, you're on the same side."

"So I keep getting told."

Agnar's lips were drawn into a flat line, and he seemed to choose his words carefully. "No, no, I understand. I'm sure it is hard to trust someone from the exact class of people you're rebelling against. I get it. Truly. I would have a hard time trusting me in your position. I am here to help, however. I hope I can prove that."

Baldr glanced between Inda and Sigrid, his fingers curling tightly around his utensils. His eyes cast down to the food in front of him, and he stuffed a bit of meat into his mouth. Taking his sweet time to chew and swallow, he did not look up.

Sigrid pressed her knee against Baldr's beneath the table. "For me, there are things about this city that feel very familiar, but more that don't. It feels surreal to be somewhere I'm not worried about guards or entitled human noblemen."

Agnar gave an awkward laugh, poking at his food. "Food's very good, though, I will admit. Such a shame my father cannot simply work with the elves. We could establish great trading routes here."

"Your father shouldn't be the one making those decisions," Baldr said tensely. "It was our land first. It should be in our hands."

Agnar bristled. "I understand my father is not a perfect ruler, but—"

Baldr interrupted. "But what? You know he cannot remain in power."

"I know." Agnar frowned, pushing aside his plate. "But there are a lot of humans in Hedeby, and you can't simply get rid of them. We should work together."

Baldr scoffed, sitting back in his chair with his hands gripping the edge of the table. "I know good humans. The good ones are the ones who don't control great swaths of land that don't belong to them. They live in small homes and live modest lives."

Agnar bristled. "It isn't my fault I was born the way I am. I didn't ask to be stuck here."

"Stuck?" Baldr threw his hands into the air with a cynical laugh. "You aren't stuck. You can choose to do what you want at *any point*. You could go back home right now, and your life would be the same. Don't think just because you've done one good thing that you will be accepted."

Sigrid exhaled a tired sigh and knocked the bottom of her cup against the wood table to get their attention. "Stop. You're both frustrated, but stop."

Baldr shot her a terse look but ultimately shrugged his shoulders in resignation. "Apologies. Perhaps I am tired."

Inda pointed toward one of the kitchens. "They have some wonderful tea there. Will wake you right up."

Baldr nodded and stood, heading off with his head down. Agnar exhaled a sigh. "I'm sorry. I'm not trying to start trouble."

Shaking her head, Sigrid reached across the table to pat Agnar's hand. "Don't worry. He's got a lot of reason to be angry if we're going to be honest. He's from Hedeby and from all his accounts, it doesn't seem like elves are treated very kindly there. He's a half-elf, so I'm sure his experience has been difficult."

Agnar's face fell, his teeth biting his bottom lip until it turned red. "No, no they're not. It was something that just seemed normal for most of my life. I ... didn't question it."

Inda smiled sweetly at the prince, her arm snaking around his shoulder. "There, there, dear. You did a great thing by coming to warn us. We don't know how the Elders will respond just yet, but whatever they decide, you came to warn us. Baldr will realize in time his own plea for help is strengthened by your revelation. His chances for success were far less before you arrived. He is passionate, and sometimes passion can make us stubborn."

When Baldr returned, he tossed down a flyer he'd found somewhere on his journey. He did not, Sigrid noticed, have any tea. "There's a tavern opening. Tavern means alcohol. Let's go."

Inda raised a manicured brow. "What?"

"Tavern," Baldr replied. "Drinks. Then you can show us the rest of the city. If you want me to relax, then let's do something relaxing."

The three at the table looked between themselves before looking back up at the rather determined man. Sigrid shrugged and broke the silence. "Sure. But you're buying my drinks."

CHAPTER FIFTEEN

The tavern itself reminded Sigrid of Inda's main room, with all the cushions and pillows in circles on the floor. Patrons sat and lounged about, drinks in hand, with short tables at the center of each circle of pillows. It was still early enough in the day that there weren't too many people present. Sigrid found herself a large cushion on the floor and flopped into it, sending Baldr off to bring her a drink. Agnar took a seat next to her.

"Aren't you going to get a drink?" she inquired.

He shrugged. "Maybe. I'm not much of a drinker if we're being honest. My father and mother would bathe in ale if they could, but I tend to shy away from the stuff. Not that I can't enjoy a drink now and again, but ... perhaps it's just a bit early for me."

Sigrid opened her mouth to respond, but Baldr returned just then with two tall clay mugs. The tops nearly foamed over. Inda approached behind him, four smaller glasses held between her fingers. "Since you're all new here," she said, taking a seat and pushing one glass toward each of them, "I thought you might enjoy our signature liqueur. It's made from the sap of a local plant."

Sigrid eyed the glass. The contents were white, almost the color of milk, and in truth, she wasn't so sure about trying it. She'd never had a liqueur quite that color before. "What is it?"

"Seco!" Inda beamed with excitement. "The sap is fermented and creates this! It's delicious. Very sweet."

Agnar exchanged looks with Sigrid before offering an awkward smile. "I suppose one wouldn't hurt."

"Shall we toast to something?" Inda asked, lifting her glass in the air. "How about we toast to the future. May it lean in our favor."

Sigrid nodded, lifting the glass and clinking it with the other three. Shooting it back, she noted the sweet flavor that almost masked the punch of the alcohol. Slamming the glass on the table, she shivered. "That's good." She nodded, tapping the rim of her glass. "I might get another one of those."

Agnar did not look quite as enthused. "Oh, it's fine," he replied politely.

Baldr followed his shot with a drink from his mug. "Too sweet," he replied.

Sigrid rolled her eyes. "Too sweet. Who doesn't like sweets? It makes it so much easier to get drunk that way."

Inda laughed, but Baldr simply pointed to her mug. "Give that a try. It's a wonderful beer."

Sigrid lifted the mug to her lips and took a sip. The drink was earthy and bold, but a little too dry for her tastes. She took a deeper drink anyway. If she was going to drink, she was going to enjoy it, she determined. "It's fine," she said. "I think I like the shot better. I could do a few of those."

"Tsk, careful," Inda said, waggling a finger. "They'll hit you hard. I wouldn't do more than one of those if you're going to have that beer. It's too early for you to be too far into your cups."

The tension from earlier that day seemed to dissipate with time. Baldr relaxed, regarding Agnar with slightly more warmth, though he was careful to avoid anything that revealed too much about the Collective. Agnar, for his part, attempted to engage with Baldr as politely as possible. He was friendly and warm, so much so that Sigrid caught Baldr slipping and laughing at Agnar's jokes. She watched the two interact as they continued to drink. Inda or Baldr eventually brought two more rounds of beer. Baldr would stop smiling when he realized he was being too friendly, but the more drinks he had, the more he simply seemed to forget Agnar was his supposed enemy.

"You're telling me you had an affair with your lady-in-waiting, and your parents didn't notice for how long?" Baldr laughed.

"Two years," Agnar grinned. He might have intended not to drink, but that first shot seemed to be enough to encourage him to join the others. "Her name was Magna and she was beautiful and plump. Of course, I loved her for far more than the width of her hips and the softness of her belly, but it didn't hurt that she was a pleasant handful. When my father found out, he sent her to be married to some nobleman with an estate outside the city."

Sigrid pouted. "Oh, how sad."

"He shouldn't have cared. If he'd accepted who I was, she would have been good marriage potential. Her family is wealthy. I may not be able to get her pregnant but ... she and I discussed it. If my father had allowed it, I would've carried a child from her brother, and we'd have raised it as our own. Of course, my father didn't go for that. Oh no. He didn't mind if I had mistresses, but I had duties as a daughter. I never dared to tell him I am his *son*, but sometimes I wonder if my mother knew. Or suspected."

Sigrid frowned. "I don't understand. I know the Heddish are far stricter in their ideas of love, but ..."

"If I weren't royalty, it probably wouldn't matter. Even most nobility has far more freedom than I do—did. But, at the end of the day, my family believes it has certain obligations."

"I'm sorry," Sigrid said softly, resting her cheek on the back of her hand. "I can't imagine what that is like."

Baldr inhaled slowly, his eyes settling on the prince. To Sigrid, he looked contemplative, his eyes seemed to bore through Agnar's flesh as if to read him to his core.

Sigrid reached her hand beneath the table and settled it on Baldr's knee. His hand dropped, finding hers, and their fingers wrapped together. She felt him relax beneath her soft touch. The familiar warm feeling that came from his touch filled her body, and for a moment she forgot all about her attraction to Agnar. When she pulled away and lifted her mug to take a long drink and hide the color that rose in her face, she briefly considered how rarely she'd ever found herself attracted to anyone. There had been men and women here and there, but to feel so viscerally in her bones the pull toward even one person, let alone two, was strange. The time they'd spent together had brought them close, and even now as she looked at him, she felt her heart begin to race. That, certainly, was not a feeling shared when she looked at Agnar, no matter how painfully beautiful she found him.

"Sigrid," Inda said. "Sigrid!"

Sigrid looked up. "What?"

"I asked you a question. What is it you do back home?"

The curly-haired elf blushed and offered an awkward laugh. "Sorry. Suppose I lost myself in thought for a moment. These drinks are starting to hit me. Back home? I am ..." She paused, wondering suddenly how her profession might be taken here. Clearing her throat, she continued, "We call ourselves 'painted women.' I don't know if that's what we're called everywhere. I am a ... ah ... courtesan."

Inda nodded, but the news didn't seem to faze her at all. Her lips turned up in a smile. "Oh, I am familiar with the work. We have our own painted women here in Uruachi, though I'm sure the position is quite different. It is more respected. The profession is too tainted by Heddish morals down south, restricting it from being what it could be."

Sigrid exhaled a relieved sigh. "What are the painted women here like?"

"They are regarded more as priestesses of Ata than the mere companion you are considered to be down south. Not to say they are never sought simply for those services, but they play a far larger role. They bless farms with fertility, and great tributes are made to have the chance to perform in a ritual with them."

Agnar coughed on his drink. "Wait, painted women? I've heard the term before. That is an elven thing, yes?"

"Well"—Sigrid pursed her lips—"it started that way. In Copper City, it sort of became a catchall for all of us. I've never met a human woman who used the term, though."

"Ah," Agnar's cheeks turned a soft shade of red. "I see. In Hedeby we just call them whores." It was Sigrid's turn to bristle, and Agnar was quick to notice. "Not that there's anything wrong with being a whore!"

"I don't like that term." She frowned. Baldr slipped his hand onto her knee. "But yes, I suppose I'm a whore. A harlot. A lady of the night. Whatever you want to call me. I'm still a painted woman."

Agnar shot her an apologetic look and bowed his head. "I meant no offense. I was just surprised. You do not strike me as a … painted woman."

"Well, I'm not wearing the paint that marks me." She looked at Inda. "Do painted women wear the paint here? I imagine they do, if they carry that name."

She nodded. "Yes, they do. The art is beautiful and elaborate. The more elaborate, the higher their ranking and importance. Because they influence fertility, the highest-ranking painted women often serve advisory roles to the Elders Council. Perhaps we will find time to visit a temple of Ata before you leave."

Sigrid perked up. "Oh, I'd love that. Back home, Ata and the painted woman are rather … separated at this point. Elven painted women will often pay homage to their roots, I certainly do, but it's not a religious position anymore."

"Such a shame," Inda replied. She tapped her fingers on the table, her eyes scanning over the three. "Well. I do believe I should be going. I still have business to attend to, and now I am perhaps too drunk to do it. Hopefully, the trip back home will sober me up. Baldr, Sigrid, feel free to remain and enjoy your evening. I doubt we have any news from the Elders quite yet."

Sigrid nodded at the woman as she stood. Baldr and Agnar both raised their mugs to their host.

"Thank you for showing us this wonderful tavern," Baldr said, perhaps a little giddy with drink. "I know you wanted to show us a lot more, but this will do for now."

Inda laughed, patting Agnar and Baldr on the head before heading out the tavern door. The three were left together, momentarily stuck in awkward silence. Sigrid exhaled a breath and shot everyone a wide smile. "We should get another one of those seco drinks."

"Sigrid, you've had, like, four beers." Baldr frowned.

"So?" She stood, nearly tripping on a pillow, and sashayed toward the bar. Returning a few moments later with a round of drinks, she plopped back into her spot and pushed a shot toward each of the men.

Baldr laughed, lifting the glass and holding it at arm's length. "I think I've had more drinks on this adventure with you than I have in the last six months."

Sigrid fluttered her lashes at him. "Oh, my dear, I am quite good at drinking. But you're right. Perhaps we've been drinking quite a bit. Let's have this last drink, and we'll walk Agnar back to the palace. We can make it back to Inda's, can't we, Baldr?"

He shrugged and brought the shot to his lips. The three of them downed their drinks in sync, each slamming their glasses on the table when they were finished. Baldr helped Sigrid off the ground, and Agnar trailed after them as they exited the building. Behind them, a man stood from his seat and followed. Had someone been following them the entire time? Of course, Sigrid thought. Agnar still needed supervision.

Outside, the sun had set, leaving the city illuminated by thousands of flickering lights. Sigrid spun around in the street, her arms raised above her head. "It is so lovely here," she said. "If I could, I think I'd stay. My legs would be so strong from all the steep hills!"

"Your legs look rather strong as it is," Agnar said, taking her hand and twirling her in a circle as if dancing. "You say you are a harlot, and yet you have the body of a shield-maiden."

"Thank you, thank you." Sigrid laughed, pulling her hand from Agnar's grasp and bowing dramatically. "I do train very hard."

"It's true," Baldr interjected, catching Sigrid by the waist and turning her in the direction of the palace. He'd had just as much to drink, but once again she found herself far more affected by it. "I've seen her skills in action and suffered defeat at her hands."

"Ah, well, I'm sure anything in her hands is sweet."

Sigrid giggled. "Such a sweet-talker, my dear prince. I'm sure there must be someone back home who would be jealous of such words."

Baldr glanced between the two of them and silently began the hike toward the palace.

Agnar bounced along next to Sigrid, a brightness in his eyes and ruby tint to his pale cheeks. "To your assumption, no, there is no single person. I have been so focused on my job I have had little room for romantic notions, save the tale I told you before." He leaned in, his lips so close to her ear she could feel his breath. She had the sudden urge to kiss him, but even she could tell that was the drink's suggestion. "It seems I have caused a bit of jealousy still. Your lover here does not like when I provide you much-deserved attention."

Sigrid giggled, casting her unsteady gaze at the man several paces in front of them. "When we met, he was a rather silly fellow. He acts so seriously around you. I don't know if it's jealousy or distrust."

Baldr spun around at that, eliciting a surprised gasp from Sigrid's drunken lips.

"I am not jealous."

Agnar snorted. "But you are! Dear Baldr, you have nothing to worry about. I am, if nothing else, a man of honor."

"Sigrid can do what she wants," he replied tersely. "Sigrid and I are close. We don't need to tell you our relationship."

"Ah!" Agnar raised a fist. "So there is a relationship!"

Sigrid giggled and patted Agnar's shoulder. "Stop teasing him. What Baldr and I are will remain between us. You're so very nosy, Aggy."

"Aggy?" He scoffed. "Now you're giving me nicknames?"

She took him by the hand and dragged him forward, catching Baldr's hand with her other. Sigrid pulled the two along up the hill, huffing and laughing. "Enough with this silly chest-beating. It's beautiful out."

Baldr exhaled. "She's my wife, you know," he said.

Agnar laughed. "So that is where this tension comes from. Perhaps this ruse has become more!"

Sigrid cast a grin over her shoulder at the blond prince. "He was very respectful, don't let him fool you. Behind closed doors, he kept his hands to himself and everything!"

"You are a stronger man than I," Agnar lamented, gripping Sigrid's hand a little tighter.

Baldr shrugged. "Probably."

"Tsk, Agnar," Sigrid scolded, shaking his hand to chastise him. "We've had a bit of a journey to focus on. Little time for anything raunchy."

"Sounds like an excuse to me," Agnar replied. "But I suppose I can understand keeping it professional."

Sigrid guided them up the long road to the palace, keeping both their hands firmly in her grasp. The tension between Agnar and Baldr subsided again, the two even cracked a few jokes at Sigrid's expense. It felt cheerful, reminding Sigrid a little of those slow nights at the brothel where they sat around and joked about each other. Baldr might not have been Agnar's greatest fan, but Sigrid found herself enjoying him more by the moment. Brigid would like him, she thought. She'd enjoy his humor. A sudden crush of homesickness washed over her, forcing her to drop their hands as they approached the palace.

"Are you all right?" Agnar asked, reaching out to retake her hand.

"I'm fine," she replied with a sigh. The alcohol had begun to burn off from their exercise, and she found herself wanting another drink. "I was thinking of Brigid."

"Who?" Agnar blinked.

"My friend. My closest friend. She's back home, but I was just thinking of her. I was thinking how she'd find you funny."

"Would she?" Baldr sniffed.

"I think so." She smacked Baldr's arm. "Agnar, thank you for coming with us today. We'll see you tomorrow. Or the next day. Or ... whenever we get brought back in for a meeting."

He nodded, leaning forward to press a kiss on her cheek. Baldr visibly bristled, which only seemed to bring a grander smile to Agnar's lips. "I'll see you soon. Good night, both of you."

CHAPTER SIXTEEN

The pair returned to Inda's. The journey back was quiet and, perhaps, a little awkward. When they returned, they found the house silent. Inda must have gone somewhere else, Sigrid thought. The two made their way to the kitchen to find a bit of coffee to brew.

"I'm sorry," he said after an extended silence, scooping coffee from a tin into a press. "I acted like a fool around him tonight. I suppose ... I have some misgivings about Agnar."

Sigrid sighed, taking the pot of hot water off the stove to pour into the press. "I understand why you are unsure about him, but I really don't think he's here to do anything nefarious. He seems to genuinely want to help. Why would he come all this way alone if he doesn't mean what he says?"

"I know it doesn't make any sense for me to be suspicious, but it's hard to separate him from his family. He might not be the one in charge, but he's still lived a spoiled existence."

"I doubt someone with a happy life would be so quick to turn on it." Sigrid placed the pot back on the stove. "Something tells me there's a little more to it."

Baldr was quiet for a moment, his face drawn and heavy. Finally, he swept his fingers through his long black mane of hair. "I promise this isn't about jealousy. I ..." He paused, carefully deciding his words. "You know I am attracted to you. But ... I just don't think it's a good idea for anything to happen. Not right now. We have a lot to do, and it would just be a distraction. This is on me, Sigrid. Don't feel like you've done anything wrong."

Sigrid leaned against the wall with her eyes never leaving him. Her heart sank a bit hearing how he felt. Knowing he felt for her as much as she did for him did not make her feel any better. It would be easier knowing he was just a flirt and nothing more. But he wasn't. He was, she felt, being responsible by not pursuing anything with her. It wasn't the right time, and relationships were all about timing.

"It's okay," she replied softly. "I know we haven't spoken about it too much, but ... I think we both knew it wouldn't be appropriate to pursue anything right now. And I appreciate you being honest with me. I want you to know that I do also feel for you, but if now isn't the time, it isn't."

Baldr moved forward and stood in front of her, one hand settling on her shoulder. She could feel the heat of him through her shirt and her heart sped up in her chest. She looked up at him and took all of him in—his soft brown eyes, his full lips, the sharp angles of his handsome face. She reached up and touched his hair, brushing back the raven-black strands.

"Sigrid, you are a wonderful woman. Maybe when things are more settled, when we aren't ... on this journey, perhaps we'll have the room for something between us."

"Maybe," she said with a sigh, her shoulders falling.

Sigrid forced a smile and patted his cheek, then stepped around him to head toward her room. She didn't bother with the coffee.

The Temple of Ata was far larger than the one in Copper City. Towering above her, the temple was painted in bright reds and blues, its rounded windows sporting beautiful stained glass. Sigrid's chest constricted. Exhaling a deep sigh, she stepped forward and pushed open the large, intricately carved front door. It led into a large room with stairs leading to the second story at the far corner. There was a large statue at the center of the room. The figure was imposing, standing tall above the women who tended to the incense and offerings left beneath. Sigrid inhaled a sharp breath as she gazed upon the statue. In Copper City, their image of Ata had been far more humble, a crude carving that had worn down over the years. This one was intricate, so lifelike in its reproduction that Sigrid wondered if her flesh would be warm upon touch. She was distinctly elven, with her tall stature and long, pointed ears. Her eyes were cast upward, her hip cocked to one side, and her arm draped over the side of her body, accentuating her curves. The other arm lifted into the air, holding a bowl with incense burning in the center. Her plush lips fell open, and the statue was so intricate Sigrid could see her teeth between. The statue's skin was painted a beautiful, deep bronze, her hair dark and cascading over her shoulders. The sheer attention to detail struck Sigrid. The temple in Copper City did its best with what it had, but it took an artist of the highest caliber to create such a lifelike creation.

A woman, her lips painted a deep red, approached Sigrid. The flower on her forehead was elaborate and glimmering gold. "Welcome," she said, regarding Sigrid warmly and outstretching her hands. Sigrid took her hands, unable to hold back a bright smile. "A new patron."

"Oh, thank you," Sigrid replied giddily. "This is my first time here. I'm not from this city, and our temple is not nearly so grand."

"I'm sure it is perfect in its own way," the woman replied. "Are you from one of the northern towns?"

"Oh, no." Sigrid laughed. "Copper City is to the south. A week by horseback. I'm Sigrid."

"Sigrid?" The woman's eyebrow raised. "It is a pleasure to meet you. I am Chimalma, the high priestess of this temple. I'm not sure we've ever had a visitor from Copper City."

"I am a painted woman back home, though from what I understand, the position is a little different here. I suppose I wanted to come to pay tribute."

Chimalma took Sigrid by the small of her back and led her deeper into the large room. Standing in front of the statue, the two looked up at it. The high priestess spoke: "The beautiful thing about Ata is she accepts her maids in whatever way is natural to them. I've heard of the painted women in the south. History took our paths in different directions, but I am sure you pay tribute to your roots."

Sigrid nodded. From a pocket in her cloak, she pulled out a lipstick. "I couldn't carry much, but I brought an offering from home." Stepping forward, she placed the lipstick at Ata's feet. "My favorite one."

"A fine offer." Chimalma smiled.

"So"—Sigrid turned to the priestess—"I'm told that here painted women and priestesses are the same thing."

Chimalma laughed. "I suppose, yes. We all have different responsibilities and duties. I understand the Heddish tend to focus on the sexual aspect of the term, so painted women aren't priestesses at all."

"Essentially." Sigrid shrugged. "The priestesses care for the temples, handle religious matters, but ... not everyone pays tribute to the original painted woman."

"That's a shame, but I cannot fault women for doing what they must to survive. How do you pay tribute back home?"

"I visit the temple. Bring gifts. I light incense to Ata and look to her for protection. I could always do more, I suppose."

Chimalma set a warm hand on Sigrid's shoulder. "I'm sure you do plenty."

"What do the painted women of this temple do?"

Chimalma cast her heavily lined eyes on the statue. "Oh, any number of things. We have those who are more akin to what the Heddish see all painted women as, who take others to their bed for the sake of a good hunt or harvest. We have those who provide counseling for married couples or those who need to better their relationships. Some tend to the temple. I rather enjoy guiding temple visitors through meditation."

"Quite the variety. So many choices." Choices that Sigrid never had and probably would never have. Options to do what they pleased. Sigrid's body was cold at the thought. How could she resent not having choices she'd never had?

Sigrid tried to take in the grandness of the temple. The scented smoke filled her lungs, and her head swam as she inhaled. Chimalma chuckled, and her laugh was so beautiful it almost sounded like music. Sigrid looked at the priestess. The gold of the woman's jewelry glimmered brighter and brighter.

"Wow," Sigrid said simply, her mouth falling open.

"Oh, my dear," Chimalma huffed, taking a folded fan from her pocket and fanning it in Sigrid's face. "Do you not use skyweed at your temples? It can be ... heady, at first."

"Skyweed?" Sigrid blinked, trying to clear the pleasant fog from her mind. "I'm not familiar."

Chimalma gestured to a bowl at Ata's feet that burned an oil, its smoke mingling with the incense. "Skyweed oil is derived from a flower. The plant on its own is used for tending to small burns and cuts, but the oil, when burned, can leave one feeling rather ... happy. You get used to it after a small while."

"Huh." Sigrid stared at the oil, her mind moving slowly. It felt similar to the dream herb she smoked on restless nights, but this she felt far more in her head. It was like a warm blanket spread across her mind, dimming her fears and anxieties. "Why do you burn it so openly?"

"It cleanses one's mind, offers clarity."

"I do not feel very clear."

"You will."

Sigrid doubted that as she wandered away from the high priestess, instead turning her attention to the paintings on the walls. Some were clearly ancient, the art on them more symbolic than literal, with sharp lines and exaggerated features. The newer ones retained the same bright colors, but the art itself had grown so realistic she wondered if she could simply step into them. Despite their beauty, it was an ancient painting that drew her interest.

"What is this one?" Sigrid asked as Chimalma came to her side.

Along the edges of the painting were hieroglyphics, each containing an image. Some of the hieroglyphics resembled people or animals, but she could not make sense of others.

"Ah," the priestess said, smiling, her painted lips parting to flash teeth set with precious stones. "The birth of Ata."

Sigrid blinked through the fog in her mind. "I can't read it."

"This is the oldest form of elven we have. Most can't read it anymore either. It tells the story of how she became a spirit."

"She was a person?"

Chimalma nodded her head. "The spirits have existed for far longer than we, and they have their own histories that have been passed on to us. This one"—she gestured to the artifact in front of them—"tells the story of how Ata was born. She sprung forth from the ground in the form of a woman at the peak of her womanhood."

The figure in the painting was certainly well endowed, her breasts pronounced and her hips wide.

"We don't have this story of her," Sigrid said.

Chimalma gave Sigrid a pitying look. "A shame. It is one of my favorites. There was a village so overcome with drought they could not make anything grow and were on the brink of starvation. Without crops, their herds dwindled, leaving them without meat. The people of the village came together, praying to the earth for salvation. They gave everything they had to the earth. Their finest wines, their grandest cloth. Whatever they could, they offered it as sacrifice. One day, a woman went to the fields to beg the earth to offer her something, anything. That was when the earth spoke to her, whispering through her mind like a gentle breeze. The earth told her that it required great passion and love from her to draw enough energy to resurrect.

"The woman thought on it for many days, not sure what she could give that brought her passion or sparked love. She only had one thing in the world she loved, and that was her wife. Knowing nothing else that she could do, the woman took her wife to the fields, where she serenaded her and offered a meager feast. It was through their passion, their love, that something began to change.

"The woman and her wife returned on several nights, and even during some days, over a few weeks. The woman did not know if her superstitions were doing anything, but in time it simply became a happy ritual between two people deeply in love. It was the energy from that love, that fiery passion for another person, that finally brought them relief. One final evening, the two returned to their little spot in the barren field and lay a blanket on the ground. They lit incense, and the two joined together one more time. Their passion summoned a great power, uniting the two as one. Ata was born from them, from their love, fully formed."

Sigrid gaped at the high priestess. "I've never heard this. We have no origin for Ata, it is a mystery. So she became a woman?"

"In a sense, yes."

"How did she cure the land?"

"Well ..." Chimalma took Sigrid by the arm, drawing her toward a newer painting. At the center was the same woman that stood as a statue in the middle of the room. "As she entered the village, the heavens opened up, pouring rain behind each step she took. Ata told the people of the village they would perform a ritual in that very rain she brought with her. She took five from the village—a warrior, a priestess, a farmer, and finally a pregnant woman and her husband. She took them to the field, where the six of them lay beneath the storm. They allowed her magic into them, and through them, she channeled her power into the earth."

"What did they do in the ritual?"

"Well, it became the basis for our practices today."

Sigrid looked up at the painting. The subjects within all lay on wet earth, their bodies writhing together. At the center, Ata sat straddling a man's hips. Beneath them, roots shot into the ground, spreading into the earth in a vibrant web, parting the dark earth.

"Do you ... do this, then? Magic like this? Our priestesses ... offer little more than prayer and words, however comforting they might be from time to time. They are not taught magic. Not like this."

"That is unfortunate," Chimalma replied, looking at the painting wistfully. "Ata is far more than her magic, but she is a powerful spirit. Her magic must be channeled properly. Even here, only those with the greatest control of magic are permitted to perform her rituals. It is a magic that can easily be abused, so it is cherished and kept safe."

"The Heddish practice some magic, but there are few humans with much of a gift, so it is rare for anyone to do more than study it academically. I did teach myself to light small fires, though."

Chimalma's eyes shot open. "You can create fire?"

"Not easily, but yes. It takes a great amount of concentration."

"All magic does, or more people would practice it. Show me."

Sigrid's eyes opened wider, and the pit of her stomach fell away. "What? No, no, I'm not very good at it. Sometimes I can't even do it at all."

Chimalma quickly grabbed Sigrid by the arm with such strength that pain shot through her muscles. Pulling her into a different room, she retrieved an unlit candle from a cabinet and held it out. "The skyweed will help."

Sigrid frowned. "I'm not sure skyweed did much for my attention span."

"Nonsense. The heady effects should have worn off by now. You can focus."

Blinking, Sigrid realized Chimalma was right. Though the calm, weightless feeling remained in her body, her mind no longer felt clouded. She was relaxed, but she could think. Sighing in resignation, Sigrid brought her hands up to the candle. Concentrating, she closed her eyes and focused all her energy into her hands. Sometimes, she could do it quickly, taking no more than a minute or two of concentration. This time, she was almost certain she would fail the request, as even after five minutes she felt nothing.

"Just breathe," Chimalma said softly, her voice wrapping around Sigrid like the arms of a beautiful woman.

Sigrid didn't know how long she stood there, concentrating on the flame, likely looking like an idiot to any who might wander past. Chimalma was patient, and eventually that patience paid off. Sigrid began to feel her palms warm, and suddenly a flash of heat between her hands indicated the candle was lit.

"Marvelous," Chimalma declared, holding the candle higher between them. "It's not impossible, but doing magic this quick takes time to learn. You must have been a very, very determined child."

Sigrid stared at the flame, her lips splitting into a smile so wide it nearly pained her. "I was."

"How long did you say you will be in Uruachi?"

Sigrid's shoulders sagged. "Not long, I don't think."

Chimalma's lips sank into a frown. "Disappointing. You have the makings of a painted woman. A true painted woman." Leaning forward, the priestess leveled her gaze with Sigrid's. "If you decide to stay, seek us out again. It is never too late to join the temple."

Those words stayed with Sigrid as she made her way back to Inda's home. She recalled the last time she was in Copper City's Temple of Ata and the emptiness she'd felt. To her great surprise, here she felt ... something. A flicker of light from a candle to illuminate a darkened room.

The Elders Council faced Sigrid, Agnar, and Baldr, boring holes in the three with their eyes. Elder Tonuac spoke first. "We believe the news you bring us is dire. We have remained distant from Hedeby for many years, content to live and let live. Over the last few days, we have spent countless hours deliberating, debating, and plain arguing about what the right course of action is. The fact of the matter is it takes time to mobilize military forces. We agree to send aid to Copper City, which we see as a city in need of freedom. Aiding you will mean war, but as Prince Agnar has kindly warned us, war is coming regardless. Perhaps it was always on the horizon and we simply wished for it to stay away while we managed our own kind. For now, we will send you back with word of our preparation. I wish we could send you with a whole army, but these things require time, planning. For now, we can send but a promise."

"How long?" Baldr asked. He vibrated with excitement, but for now, kept his face plain.

Elder Xochitl answered, "A month, at the absolute earliest, I expect. Two or three is more likely."

Baldr exhaled a sharp breath. "I understand, though that is not ideal. Still, thank you. I cannot tell you what it means to hear we have your support."

Elder Xochitl smiled. "You've been a wonderful reminder of what it is to love your people, Baldr of Hedeby. It is time we send aid."

Elder Tozi spoke up, "And it was not an easily won victory. Though in the end, we decided this was for the best. Please be understanding of those who did not wish to engage in this conflict. It is likely that without Agnar's warning, some may have been far harder to convince."

Baldr's lips set into a hard line, but he nodded in agreement. "Then we have much to thank him for," he said, offering Agnar a polite nod. "We will deliver this news at once to the Collective. We should leave as soon as possible."

Tozi nodded. "We will send a messenger ahead of our arrival, though I can imagine word will spread quickly of an army marching south." She offered a wry smile. "Sigrid, I will have research done into the creature you killed. Should we find anything of importance, I will ensure we send word on what we find. I'm sure you will want to know."

Sigrid blinked, surprised. "Oh! Thank you. I'm glad you find this matter as serious as I do."

"Of course. I spoke with a good friend of mine at the Temple of Ata. She mentioned you visited. I know you turned down her offer to stay already, but should you ever wish to return to study at the temple, all you need to do is send word."

"I did not know you were friends with High Priestess Chimalma," Sigrid said.

"There is great strength in Ata, and it benefits the Elders to pay our tribute from time to time. Chimalma has trained many in magic. It would be difficult, but you strike me as the sort who would be a good, disciplined student. I hope you will consider returning when the world is peaceful enough to do so," replied the Elder.

Sigrid found herself speechless. Her encounter with Chimalma had been memorable and rather brief, but she'd felt an instant connection to Chimalma and the temple itself. In her heart, she wanted to stay, but she couldn't run away from her life. The thought of not telling Brigid, of abandoning the Pearl without so much as a goodbye, was too heavy in her chest. No matter how much she desired to learn magic in a way she could never learn in Hedeby, there was still business to finish. Maybe one day.

"I will consider it," Sigrid said, nodding.

Baldr eyed her curiously. She'd mentioned going to the temple, but they hadn't discussed it after she returned. She'd been in good spirits, if a little distracted, but it was news to him that she'd been offered to be trained. Sigrid gave him a shrug.

"Another thing, Prince Agnar," Tonuac spoke up. "Some of our scouts have sent word of a small troop of Heddish soldiers along the border. They have not dared cross into our territory, but the lower villages say they've been looking for a woman who may be dressed as a man."

Agnar tensed, his fists clenching so tight his knuckles turned white. "Did your scouts offer any description?"

"Only that though the group was small, they were calculated. They rode with a red-and-gold banner."

The prince's jaw tightened. "I have a suspicion of who it may be. My uncle, Commander Sigmund Gorm, heads a troop known as the Gryphon's Claw. If Gorm is this far north, then he found my trail. He'll know I'm here eventually if he doesn't already."

"You should stay," Tozi suggested, crossing her arms. "They will not venture this far north with so few numbers. You'll be safe here."

"No." Agnar shook his head and squared his shoulders. "If it is all right with them, I would join Sigrid and Baldr and return to Copper City. I wish to be of aid to their cause."

Tonuac frowned. "With all due respect, it is not safe to travel if they know where you are. Do you think your father knows you've come to warn us?"

"Probably, at this point, though he will likely deny it until he has physical proof. War is coming whether I stay or go, and you'll be sending aid to Copper City soon anyway. Whatever information I can provide I can give it to your generals when they arrive. For now, I think I am best used elsewhere. I think I can appeal to some lower Heddish nobles who may sympathize with the cause and provide aid, but I can't convince them from here."

Baldr laughed. "What would they gain from helping us?"

"Plenty," Agnar replied tersely. "You will need more allies than Uruachi can provide."

"We do not need the Heddish." Baldr scoffed, turning fully to Agnar. "The only Heddish who have supported our cause thus far have been the poorest, most forgotten of your kind."

"But they don't have to be, Baldr. Some of them will never be on your side, but some can be convinced. I can convince them. I've trained my entire life to negotiate with nobility. There are those with elven connections who are more likely to sympathize with your cause, particularly in Copper City where having children with an elf is far less frowned upon. Lesser noble houses have a long noble bloodline, but their families were never the most prominent, so their attachment to the royal family isn't as strong. Baldr, there is much insight I can provide. You need me."

Baldr crossed his arms, his eyes shooting to Sigrid to seek her opinion. She looked between the two men and said, "If you want to return with us, you will find not everyone is as welcoming as I am, and many will regard you with distrust. You will have to earn their trust in a way you've never had to in your life. Your royal status will not gain you favor. It will be a barrier. I trust you, but I am nobody of power. Are you sure you want to come?"

Agnar looked her square in the eyes, his expression determined and firm. "Yes. I can be useful. I can't go at this with half my heart. I made my decision, and it is up to me to see it through. I want to come with you if you'll have me."

Baldr looked to Sigrid, his expression cheerless. Finally, he sighed and raised his palms in defeat. "So long as you understand you will not be as readily accepted as you were here, then ... you can come back with us. Sigrid trusts you, and I trust her."

Sigrid smiled, her chest swelling. The Elders looked between themselves with uncertainty, but Sigrid was sure Agnar was making the right choice. He was right—he could be useful. Sigrid knew from experience that some Heddish had more private elven sympathies than they publicly expressed, and if anyone could convince them to make those sympathies known, perhaps it was Agnar. Surely Baldr would realize this eventually.

Tozi exhaled a long sigh. "Very well. We will send you with supplies for the road back, as well as a donation for the Collective's coffers as a show of good faith. We will prepare our troops as quickly as we can. In the meantime, do stay safe. Things sit at a tipping point. Keep the needle balanced until help has arrived."

CHAPTER SEVENTEEN

Sigrid's heart sat heavy in her chest when they departed Uruachi a day after their last meeting with the Elders. True to their word, the Elders had given the trio a third horse for Agnar and plenty of supplies for the journey ahead. Sigrid's and Baldr's horses had been treated like royalty. They were fully refreshed and more pampered than they'd ever been in their lives. Sigrid almost felt bad taking them back to Copper City, but she was sure their owner would be happy to see their return. They'd been good horses. They were owed some pampering.

Sigrid felt she could use a little pampering herself and looked forward to visiting the bathhouse upon her return. As much as she enjoyed Uruachi, there were things about home she found herself missing. Going to the bathhouse with Brigid felt painfully normal, and with all the adventure she'd had, she could use a day of normal. Uruachi had its own bathhouses, but Sigrid missed the little ritual of attending with her closest friend. Thinking of Brigid tugged at a painful string in her heart. She hoped things were calm in Copper City and that Brigid was safe. She hoped Cualli and Zuma were well. If they traveled quickly, she'd see them all soon. The thought of home squeezed her chest.

Once out of Uruachi's territory, the three made their way off the main path toward the river to stay out of sight. With Agnar along for the journey they had to be more careful, and staying in villages was no longer an option with Gorm's forces so close. If they needed supplies, Sigrid or Baldr would head to a nearby town, but they had been gifted enough supplies that they were certain they would not need to stop for necessities. Upon returning to Copper City, they'd hide Agnar in the brothel just as Sigrid had done for Baldr at their first meeting.

"Tell me about your friend Brigid," Agnar said from atop his horse. He rode next to Sigrid, keeping close.

"Hmm?" She blinked, her mind wandering the longer they rode.

Agnar sighed. "This is the most boring this journey has been so far. Indulge me in some conversation, my dear."

Sigrid laughed. Baldr, he and his horse in front of them, turned his head to peer at them out of the corner of his eye. He said nothing and turned his attention back to the path before them, once again acting as their compass through the dense woods that lined the river.

"She's lovely," Sigrid said, watching Baldr from behind. "Brilliant. So good with numbers it is scary. She handles all the finances."

"Of your brothel?"

"Yes. The Golden Pearl. We've been open, oh ... two years now?"

"And what of you?" Agnar called to Baldr. "Do you have a great friend as well?"

Baldr was quiet for a long moment. He'd spoken only when necessary since they'd left, choosing mostly to speak in whispers to Sigrid whenever Agnar was out of earshot.

"Not anymore," he said. "Once."

Sigrid's eyebrows raised, her eyes growing round. She listened carefully. Baldr continued, his words strained. "Eztli. We were conscripted into the army at the same time. We knew each other before, but it wasn't until then that we became friends."

"Ah, a comrade," Agnar said with upturned lips. "My father says that's a strong kinship."

Baldr bristled and turned to shoot a scathing look over his shoulder. Seeing the surprise on Agnar's face, he softened, though his fingers still gripped the reins tighter than necessary. "I suppose even he is capable of being correct."

"Sorry," Agnar sighed.

"No, I get it," Baldr said, turning his head forward. "He's still your father."

Agnar spurred his horse forward. "You speak of your friend as if they are no longer here."

Baldr's shoulders rose with his deep breath. It was a long moment before he answered. "He's dead."

"I'm sorry. May I ... ask how he died?"

Baldr cast a suspicious gaze on Agnar, but seeing no malice, turned his eyes forward again. "Treason."

Agnar's face went pale. "I'm sorry," he said, breathless. "I'm sure he did not deserve it."

Baldr considered this for a moment before offering a snort in response. "No, I don't think he did, but your courts certainly thought so. If you can call them courts. He was found guilty of sedition, and since he was in the army ... well, they just couldn't have that."

Agnar's face was drawn in pain, his blue eyes filling with water. "That isn't fair."

Baldr looked at Agnar, his own face ashen and contorted in grief. "No. No it isn't."

They rode in silence after that, but Baldr softened. When Agnar asked a question, he hesitated less, and his words became less tense. They stopped only when the night threatened to obscure their path.

Agnar took a seat next to Sigrid. The fire in front of them roared in its pit. A pot hung over it, the contents within stewing and greeting them with the pleasant scent of dinner. Sigrid smiled at their companion and lifted the ladle from the pot and offered it to him. "Stew? We are lucky to have been given spices. Makes traveling food far less bland."

"Yes, thank you," he replied happily, leaning forward to sip the stew from the ladle. His lips parted in a wide grin. "You are a talented chef, Baldr."

Baldr offered a polite nod in response. Breaking off a piece of bread, he dipped it in his bowl and ate quietly. Sigrid and Agnar were content to chat, passing the time with idle, meaningless conversation that nonetheless brought them comfort.

"I'm going to … relieve myself," Baldr said awkwardly, standing and heading into the dark of the woods.

Sigrid waved at him as he left. "Believe it or not, I think he's warming up to you," she said, cleaning out the inside of her bowl before stowing it back in her pack.

"It's hard to tell, but I hope so. Admittedly, it is nice to have the two of you for this leg of my journey. On my way north I was so afraid of getting caught I couldn't stop and think. I had one goal: get to the Kingdom in the Mountain. That night we met was the closest I'd been to being caught and it was the most scared I've ever been too."

Sigrid smiled, reaching over and settling her hand on his knee. "I'm glad to have you. You know, you're one of very few human men that I can tolerate being around."

"Oh, well, thank you," he laughed, bowing his head and gesturing dramatically with his hands. "I don't know many elven women, but you have been my favorite so far."

"Oh, wait until you meet Brigid, she'll take your breath away."

"I look forward to it."

The two laughed, their faces lit by the fire before them. Baldr burst through the trees, his face drawn in panic. He held a finger to his lips and quickly doused the fire in water, steam rising as the coals hissed.

"What's happening?" Sigrid whispered, crouching next to where the flames had been.

"Soldiers," he replied. "Get to your horses. Quietly. If we're lucky, they didn't see the flames."

Sigrid and Agnar nodded in silent response, each gathering their bags and saddling their horses as quickly as was possible. The animals sighed in protest.

"Lead them on foot for now," Baldr said, his voice low and tense.

Quietly, with three large animals in tow, they crept through the forest. The sun was quickly setting, casting long shadows that made it difficult to navigate the trees. They listened for the rushing of the river water, not straying too close, but still using it to find their way.

It wasn't long until they could hear the shouting of men and see the glow of torches between the trees. "Shit," Baldr whispered. "Shit, shit, shit."

Agnar frantically pulled his hair out of his face, tying it into a tight knot at the back of his head. He pulled his hood forward, obscuring his face. Sigrid and Baldr followed suit, pulling their hoods up over their heads.

"What do we do?" Sigrid said, her words hushed but urgent.

Agnar flexed his fingers. Sigrid could see he was shaking. She reached out and took one of his hands, holding it tight.

"Let them take me," Agnar said, his voice low and tinged with fear.

"What?" Baldr huffed. "No, we're not doing that."

"If they take me, then you two can get away. They don't have to know we're together."

"We're not doing that," Sigrid replied firmly. "We're not leaving you behi—"

Baldr reached out and placed his hand over her mouth, the shouting growing louder. They crouched low, their horses shaking their heads knowing danger was nearby.

The sound of hooves grew louder and louder until a horse broke through the trees. The flame from the rider's torch illuminated the area, revealing the three crouched next to neighing horses.

The rider looked at them, dumbstruck, before opening his mouth and calling for the others. Not waiting for anyone else to show up, the three rebels jumped up and mounted their horses.

"Hey!" the soldier called out, but it was too late.

They took off into the dark trees. The sun had completely set now but their eyes had begun to adjust, and the horses narrowly avoided colliding with trees. Sigrid's heart beat so fast she was sure it could be heard by their pursuant.

Soon enough, there were three riders on their tail. "Princess Agnes!" they called out, pleading with Agnar to stop.

"How did they find us?" Agnar cried, his eyes glued firmly ahead.

"Fuck if I know," Sigrid shouted in response.

In front of them, a man on a horse burst through the darkness. Surprised, Sigrid's and Agnar's horses reared. Crying out, Sigrid was thrown from the saddle, landing on her back. The wind rushed from her lungs and she gasped for air.

Agnar managed to hold on to his horse, but quickly dismounted when Sigrid was tossed. He knelt at her side, frantically checking for injury as she struggled to regain her breath.

Two riders came up from behind, trapping them.

"You have companions now," one of them said.

That voice. Sigrid knew that voice. Pushing up from the ground, she looked at the man who had spoken. The other grizzled soldiers were unremarkable, reminding her of every old warrior she'd met over the years, but this one was different.

Commander Gorm grinned from atop his horse. "You've been remarkably difficult to find, Princess. You should be proud of your abilities. If you weren't a princess, I'd say you'd make a good spy."

Agnar glared up from where he knelt, his hands still on Sigrid. His fingers dug into her, but they shook. "Good to see you, Uncle."

Gorm dismounted and motioned for his two thugs to do the same. Baldr jumped from his horse, putting himself between Gorm and Sigrid. Gorm cocked his head to the side, lifting the torch higher in the air to illuminate Baldr's face. "You look familiar," he said.

Baldr said nothing in return.

Finally able to breathe, Sigrid pushed herself to her knees. "Baldr, don't," she said.

He ignored her.

Gorm handed off his torch and stepped forward. "How sweet. You have some loyal servants, Princess."

Baldr spit at Gorm's feet. "We're no one's servants."

The commander's eyebrows raised. "So lively, this one. You must think highly of yourself. If not servants, then what? Captors? I'm sure my brother-in-law would be more than happy to hear you hadn't run off after all but instead were being held captive by elves. It'll give him a nice enough excuse to crack down on every elf in all of Hedeby. Not that he needs much of an excuse, you are a rowdy lot."

"Oh, shut up." Sigrid gritted her teeth. "We've heard it all before. We're savages. Hardly civilized. Good for nothing, a drain on the system. Just shut up. Whatever you want, you're not getting it."

"I just want my niece. She's dearly missed."

Agnar tensed and raised his chin. Standing, he pushed back his hood and gave the commander in front of him a heavy gaze. "I'm not Princess Agnes."

"Enough of your games. I'm taking you home."

"No," Agnar said. "You aren't taking me anywhere, and my name isn't Princess Agnes. My name is Agnar, and I renounce my title. I want nothing to do with the crown."

Gorm's eyes grew wide. "What is this? What trickery have they put in your head?"

"This is no trickery," Agnar replied, moving to stand behind Baldr. He placed his hand on the half-elf's shoulder. "You will not hurt my friends, and you will not take me home. You can return with a message to my father: Leave me be. I do not wish to return home, and I am not going to."

Commander Gorm's expression darkened as he took a step forward. "I don't care what you think your name is, I am taking you home. You can sort out your issues with your father later. I have a job, and I am going to finish it."

"No." Agnar stepped in front of Baldr.

"If you don't come with us, I'll have your friends here killed. You want that? Come with me, and we'll let them serve in the kitchens."

Agnar shook his head. "No. I'm not going anywhere. If you want a fight, we will fight. But I'm not going home."

Before swords could be drawn, Agnar rushed forward and tackled his uncle to the ground. His fists connected with Gorm's face over and over as the commander tried desperately to push the younger man off him. His henchmen rushed forward, but they found themselves at the end of Baldr's sword.

One of the men laughed, and as soon as he did, Baldr's sword swung through the air. The man barely had a chance to jump out of the way.

Sigrid felt around for the hilt of her dagger, but her horse was too far away to grab her sword from her pack. Her eyes moved frantically between Agnar and Baldr. On the ground, Agnar rolled around, his face bloody as he furiously pummeled Gorm. Baldr deftly dodged blow after blow, keeping the two soldiers occupied.

Baldr whipped around as a soldier tried in vain to thrust his large sword through Baldr's stomach. He stumbled forward before turning, leaving his back exposed to Sigrid as the other soldier closed in on Baldr from behind. Before she could think, she darted forward and grabbed the man by the back of his head. He cried out in surprise, but his cry soon turned into a gurgle as she drew the blade across his throat. Blood spurted forth as he dropped to his knees, frantically pawing at his throat.

Baldr looked on in surprise.

"Behind you!" Sigrid cried out, pointing.

He was not quick enough to move completely out of the way as the soldier thrust his sword forward, slicing open a wound on Baldr's hip. With adrenaline pumping through his veins, it didn't slow him down, and the half-elf spun to sink his sword into the soldier's stomach.

Sigrid turned to Agnar, finding him on his stomach. Gorm was straddling his back and tying Agnar's arms together. Rushing forward, Sigrid tackled the commander.

"Bitch!" he roared, rolling over on top of her.

She thrashed at him, dagger still in hand, and brought it down into the meaty bit of flesh exposed at his armpit. She felt the hot blood splash on her as he screamed. His fist connected with her face as he shouted obscenities at her. The dagger was still sticking out of his body as she managed to slither out from under him and dart for her horse. She could see the gleam of her sword's hilt sticking out of the pack.

Gorm grabbed her by the foot, tripping her. As she turned to kick him in the face, Agnar was quickly on him. He held a rock in his hand and brought it down hard on the back of Gorm's head. The commander fell face-first into the dirt.

Sigrid breathed heavily, struggling to catch her breath, but there was no time to dawdle. Kicking herself free from Gorm's hand still wrapped around her ankle, she and her two companions quickly made for their horses. Leaping onto the saddles, they took off into the forest.

CHAPTER EIGHTEEN

They rode until it hurt to sit in their saddles. Not stopping for so much as a water break, they moved as quick as their already-tired horses could take them. It wasn't until they were afraid of their horses collapsing from exhaustion that they finally came to a stop. They'd made it out of the forest and into fields of corn. Hoping the tall stalks would provide them cover, they waded through the corn until they found an area large enough for the three of them and their horses.

Nobody spoke. Agnar offered no words, and Baldr looked as if he'd seen a ghost. Sigrid could find nothing to say.

Even with her exhaustion, Sigrid found it impossible to sleep. Fear pricked at her muscles every time she felt herself begin to fade into dreams. Sigrid knew she'd get no sleep until they were safely back in Copper City.

She thought of the man she'd killed. *Killed*. Slit his throat from behind. She turned over in her blanket and pulled it tighter around her body. Tears stung her eyes and wet her face as she recalled the moment over and over. She could still feel the way his flesh sliced beneath her blade. It was too easy, she thought. Too easy to simply cut into flesh.

No matter how many times she ran through the scenario in her head, she could see no way to avoid bloodshed. They were never going to leave without Agnar. They'd made a commitment to each other. This was their journey now, as a group. He was officially a rebel. A revolutionary. He was fighting for them, so it was only fair they fight for him too.

They were only allowed a few hours of rest before they saddled up and took off again. They were so close now, they couldn't waste time. Sigrid fed the horses what spare vegetables they had, and she hoped they knew, in their animal way, that it was an apology for making them work so hard.

The gates to Copper City were within view before long. Sigrid almost cried from relief, her heart aching at the mere sight of her home. She recalled all the times in her life she wished she could be anywhere else. Seeing Uruachi was spectacular and she hoped to return, but at the sight of home, all she wanted was the familiar. Tears welled in her eyes as they crossed through the gates.

Tying the horses up outside the Collective's safe house, Baldr helped Sigrid from the horse. She stumbled; her legs were ready to give out. Steadying her with strong hands, Baldr gave her a concerned look. "Are you okay?"

"I'm just tired," she responded.

"Well, let me check in. I'll escort you and Agnar back to the Pearl. They'll want to see us as quickly as possible, but none of us is in any shape to talk right now. Wait here."

Sigrid nodded as he turned and disappeared into the dark building. Sigrid felt her mind drift away and wasn't sure how long he was gone, but eventually, he returned with Cualli. Sigrid almost burst into tears at the sight of her and found the strength to throw her arms around the tall woman's body. Cualli gasped in surprise but returned the gesture, giving Baldr a confused look over Sigrid's shoulder.

"It is so good to see you," Sigrid said in a breathy voice, pulling back to hold the beauty at arm's length. Emotions surging in her chest, she took in the woman's features, from her angular face to her narrow, amber-colored eyes.

"It is good to see you too," Cualli replied with wide, curious eyes. "You seem tired."

"Oh, exhausted." Sigrid smiled. "I just want to go home."

Cualli pressed her lips to Sigrid's forehead. "I'll take these three," she said, gesturing to the horses. "They look like they could use some care. Can you get home fine?"

Sigrid groaned. On the one hand, the thought of getting back on the horse made her want to throw up. On the other hand, walking back to the brothel made her joints scream in protest. "Oh, we'll be fine," she replied.

"Anam will want to see you three first thing in the morning. You're lucky it's late or you'd be in for some questions." Cualli's eyes turned to Agnar, her manicured brow lifting.

"You have my gratitude," Agnar replied, taking her free hand and bringing it to his lips for a kiss. Cualli laughed, but she didn't seem to mind the gesture.

Sigrid watched Cualli take the horses down the street toward the stables, then she turned and immediately headed in the direction of her brothel. Agnar and Baldr hurried to catch up to her.

"I thought you were tired," Agnar teased.

"I'm too close to home to slow down now."

Agnar laughed with a nod of his head. "Fair enough. I've never been to a brothel before. This will be a first for me."

"Really?" Baldr raised a skeptical brow. "You're telling me you've never visited one? Not even once? Some royal you are."

"Not even once. I suppose I could have, but I'd had enough on my plate. Not that I think there's anything wrong with it," he said pointedly, looking to Sigrid with an awkward smile.

Sigrid did not have the energy to unpack what he said. She was determined to get home, to see Brigid, to see her bed, all of it. She missed her incense and her books. She missed going to the gymnasium. Now that she was back, she realized just how much she'd missed her home. The thought brought tears to her eyes, which she batted away before either Baldr or Agnar could see.

The windows were lit, and a green flag hung on the door, indicating that they were open for business. Though she wanted to burst through the front door, she opted to instead lead the two men around the building to the back door facing the alley. The kitchen was empty when they arrived, but she could hear voices coming from the front room.

Pressing a finger to her lips, she led Agnar into the small room off the kitchen that Baldr had once occupied. Grabbing a candle from the wall as she entered, she ushered the men into the room. She lit the candles within and slowly closed the door behind her.

"So this is the ... what did you call it? The Golden Pearl?" Agnar asked, lying down on the bed and removing his boots.

Baldr took a seat in a chair against the back wall. "Sigrid was kind enough to let me stay here for a time when we first met. I needed a safe place to lie low, and she was willing."

Agnar placed his hands beneath his head. Whether he intended to fall asleep, she didn't know, but soon the prince was snoring softly. Baldr smiled in amusement, but he, too, looked close to sleep. "I should go," he said as his eyes closed.

"You can stay here. No need to go anywhere. You can check in tomorrow."

He shook his head and stood. Moving across the small room to stand in front of her, he lifted his hand and brushed hair from her face. "You were spectacular," he whispered, leaning forward to press his forehead against hers.

Her heart sped up, and she leaned against him without a second thought. His arms wrapped around her, and he pressed his warm body into hers. She melted into him. They stood for a time wrapped in each other's embrace.

"I'll be back in the morning," he said, his lips not far from hers.

She wanted to kiss him. She wanted to tell him to stay. Instead, she nodded and escorted him through the kitchen.

It was late before Brigid was done with her final cull. Creeping into the receiving room as Brigid closed the door, Sigrid took a seat on the couch and spread her arms across the back. Upon turning around, Brigid yelped, "Sigrid!"

Sigrid grinned and stood, moving across the room with her arms spread. They met in the center, staring at each other, before finally tangling themselves in each other's arms.

Sigrid was totally and utterly unaware of anything in the room but Brigid. She wrapped her muscular arms tighter around the shorter woman, tugging her closer and inhaling the scent of her rose-infused oil. It felt so familiar, so comforting. Sigrid's heart threatened to burst out of her chest as the two held tight.

"Gods," Sigrid whispered as the tears she'd felt earlier began to freely flow. "I know I haven't been gone that long, but it felt like forever. I have so much to tell you."

"Oh, me too." Brigid laughed, pulling away and grasping both sides of Sigrid's face. "You look thinner. And tired. Get some rest tonight, and we'll talk about this tomorrow."

"Just let me hug you," Sigrid whined, tightening her arms around Brigid's body.

She buried her nose into Brigid's halo of coiled hair, inhaling her oils and perfumes. For a time, they stood there silently, content to be in each other's arms. Eventually Sigrid pulled back and brushed the tears from her eyes, her mouth pulling into a wide smile. "Oh, I should warn you, there's a prince in our guest room."

"I'm sorry, a prince?"

"Mmhm. I'll explain it in the morning."

The next morning, Sigrid woke to the sound of Brigid's laughter. It was loud, unrestrained, and coming from the kitchen. In nothing but her nightgown, Sigrid stumbled through the brothel until she found her way to the kitchen. She found Brigid and Agnar at the counter, laughing over the metal contraption they used to brew coffee.

"Good morning?" Sigrid blinked and rubbed her eyes of the sleepiness still in them.

Brigid turned and laughed. "Agnar has never made coffee before."

"Ah," Sigrid said, laughing hesitantly and taking a seat at their small table. "Good thing he has you to teach him."

"Oh, she is making a marvelous teacher," Agnar said, turning his eyes to look at Brigid.

He was enchanted. Sigrid had never seen him so bedazzled. He looked at Brigid with total admiration and desire, doing nothing to conceal his attraction. He laughed and flirted as she attempted to teach him to make a proper pot of coffee.

She laughed at every joke. Sigrid fell silently into the background as she watched, the two of them quickly forgetting Sigrid was in the room. Brigid's cheeks were dark and her eyes bright. She touched his arm, then his hand, and leaned in close when he was listening to her instruction.

Sigrid had never seen Brigid like this. In the years she'd known Brigid, the woman had only had one relationship. He'd been a Heddish boy, the son of some merchant, but they were both young and foolish with their affections.

Once he'd left her heartbroken, she never seemed to take much interest in affairs of the heart.

Their flirtation was interrupted as Baldr opened the door with a dark look on his face. Everyone quieted, their eyes turning to him.

"We need to go," he said.

Sigrid nodded and stood, leaving the room to dress. When she returned, they followed Baldr through the streets to the Collective safe house.

Brigid and Sigrid sat outside of Anam's office as Agnar was interrogated inside. Only Baldr was allowed in the room with them, which Sigrid protested to. Sitting with a deep frown on her features, the painted woman crossed her arms and audibly huffed.

"Calm down." Brigid rolled her eyes. "You brought the royal prince to the rebellion. You're lucky they didn't immediately take him hostage."

Sigrid huffed again. "I have been on the road with both of them for weeks. I was there for everything. I should be in there."

"I'm sure she'll call you in soon," Brigid soothed, setting her hand on Sigrid's knee. "Just calm down."

Sigrid's scowl deepened. "They better."

"I still can't believe he's the prince. I didn't know we had a prince."

"Guess we've always had one, even if we didn't know it."

Brigid nodded. She lifted a dark hand and unfolded Sigrid's arms, forcing her to drop them to her sides. Holding Sigrid's hand, Brigid leaned to the side and rested her head on Sigrid's muscular shoulder. "He was very funny at breakfast. Doesn't know how to make his own cup of coffee, but he's funny."

"Well, I suppose when you grow up as royalty, you have someone to make coffee for you."

"He's very handsome."

"He is."

There was a silence between the two of them. Sigrid swallowed, the fingers of her spare hand digging into the fabric of her skirts. It felt nice to be in her old clothing. She felt as if she were back in her own skin. "Baldr has had a hard time trusting him."

"They seemed fine this morning."

"That's good. At first, Baldr was ... definitely not a fan of Agnar or anything he had to say. He was extremely suspicious. I think he's eased up, but ..."

"He seems like the sort who is good at winning people over."

Sigrid nodded. "He has proven to be that way."

"Will he be staying with us?"

"I don't know. He could take the spare room we gave to Baldr. Anam may want to keep him close. I'd rather keep him near me, though. I feel like I've earned that."

Brigid nodded and squeezed Sigrid's hand. The door in front of them swung open, startling the two, and Baldr stood in the doorway. He appeared tired, but otherwise in good spirits. "You can come in, Sigrid."

"What about me?" Brigid sat up.

"Well, since you live there, come on." He waved the two into the room.

Agnar sat at the end of the room in a cushioned chair. Anam stood at an angle in front of him. Her arms were crossed, but she didn't appear to be upset. "Well, good to see you, Sigrid," Anam said. "According to Baldr, you were quite the asset on the journey. You did far more than provide a sword."

Sigrid smiled, but she could not mistake the skepticism in Anam's voice. "Thank you," Sigrid replied. "How ... are things?"

"Good," Anam replied, reaching out a hand to settle on Agnar's shoulders. "I was skeptical at first, but Baldr assures me Agnar has been nothing but honest. He also tells me the warning, that the king intends to move north toward Uruachi. We are lucky to have this warning, otherwise we'd be met unprepared. We have been preparing for further assault within the city, and the guard has all but left this side of the city."

Sigrid gaped. "That's why they weren't at the gates! What—what happened?"

"Quite a bit. There was more unrest after you left, morale among the guard was low, and many have abandoned their positions. This allows us to prepare for reinforcements. It looks like we may actually be able to take the city."

The thought made the blood in Sigrid's body run cold. "Gods, that's ... a lot."

Anam smiled proudly. "This could not have worked out better if we wanted it to. Within a few months, we should have an army at our back, no longer just a network of rebels. No revolution is won without allies, and you two hand-delivered one for us. Both of you should be proud of yourselves."

Sigrid nodded and forced a smile, but Anam's words continued to ring through her head. Take the city. They were going to overthrow the government. It suddenly felt far more real than it had so far, which caught Sigrid by surprise. The entire journey had been painfully surreal compared to this icy realization. A sudden queasiness clenched at her stomach.

Baldr, sensing something was amiss, reached out a hand and settled it on the lower part of Sigrid's back. He could feel the tension of her muscles through the airy gown. Sigrid did not miss Anam's disapproving gaze.

"Baldr failed to tell me before you two left that you run a brothel in town. The Golden Pearl, is that right?"

Sigrid looked to Baldr, then back to his mother. Swallowing, she nodded. "Ah, yes, that is correct."

"I was surprised. As far as I knew, you were garment workers. Curious."

Sigrid licked her dry lips. She couldn't tell if she saw disapproval in Anam's eyes because of what Baldr had said about her opinion on painted women or if there was something else there. She felt small beneath Anam's gaze.

"I wonder, do you think your *profession* aids you in your work with the Collective?"

"Oh ... I think so, perhaps. I've learned many skills. I like to think I've proven myself at least a little bit."

Anam clicked her tongue. The sound was like a hammer on Sigrid's ears.

"Even I cannot deny that." With that, she waved a dismissive hand. "I have a lot to discuss with the others. We must keep Agnar's presence as quiet as possible, even within the Collective. For now, he will remain at the Pearl, if that is okay with you." Anam strode back to her desk and took a seat behind it.

Sigrid blinked. "Oh! Yes. Good. He should stay with us."

"Glad we agree. Baldr will maintain contact and will shepherd the prince wherever we might need him, in secret. Just because the guard has retreated for now doesn't mean we can get sloppy. Stay under the radar, and we'll reach out to you with instructions soon. You may go."

Sigrid blinked. "That's it?"

"That's it. For now. I need to go over a few things with the Council. When I need you, I'll call."

The four of them were shuffled out of the room, and the door closed firmly behind them. Standing in the hallway, they glanced between each other before shrugging and returning to the brothel.

CHAPTER NINETEEN

There was laughter coming once again from the kitchen when Sigrid made her way down the stairs. Her hair pulled back in a lazy ponytail, Sigrid had barely rubbed the sleepiness from her eyes when she came to find Agnar and Brigid giggling at the breakfast table. At first, they didn't notice her enter. They were wrapped up in each other's attention, their eyes locked on each other. Brigid popped a piece of bacon into her mouth as Agnar seemed to finish a joke, and she burst into a fit of laughter once again.

"Gods, it's so early," Sigrid groaned, standing in the doorway and looking at the two as if they were aliens. Neither Sigrid nor Brigid had ever cared for mornings, both often worked far too late into the evening to wake before the sun rose to high noon. Sigrid's sleep schedule had shifted on her journey to Uruachi, but she wasn't sure she'd ever get used to mornings. Sigrid stumbled around looking for the coffee.

"If you're looking for the coffee, we finished it," Brigid said as she took a rather smug sip from her mug. "I can go get some later."

Sigrid turned her tired gaze to the two that were still giggling away. Crossing the room, she took the mug from Brigid's hands and stole a long drink. It was still hot and burned her tongue. "Ow, ow, ow." She winced.

"That's what you get," Brigid replied haughtily and took her mug back. "Run to the market and buy some more."

Sigrid shot Brigid a dirty look and opened her mouth to respond, but the rear door swung open with a loud bang. Baldr came striding in. "Ah, good, you're all awake."

Sigrid exhaled a tired sigh. "You don't live here." Why was everyone so noisy this morning?

"My, grumpy," Agnar quipped.

"I just want some coffee," Sigrid whined.

Baldr looked at Sigrid with an amused grin. "Are you out?"

"Yes, Brigid cruelly drank the rest."

"I had some too!" Agnar replied proudly, ignoring the look Sigrid shot him.

"I'll run and grab you some," Baldr offered. "I know how useless you are in the morning."

"I am not useless. I am actually very useful!" Sigrid crossed her arms.

Baldr smirked. "The most useful. Do you want me to go grab you coffee or don't you?"

Sigrid pursed her lips. "Yes," she finally replied sheepishly, tapping two fingers together.

As quickly as he'd arrived, Baldr turned and strode out of the kitchen.

Sigrid took a seat next to Brigid, reaching for her cup of coffee.

"Ah, no." Brigid swatted Sigrid's hand away.

"Oh, come on," Sigrid whined. "You don't need it as much as I do."

"Oh, is that so?" Brigid held the mug out of arm's reach.

Sigrid lifted her chin defiantly. "Yes. I was going to go to the gym today. I'll need the coffee to keep me energized."

"Sounds like a personal issue," Brigid replied as she inhaled the sweet cinnamon scent of her drink.

"Now, now, ladies," Agnar said, slipping his mug of coffee toward Sigrid. "I'll make more when Baldr gets back. I'm a guest, take mine."

Sigrid laughed and pushed it back. "No, no, I'm playing. Brigid has a bad habit of using something and not replacing it."

"I do not!"

It did not take long for Baldr to return with a small sack of coffee beans. Baldr tossed them in the little grinder they kept, then set the kettle on the stove. Sigrid watched him as Brigid and Agnar continued to chat. Whatever they were talking about went right in one ear and out the other as she kept her gaze on Baldr. Now that they were home, she saw a little less of him every day. Anam sent him on tasks, and Sigrid couldn't fault him for doing his job, but she found every day she missed him a little more. He came by to check on them and pass on information as necessary, but he'd become so busy. Having him there now pulled at her chest. They'd been through so much together, and it pained her that now they saw so little of each other. Being his friend and comrade was wonderful. Still, as she watched him busy himself with making them coffee, she found she desperately wished they had more. He'd made his position clear, though, and she had to respect that.

Turning her attention to Brigid and Agnar, her heart sank a little more. Agnar was a flirt, but there was no denying that the two had found something in each other. Though they'd only been home a little over a week, Sigrid found Brigid and Agnar lounging around late into the morning hours simply talking. A pang hit her in the heart. Perhaps it was jealousy? she wondered. What was she jealous of? Was it that someone had captured Brigid's attention? No, she could feel in her chest that wasn't it. The jealousy she might have once felt when Brigid took interest in another did not rear its head. That desire was long gone. This jealousy was something different. A longing for something Brigid and Agnar didn't necessarily have. They'd known each other such a short amount of time.

This seemed so different. Time seemed to slow around her as she watched the way Agnar interacted with the elegant woman next to him. His attention was rapt, and his eyes never left her unless necessary. His smile was wide and genuine, and every time she made him laugh, he seemed to melt a little. As she looked at them, she hoped whatever this flirtation was would lead to happiness for her dearest friend.

Sigrid averted her eyes to her hands, picking at her ruby-red nails.

"Here you go," came Baldr's voice as he set a steaming wooden mug in front of Sigrid.

A smile lit up the woman's face. "Ah, finally," she said, lifting the mug to her face and inhaling the deep scent. He'd put cinnamon in the grounds too, it seemed. Brigid must have told him that's how they drank it.

Baldr took the fourth seat, the light from the sun illuminating his bronze face. Sigrid's chest tightened as it now always seemed to around him.

"Anam wants to see you tonight," he said to the three in front of him.

"Oh, good." Agnar finally tore his gaze from Brigid to look at the man to his side. "I've got something I've been wanting to talk to Anam about. Since you're all here, I thought ... I would run it by you three first."

"What is it?" Brigid asked, getting up from the table to pour herself a fresh cup of coffee with a splash of cream.

Agnar chewed his bottom lip for a while, twiddling his thumbs on the table. "Well ... I've been doing a lot of thinking since we got back. Right now I'm being stowed away like a fugitive, and I understand. If anyone knew I was here before we were ready, it would be chaos. But ... I've made up my mind." He sucked in a deep breath and cast his gaze down at his hands, tightly gripping the mug in his hands. "I want to join the Collective. Officially. I can do more good than I'm doing right now. I want to bring it up to Anam."

The three of them stared at him. Baldr was the first to speak and reached out a hand to pat Agnar's back. "Well then, I hope she brings you into the fold. You've earned it."

Sigrid nodded, reaching across the table to touch Agnar's arm. "Are you sure?"

"Why wouldn't I be? I escaped to the Kingdom in the Mountain, betrayed my own family, and came to Copper City to keep passing on the warning. I've committed treason on multiple occasions now. There's no going back. This is what I choose. I ... see a very different life now." He furrowed his brows and leaned back, drawing a hand down his cheek. "Picturing a life I want to live has always been difficult for me. I knew when I was young what I didn't want, of course. I wasn't a girl, and I didn't want to pretend I was. I couldn't see what kind of life that left for me in the future. My father refused to accept me as a prince, insisting I marry a man to secure an alliance good for the kingdom. I knew I didn't want that life either. I knew I didn't want to see my father initiate a needless war just so he could call himself a conqueror. My life has been a line of things I don't want without always knowing what I do want. Now ... I can see something. It might just be an outline of something in the distance, but I can see it now. I can see a life where I'm not ... not a prince. Where maybe I can do something else, like ... bring the Heddish and the elves closer together. Help create a different world. I can finally see what I do want, not just what I don't."

Brigid reached down and took one of his hands in hers and squeezed tight. "That's wonderful, Agnar. I'm glad you've found this clarity," she said softly, her thumb rubbing over the back of his hand.

Baldr beamed. "You've surprised me at every step. Are you sure you were born royalty?"

Agnar laughed. "Pretty sure, if how difficult it was to learn to build my own fire is any indication. Honestly, I'm not entirely sure how I managed to survive all the way to Uruachi."

"Looks like you'll be sticking around for a while," Sigrid said with a gentle smile.

Agnar nodded. "I hope so." His eyes shifted to Brigid and held her gaze. Sigrid looked away as the moment dragged on, feeling somehow like she was intruding on something private.

Baldr broke the silence with an awkward clearing of his throat. "Well, if you'd like, I'll let Anam know you want to speak with her tonight."

Agnar hesitated. "Yes ... I would appreciate it."

Baldr squeezed Agnar's shoulder, stood, and moved to leave. He stopped momentarily behind Sigrid and opened his mouth as if he were going to say something, but he decided against it and slipped out the door.

Four pairs of eyes landed on Sigrid.

"What was that?" Brigid prodded.

"What was what?"

"That ..." Agnar replied. "This weird ... energy between the two of you. I mean, the energy between you two has always been weird, but now it's even weirder."

"Yeah," Brigid frowned, reaching out and forcing Sigrid's chin up. "You two were always ... touching and stuff before you left. Flirting. Now he comes by every day but he's always at a distance. Did something happen?"

"They were like that back in the Kingdom in the—in Uruachi," he corrected himself.

"Didn't stop you from being a huge flirt," Sigrid said testily.

Agnar laughed. "But that's it, see? He cared. Ever since we've been back in the city, he's been ... strangely distant. Present, but not."

Sigrid frowned and crossed her arms tight over her chest. She wanted to get up and simply leave the room, but she knew they'd both chase her down anyway. She inwardly cursed bringing Agnar around since it meant giving Brigid backup. When she didn't answer, they leaned in together, and she felt their collective gazes boring into her skin. Shrinking into her chair, she waved them back. "I don't know what is wrong! He's been weird since we got attacked by Gorm. But he's busy! His mother is the damn leader of an entire rebellion. He probably has a lot on his plate, and we shouldn't read too much into it."

Agnar and Brigid looked at each other for a moment, exchanging a glance that only frustrated Sigrid further. She did not like someone else having the same silent conversations she used to have with Brigid when gossiping.

Brigid turned in her chair and reached over to take Sigrid's hand. "It bothers you, though."

Sigrid sunk further into her chair, hoping to disappear entirely. "Of course it bothers me, but I have no right to be bothered by it. It isn't the right time for him."

"But it is for you."

Sigrid shrugged. "I suppose. I don't have the same holdups as he does on the issue, but it doesn't matter, he's allowed to prioritize other things. I can't force someone to put those things aside."

"I know," Brigid replied softly, trying her best to sound comforting. Sigrid just felt annoyed. "I'm sorry. There'll be others. Baldr's a great guy, but you're right. You can't force him. You just don't seem very happy having him around."

"What do you mean?" Sigrid pushed herself up in the chair. "He's still my friend."

"It's clearly hard on you."

"It is not!"

"Yes, it is. You might not feel the energy, but we do."

"Oh, it's *we* now," Sigrid snapped.

Agnar held up both hands. "Whoa, listen, we're just worried about you. You've spent a lot of time in your room since we got back. You haven't seen one cull, which isn't weird to me, but Brigid thinks it is very stra—ow!" There was a thump beneath the table, and Agnar quickly bit his lip, his cheeks reddening.

Brigid gave Sigrid a sweet look, but Sigrid cut her off before she could speak. "I appreciate the concern, guys, but if you haven't noticed, we've had very few culls even walk through our door right now."

"You haven't picked up your sword. Normally you'd be at the gym when things are slow. You work harder than anyone here on your physique."

Sigrid nearly stood and stalked out of the room. A voice deep in her mind reminded her not to let her emotions get the best of her. If she lashed out, she'd regret it later. Even as bubbles began to boil beneath the surface, she worked diligently on keeping her anger at bay. She drew upon years of practice at keeping her outbursts inside when her moods rapidly shifted. Suddenly, the pungent herb sitting in a jar in her room called her name. "Listen," she finally said, leaning forward against the table. "I appreciate the concern. I'll get over whatever funk I'm in, okay?"

"You can talk about—" Brigid began to say, but Sigrid cut her off again.

"Brigid. I appreciate it. I just … I just need to let my emotions simmer for a while, okay?" She conceded just a bit of how she felt, knowing it would satisfy Brigid enough to get out of the conversation. "I'll come to you if I need help figuring it out. Now, if you don't mind, I'm going to go to my room and smoke. Then maybe take a nap. If Baldr comes to collect us, let me know." With that, she stood and swiftly exited the room, her hands clenched into fists. With every step she took up the stairs, she inhaled deep into her chest, letting the frustration that wanted to lash out be soothed with her breath.

In her room, she shut the door hard behind her. Crossing to her vanity, she popped open the jar of the dream herb. It was ground down, easy for her to roll into a cigarette. Lighting the end with a match, she inhaled deep, allowing the smoke to fill her lungs. Holding her breath, she let the herb seep into the fibers of her body. Immediately she felt herself begin to relax, her head swimming. Crossing the room to sit in her window, she pushed open the glass and blew the smoke out toward the street.

Anam sat behind her desk and stared at Agnar with a flat gaze. Twiddling with the pendant hanging down her chest, she didn't say anything. Her eyes bore into the man as if trying to read his very soul, and her gaze seemed to find him wanting. "Don't get me wrong, Agnar, we appreciate the information you've brought to us. You are an asset to have on our side. But ... joining? That will cause quite a stir. Not many accept humans so readily, and those within our ranks spent much time gaining trust. You've been here barely a week."

Agnar clenched his fists but remained calm. "I know, but have any of those humans sacrificed what I have? Committed treason the way I have? I risked my life to take information to Uruachi. You say I'm an asset, but so far all you've done is hide me away. I get it, you probably don't know how to use me yet, that's fine. We can figure things out. But I'm here to dedicate myself to this cause. Listen, I'm well educated, and I know the countryside. If I hadn't been taken on so many tax-collecting trips as a child, I doubt I would have made it as far north as I did. I know every noble family, and I know who has power in which region. I know which jarls are in favor, and which resent the crown. I know who might harbor elven sympathies. While you hide me away, my father is readying his army to move north, which means Copper City will be in their path. I left home four months ago. In that time, I'm sure my father has made quite a bit of progress, and he most certainly knows about the unrest here. You have an advantage right now in that the guard here is far less organized and not nearly as well-trained as the army, which is why they've backed off to one part of the city. You're making good progress, but you don't yet have the forces to defend yourself when he arrives. The Uruachi soldiers won't arrive for another month at the very least. In the meantime, you need to be making more allies than you are right now. You're good at agitating. You're good at getting the people into the streets, and you know how to give a good speech. What you don't have is a great backing of wealth."

"Are you saying we need the Heddish to defeat the Heddish?" Anam frowned.

Agnar nodded defiantly, his shoulders squared. "I'm saying you need wealth. You need money. What you collect now won't sustain you in the long run. I will help you negotiate with those in the city and surrounding land who might be able to help us."

"They'll want things in return. Nobody is going to help us for free."

"No, they won't," he admitted. "But some may be amenable if they are fairly certain the alternative is the loss of their status entirely. Some of them will back who they see as the winning side. Some are nobility in name only and can easily be convinced of a new world if you give them a world they want to be in. Madame, with all due respect, you need me. I am your most powerful ally yet."

There was a great silence in the room. Sigrid shifted awkwardly, but she had to admit she was rather impressed. Agnar was a diplomat through and through. Pride surged in her chest.

Baldr spoke up after the pause in the room grew too much. "Mother," he said in a steady voice. "I didn't trust him at first, but Agnar has proven himself to me. I think he's right. We need him."

Anam shot Baldr a stern look and flattened her lips into a thin line. "Very well. He'll be your responsibility, Baldr. Everything you do will need to be run through me first. And, Agnar, I want you to tell me everything about your family that you can. Every bit of inside detail that we can use to our advantage. What you know is now what we know. Can you do that?"

Agnar swallowed but ultimately nodded, his jaw set hard. "Yes, madame. I know what this means."

Anam leaned forward over her desk, her fingers forming steeples as she rested her elbows on the dark wood. "Tell me something then. Anything. Show me you have anything useful at all."

Sigrid glanced at Brigid uneasily, but the woman next to her never took her eyes off Agnar. A fist was set against her chest as she watched him.

"Well ..." Agnar seemed caught off guard. "Well ... my father ..." He looked around at his friends as if they held the answers that suddenly seemed absent from his mind. His eyes settled on Brigid, and an uncomfortable look of dawning comprehension seemed to overtake his face. He turned back to Anam. "My father has a weakness for elven women. It is well known that he keeps mistresses. Kings long before him have done the same thing. What they don't know is that my father often takes elven servants as his mistresses. They don't get official positions at court the way a Heddish noblewoman might if she were his mistress. They often get their own suite where all their needs are met and they are lavished upon, but nobody can know. My mother prefers it because it means she does not have a public mistress to contend with, and they are stowed away where she doesn't have to see or think about them. This would be quite a scandal if anyone knew."

Anam stared forward, unmoving, for an extended silence. Finally, a smile crept across her features. "This is good. This can be used. Perhaps this could be how we infiltrate a spy. Yes!" Her eyes widened as a million different ideas seemed to pour into her brain. "Yes, good. There are many possibilities here. Stay for a while, Agnar. Baldr, take the women and go. You can return for Agnar later."

"What?" Brigid protested, stepping forward. "He didn't come here to be interrogated."

Agnar held up a hand and turned to give Brigid a reassuring smile. "It's fine, I want to talk. You go. I'll be back later." He turned back to Anam. "Right? I'll remain where I am?"

"If you're happy at a brothel, then sure."

Brigid and Sigrid both bristled. Baldr, immediately noticing, spoke up. "Mother. Sigrid and Brigid have been a great help. There's no need to speak to them like that."

"Apologies," Anam said in a tone that suggested she wasn't actually sorry. "Regardless, you three are dismissed."

Baldr herded the two women from the room, closing the door behind them. Both were still tense and did not wish to move, but he guided them both down the stairs. "Agnar can handle himself. This is what he wants."

"Your mother is kind of a bitch." Sigrid frowned. "No offense."

"None taken. I know she can be ... a lot. She won't mistreat him. And don't worry about what she said. She respects you even if she doesn't quite understand you. Even she isn't immune to Heddish propaganda."

Sigrid placed her hand on her hip and turned to look at Baldr. "I can tell."

He gave her an apologetic look and reached out to touch her arm, dropping his hand just before he touched her skin. "Go head home. I'll bring Agnar when he's done. I'll make sure he's in one piece too."

Sigrid's heart sank a little, but she gave him a nod anyway. "Fine. I guess I'll see you later."

He nodded, walking the two to the door. Sigrid headed off without so much as looking back at him. The conversation she'd had that morning with Agnar and Brigid was still fresh, and the anger in her chest began to boil once again. She worried if she did not leave, she would say something petty, and he did not deserve that from her. Instead, she took Brigid's hand and walked home in silence.

CHAPTER TWENTY

Sigrid's fingers knocked against the door to Anam's office. There were voices inside that stopped at the noise. A moment later the door opened, revealing Baldr. His eyes widened.

"Sigrid," he said. "What are you doing here?"

What was she doing there? Her lips drew into a frown heavy with disappointment. "I came to speak with Elder Anam."

"Let her in," the Elder's voice rang through the room.

Baldr stepped out of the way and let Sigrid through, his eyes following her every movement. She knew he was inspecting her attire, but she'd worn it on purpose. Her white skirt was tight, and her stomach was bare save for the string of beads around her middle. Her top was white and gold, and a large gold necklace sat across her chest.

The Priestesses of Ata had once worn something very similar, though the dress had become far more modest as the Heddish asserted control. Now it was no more than a costume for many, but for her, it was a statement. She wore it when working—and the Collective was her job too.

Anam's lips tightened into a thin line. "How can I help you?" Her eyes traveled across Sigrid's body, her distaste evident.

"Elder, I have come to ask why you have not asked anything of me. You send Baldr to do your work but have asked nothing of me."

"You have done your duty. You are harboring the prince. Is that not enough for you?"

Sigrid frowned but held her head high. "With all due respect, I believe the only reason you're allowing Agnar to stay with us is because it is the last place anyone would look for the prince. You're happy to use us when it suits you, but you see no other use for us."

Anam sat back in her chair. Her hands were folded in her lap, and one leg was crossed over the other. With a steady gaze, she tilted her head from one side to the other. "It seems to me there are few uses for painted women outside of espionage. Have you anything of use to bring to me? Secrets from a cull? Are any of your men powerful enough to be of note?"

"Mother," Baldr interjected. "That isn't fair."

"It's fine, Baldr," Sigrid said, holding up her hand. "I have far more to offer than pillow secrets. I helped earn Uruachi's help as much as Baldr did."

Anam stood up and leaned forward, her hands on her wooden desk. "Had I known more about you when Baldr told me of you, I would have objected."

Baldr huffed and took a step forward, a fire blazing in his eyes. "I told you all you needed to know about her. Sigrid is such an important addition to the Collective, and you can't even see it."

"The other one seems happy in her position," Anam said in dismissal. "The tall one."

"Cualli?" Sigrid's brows furrowed together.

"That's the one. She's brought us tidbits of information here and there, and we're more than happy to send her to entice a target should we need it."

"I am not Cualli. She helps in her way, and I will not speak for her, but you cannot believe my only use is the same as any other painted woman."

"Be happy with what you're doing. Keep the prince inside and safe. If you get any important information, bring it to Baldr, who can bring it to me. Until then, *go away*."

"You can't speak to her that way," Baldr said. "I won't let you."

"You," Anam hissed, pointing her finger in Baldr's direction. "You need to look past your infatuation. You are better than this."

Sigrid felt the heat rise in her chest. It began to bubble and boil, threatening to spill from her mouth, but Baldr's hand on her wrist brought her back to reality.

"We're leaving," he said. "I'll be back to talk to you."

Sigrid glared at the woman in front of her. "You're no different than they are if you can't see more than my position," Sigrid said as she turned to leave the room. Her words were heated, but she kept the most aggressive of her thoughts to herself.

Sigrid was startled awake by the feeling of a body throwing itself on her. She grunted as someone's arms wrapped tightly around her body. Brigid's voice was loud in her ear as she exclaimed, "There's a festival in town!"

"What?"

"A festival! The Festival of Kings! Honestly, with everything that has been going on, I kind of forgot it was coming."

"That festival is all about the royal family. Why would we want to go?"

"Because it's a festival," Brigid replied, yanking the blankets off Sigrid's body. "Get up. At the very least we can try and see if we can collect any culls."

Sigrid groaned. Even though they were beginning to run low on savings, it had been so long since she'd seen a cull that the thought made her want to stay in bed. "Do we have to? I'll go if you want me to, but please don't make me work today. I'm just not feeling great these last few days."

"What's wrong?"

"Just … emotions. You know how I get sometimes. Where … one moment I'm fine, the next moment it is like my head will pop off with anger or I want to drown myself in tears."

"You've been managing it well then. I hadn't noticed. I'm sorry."

"Don't worry." Sigrid sighed, sitting up and pulling the blankets back over her legs. "I've been managing well. Smoking when I need to. The dream herb still helps. Honestly, I think I've been feeling like this for a little while now, but with everything going on I just didn't have time to notice."

"Is it because of Baldr, maybe?"

Sigrid shook her head. "No, it isn't his fault. It does explain why I've been so emotional about him lately."

"Well, he has been weird. That's not in your head."

"I know, but I'm usually so understanding about these things. I accept it, I move on. That's how I am. I've never … pined after someone this long."

Brigid cocked her head to the side and frowned. "Sigrid. That's a lie."

"What? No, it isn't!"

"Wouldn't I know?"

Sigrid blushed, her neck sinking into her shoulders. "Brigid ..."

"I'm not trying to make you feel bad, but you have to know you get like this when you're into someone. It isn't often, which is why you think you don't."

"I do not pine!"

"Yes, you do. It's okay. You're a secret romantic."

"I am not!"

"You are! That's why we need to go out tonight. Have fun. Fine, we don't have to work, but maybe we'll find you someone cute to flirt with anyway. I'm going to make Agnar wear one of my wigs as a disguise so he can come with us. It'll be fun! With everything going on, when was the last time you had fun?"

Sigrid thought back to the small town and the inn she'd danced at with Baldr. Her heart clenched in her chest. "Fine. Perhaps I am pining. I'll go, but you're not allowed to make goo-goo eyes at Agnar the whole time."

"I do not make goo-goo eyes!"

Sigrid threw her pillow at Brigid, hitting her square in the face. "Now who is the one in denial?"

Brigid laughed, hugging the pillow to her chest. "Fine, fine, no goo-goo eyes. I promise. Just come out."

"I will. Why don't we go to the bathhouse now and get ready when we get back? We'll be the nicest-looking women there. We'll wear our best."

Brigid giggled and popped up from the bed. "Come on! No time to waste!"

By the time they returned to the Pearl from the bathhouse, Sigrid was feeling far better than she'd had in a few days. She let her hair dry in the wind as they walked home and enjoyed the feeling of the sun on her face. Brigid carried the conversation, telling Sigrid the little things about Agnar that intrigued her. Sigrid tried to listen for the most part, happy that her friend was infatuated with someone that seemed to return the sentiment, but she felt her mind wandering to the journey she'd been on. Perhaps only a few months had passed, but it could have easily been six months crammed together. Some days felt tortuously long and some were going so quickly she barely had time to breathe.

Sigrid hardly noticed Brigid disappear into her room to get ready. Sitting down at her vanity, Sigrid stared into the mirror. She looked the same as she had when she'd left. Her hair, now frizzy from drying in the sun, was as curly and dark as normal. Her arms were as muscular, and her skin was as warm as it always was. She felt different, though. Aged. She found herself increasingly wanting to be busy, and not with her usual work. If anything, she didn't want to work at all. It felt absurd to work and pay rent as if things weren't growing darker around them. Her obligations hadn't disappeared. She simply had more of them.

Her jaw tightening, Sigrid banished those thoughts from her mind. No dwelling. Lighting the end of a cigarette, she inhaled the fragrant dream herb deep into her lungs. Holding her breath, she felt her muscles relax. The knot that had begun to form in her stomach when she was alone began to unravel, and she found herself able to smile. Tonight she would enjoy her evening. She lit incense and lined her eyes in kohl. Her lips she painted a deep red. Admiring herself in the mirror, she turned her face from side to side and posed.

"You look stunning," came a voice from across the room.

Glancing up, she saw Baldr standing in her doorway with a soft smile on his face. "Hey," she said. "If it isn't my fake husband."

He laughed. "Yes, it is I, your husband. Are you working tonight?"

She shook her head. "No. Brigid, Agnar, and I are going to the Festival of Kings."

Baldr frowned. "Is it really wise to take Agnar to a festival?"

Sigrid shrugged. "He'll be wearing a wig. Remember, everyone thinks they've got a princess, they'll hardly be looking for a prince. Agnar deserves a little fun. He's risked a lot."

"He has." Baldr sighed. "I don't think Anam will be very pleased to hear of this."

"Good thing she doesn't know!"

Baldr exhaled. "Well ... just don't tell anyone. She won't understand."

"I'll take your word for it."

The air hung tensely between them for a long moment as neither of them was able to find words. She could feel his eyes boring into her, and her heart skipped when she met his gaze. "You could come with us. Make sure he stays out of trouble."

"You don't have to invite me, Sigrid."

"No, you should come. We haven't spent much time together since we got back."

"I've been pretty busy. I'm sorry I haven't been around as much."

"It's fine. Would you like to come to the Festival of Kings with us?"

Baldr eyed her as a soft smile spread across his lips. "Sure. I could use some festivities. Things have been far too serious."

"Good, good."

"I'll be back around six then?"

"Oh, I still have to do my hair. Seven at the earliest."

Baldr laughed. "Understandable. Seven it is. I'll see you then."

The festival was crowded. It was always a spectacle when there were festivals and holidays, but extra care had been put into these festivities. Sheets of paper with elaborate designs spanned between buildings, a decidedly elven touch to a Heddish festival. Parts of the festival spilled from the streets into the large park near the city's central palace. People littered the grass, some sitting on blankets and watching the festival's music from a distance.

The crowd was as mixed as all their festivals. Unlike some of the wilder celebrations, the Festival of Kings was painted as wholesome and family friendly. Children darted through throngs of people, their screams nearly drowned out by the music that filled the air.

Sigrid unfolded her fan and waved it at her face as sweat beaded her brow. Autumn was just around the corner, but summer's heat was in full swing.

"This festival happens in Hedeby once a year, though it is usually a bit later in the year." Baldr brushed his fingers through his hair just as it began to cling to the side of his face, which was wet with sweat. "The king participates."

"We all did," Agnar cut in, his arm around Brigid's elbow. "I enjoyed it as a child. As an adult, it became a chore. This will be the first I've ever attended where I'm not ..." His voice faded as if he were suddenly remembering the need for secrecy.

Baldr nodded as he pulled his hair into a knot on the top of his head and tied it in a leather thong. "Now that you mention it, I got close enough to the dais one year to see you. I was probably ... thirteen at the time."

"Ah, so many moons ago," Agnar teased.

Baldr gasped. "Aren't you only two years younger than I?"

"Two very, very long years."

Agnar dodged a playful punch from Baldr, the dark bangs of his borrowed wig all but obscuring his eyes. It was a real enough wig, but knowing what he looked like without it, Sigrid thought he looked comical with it.

Brigid pulled away from Agnar's grasp and pointed toward a tent not far away. "Beer! I would like a drink. Baldr, go get us drinks."

"Excuse me?" he responded, scoffing. "Why do I have to?"

"Because you're the one most in need of one. Here." She reached into the bag at her side and pulled out a few silver coins, slipping them into his palm. "Something dark, if they have it, please."

He did not protest but gave her a narrow look before disappearing into the crowd.

"That'll be good for him," Agnar said, retaking Brigid's elbow. "He's been all too sullen lately."

"He has much on his mind," Sigrid said, slipping her arm through Brigid's other arm.

Brigid shrugged. "Perhaps, but I don't like how distant he's been from you."

"He's not my keeper."

"He's got someone stunning in front of him, and he's dawdling." Brigid gave Sigrid a matter-of-fact look and cocked her head to the side as if she were daring her friend to disagree.

Sigrid gave Brigid a sheepish grin. "You're very cute when you're protective."

"I agree," Agnar replied. "Though I think she is cute at all times."

Sigrid imitated a gag just as Baldr reappeared with four mugs in his hands.

"What?" he asked, handing out the mugs.

"Agnar is simply telling the truth," Brigid said with a wink, happily plucking her mug from Baldr's hand.

When Sigrid was finished with her drink, another one replaced it. Baldr said little at first, and his eyes constantly scanned the crowd. He remained close to Agnar for much of the night, always more focused on guards when they grew too close than his two companions.

As the night progressed, Sigrid could see Baldr begin to relax. She could see the man she'd known when they were alone on the road. He stopped watching every guard that passed, and his cheeks darkened with every refill of his mug. For a time, he seemed to allow himself to live in the moment and not the potential dangers.

Together they wandered toward a group that had been playing music for some time. Two played the same Heddish instrument the bard in Njarovik had played, and a few others beat on elven drums. The music, a mix of styles, was strange on Sigrid's ears, but it was lively and fun. Sigrid found herself tapping her feet to the beat of the song.

"Would you like to dance, my lady?" Agnar said to Brigid, sweeping his arms out wide with one leg crossed behind the other. He gave a dramatic pose before holding out a hand for Brigid to take. She giggled, took his hand, and disappeared with him into the throng of dancing bodies.

Sigrid stood silently, watching the musicians as they beat their drums and turned the levers of their Heddish instrument. Sweat dripped down their faces, glistening in the light of the hundreds of torches that lit the square. Shadows danced across them, giving them an ethereal quality.

She felt someone take her hand. Looking down, she saw Baldr's fingers intertwined with hers, and she looked up at him with a raised brow.

"Let's dance too," he said, setting his mug on a cart of dirty mugs as it was wheeled past them for the cleaning tent.

Flashes of the night they'd danced together in the Njarovik tavern filled her mind, and her lips widened. "Of course," she replied breathlessly, and pulled him to the dance floor.

His hands were on her hips in an instant. Together they twirled around, weaving in and out of dancing couples. He was light on his feet, spinning her out and drawing her back into his embrace. The night air around them was throbbing and hot, but now and then a cool breeze broke through the crowd and across Sigrid's face. She laughed as Baldr lifted her off her feet and set her down a few steps away. His lips were pulled tight across his face, and his white teeth flashed in the firelight as he tugged her close.

"We should go dancing more often," he said above the swirling music. "I forgot how good you are."

"I'm the one who didn't expect dancing from a Heddish boy!"

He bellowed, sweeping her off her feet and dipping her so low the tip of her sleeked-back ponytail nearly touched the dirt.

"Half Heddish," he replied as his fingers dug into her hips.

She turned, pressing her back against him as the song changed. This one was just a bit slower and was suited to dancing close to a partner. His arms curled around her waist, and their hips moved in unison. Sigrid's heart, beating against her ribs, sped up.

"It's so hot," she said as they swayed from side to side. She fanned herself, but it felt as if she were just moving hot air.

"Come." He pulled away, taking her by the hand to guide her through the dancing crowd, and it was nearly painful to part her body from his.

He led her toward the park, the air growing markedly cooler as the people around them began to disperse. Near them was a large tree split in two, one part bent to the side near enough to the ground that the two of them could climb onto it. Their feet dangled above the grass, the music was quieter and chatter distant.

"Thank you," he said, dragging his fingers through his hair.

"For?"

"Inviting me. I've had so much fun tonight I can hardly believe it."

She smiled, her fingers dancing across his. "We've had some fun together these past few months when time allows for it."

"We have. As dangerous as our trip was ... there were moments I would not change for anybody."

"Like what?" Her words pierced through the air, her stomach knotting up.

He laughed. "Like the tavern."

"That night at the tavern might be one of the most fun nights I've ever had."

"We should go dancing more often. You're an entrancing dancer, Sigrid."

Her cheeks burned. In her chest, her heart pulsed quicker as he flipped his hand and allowed herself to draw her fingers across his palm. She pulled it into her lap, the tips of her fingers tracing every line. Touching him was so easy. "I ... love dancing. I have to dance for work often, and it is one thing I truly enjoy about my job."

"You can dance for me," he said, his eyes piercing through her flesh. She felt naked in front of him.

Sigrid swallowed hard and curled his fingers inward until he'd formed a fist, then set it back on the branch beneath them. "Just for you?"

"If that's what you wanted." He reached out, taking her hand and lifting it to graze his lips against her knuckles.

They'd always found touch easy. Ever since they'd met, she found herself holding his hand or reaching for his arm. He'd settle his palm against the small of her back, or she'd lean against him when they sat together. Lately, those moments had grown rare, so to feel him again ...

She shivered. "Baldr ..."

"Hmm?" He tried to meet her gaze, but she could not look anywhere but her lap.

"I've missed you coming around."

He was quiet for a moment. "Me too," he said finally. "I'm sorry. I should be around more."

"You should be where you're most needed," she replied, shifting her gaze to look toward the crowd.

Warm fingers curled beneath her chin and turned her face. His eyes met hers, melting the part of her that was afraid.

"I need to be around you. I've seen something in you that lights me on fire since the moment I saw you. I thought there was no way such a beautiful woman would be so kind to me. Then you tore open my heart and let me stay until it was safe."

"It was the right thing to do," she said breathlessly, lost in his eyes. Oh, those beautiful eyes, she thought. Brown, but lit from beneath by the sun. Even in the dim light they held her captive.

"I don't know if it was. You took a risk. Sometimes I think it would be easier if I never introduced you to the Collective. I should have simply pursued you and not complicated your life as I have."

She frowned. "I'm glad you did. Things would have happened whether or not you brought me in. Now I get to be part of it, instead of living in fear. Even if Anam has feelings on who I am."

"She's ignorant," he replied as lines creased his forehead. "She was wrong for what she said the other day. You are incredible. I told her ..." He paused, glancing toward the crowd before bringing his attention back to the woman in front of him. "I told her she's wrong about you. Not just you, but women like you. I wanted to protect you from her ignorance, and I thought … Stupidly, so stupidly, I thought if I kept away, then she'd see that my insistence isn't just about my feelings for you."

He simpered, and his lips drew into an awkward smile. She wanted to trace her fingers along them. Silence spanned between them as they sat there, trapped in each other's gaze. Electricity seemed to buzz through the air. If she just looked down, she was sure she'd see lightning.

"Sigrid," he said softly, his voice like honey.

"Hmm?"

"I'd like to kiss you."

She felt as if the wind were being knocked out of her. "All right," she replied slowly, leaning closer to him.

His fingers curled beneath her chin and lifted it. He was so close she could feel his breath against her face. He smelled of beer and the fried sweets they'd shared. Slowly his lips found hers and pressed in. He was gentle at first, his lips parting for hers. His fingers uncurled and spread across her throat, sliding around her neck to pull her closer.

She leaned into him, one arm slipping around his waist. He pressed against her with heightened ferocity, and suddenly she was in his arms. He held her tight, his kiss deep and full of a hunger that surprised her. As she felt his tongue dance across her lips, she parted them to invite him in.

With each exchanged kiss, the two grew bolder. Wrapped in his arms, Sigrid whimpered, heat pulsing through her core. It buzzed and beat, spreading through her limbs. For a moment, she almost forgot they were in public, and her fingers danced beneath his shirt to feel the hard muscles of his stomach.

When they finally parted for air, Sigrid was ready to combust. Slowly, she opened her eyes to look at the face of the most handsome man she'd ever seen. He was perfect. She wanted to kiss him again and again, no matter how many people were around them.

"You are truly a being of art," he whispered, his forehead pressed against hers as he panted.

She beamed and stole a quick kiss. "I think I've been waiting for that kiss for as long as I've known you."

"I was a fool not to have done it sooner."

"No." She sighed. "You were not a fool."

He pulled back and quickly shook his head. "I have not felt like this in quite some time."

"Neither have I," she said in a firm tone, straightening her spine. "I have wanted you, Baldr."

"I ... I know. And we'll talk about it. Figure it out. That is, if you'd like to figure us out."

"Of course I would."

He smiled and brushed his thumb against her bottom lip. "You are a goddess."

"Stop." She blushed, butterflies beginning a whirling frenzy in her stomach.

He simply grinned and pulled her into another kiss.

CHAPTER TWENTY-ONE

Sigrid smacked Brigid in the arm and howled with laughter. "Sometimes you're such a bitch," she snickered, leaning back in the cushions she occupied.

The two sat at the Collective's headquarters as Baldr helped his mother with ledgers or maps, Sigrid couldn't quite remember.

"I'm just being honest," Brigid replied innocently as if she had not just insulted one of Sigrid's most devoted customers.

Brigid had spent the day poring over books on herbs and what medicinal qualities they might have, but Sigrid had spent much of it with Baldr at the gym. When she'd returned, most of the Collective had already cleared out for the evening, leaving the main room free.

As Brigid leaned in to whisper a rather vulgar joke into Sigrid's ear, Cualli burst through the door. Her hair was windswept as if she had run from wherever she'd come from, and sweat glistened on her brow. She slumped forward with her hands on her thighs, heaving in deep breaths. "Kings-*gasp*-army-*gasp*-at the gate!"

Sigrid and Brigid glanced at each other, then back at the petite woman.

"Care to say that again?" Brigid said.

Cualli groaned and straightened up, her hands on her narrow hips, her brown face flushed. "I was out at the market, the one near the city gates, with Zuma."

"As you usually are," Sigrid said.

"Yes. A company of men came through. They were soldiers, and all were wearing the king's colors."

"Soldiers come and go all the time." Brigid shrugged.

Cualli shook her head frantically. "You didn't see them. These men were in finery. These were not your usual soldiers. I think they are here for Agnar. They have to be."

Sigrid's stomach turned to stone. "Are you sure? Did you overhear anything?"

"No," Cualli admitted, biting her plump bottom lip. "We did try to follow them for a while, and they are definitely headed toward the palace. There was one man in the middle. He looked fancier than the others, and I can spot a nobleman from a mile away. He was someone important. More important than we've had in the city in a while. It can't be a coincidence that he shows up now. It wasn't a regiment of soldiers, just a small group. They probably thought they were unnoticed."

Sigrid clenched a pillow in her lap, her fingers threatening to rip through the fabric. It had always been only a matter of time until people started looking for Agnar in the city. Who could it have been? "What did the man look like?" Sigrid asked with caution in her voice.

"His clothing was very clean. He was a little older, I think."

Sigrid exhaled, but the tension in her chest did not release. Could it be Gorm? Gorm had a beard, but that was easily remedied. He had been wearing well-made armor when they'd met. He'd last been seen so far away, and as far as she had heard, no spies had reported he'd moved closer to the city.

"We should tell Anam no matter who or what they're here for," Brigid said, reaching out to squeeze Sigrid's hand. Her face was stricken, with worry written in every line.

Together, the three of them quickly hurried up the stairs toward Anam's office. She'd been there for a while, meeting with various people, but now her door was open and she sat alone at her desk. When the three women entered, she looked up with surprise, looking very much like Baldr when he was caught off guard. "Is something wrong?"

Sigrid nodded. "Cualli says she saw some men in town wearing the crown's colors."

Cualli nodded, quickly recounting what few details she'd been able to provide to the others.

Anam frowned, sitting back in her sturdy desk chair. "I've not heard anything about soldiers being near the city. They must have avoided detection somehow."

Sigrid frowned. "Perhaps they simply did not have good information," she said.

Anam gave Sigrid a narrow look. "Regardless, this comes as a surprise. And you didn't overhear anything important, girl?"

Cualli shook her head. "I'm sorry, I wish I had. I didn't want to be detected. At one point one of them saw me following, so I had to make it look like I wanted to flirt. Men are stupid, so they seemed to buy it. A few batted eyelashes and they laughed at me and kept going."

The elder woman nodded, her mix of stark-white and deep-black hair framing her face in a tight bob.

"And they were headed toward the palace. Thank you, Miss Cualli, this is valuable."

"What shall we do?" Sigrid asked, glancing away from Anam toward Brigid.

Anam shook her head. "I'm not sure yet. I'll need to call on friends in the palace to see what they know."

"There's a parlor just outside the palace that nobility often frequent. Brigid and I could go there and see if we can gather any information," Sigrid said.

Brigid frowned. "I don't think we should put ourselves at risk like that."

Sigrid waved a dismissive hand. Every fiber in her body was tense, and she itched to run home to ready herself. She wanted to find out if Gorm was in the city. If he was, they needed to get Agnar out of harm's way. What would they do with him? Fear of the unknown made her muscles clench.

Anam considered the suggestion for a moment. "No. My answer is no."

Sigrid restrained herself from pounding her hands down onto the desk. "Didn't you just tell me that one of my few uses is gathering information? Let me go."

Anam's eyes tore through Sigrid like ice. "Prince Agnar was kind enough to tell us of his uncle, Commander Gorm. The three of you left your tussle with him before you could confirm his death, so if anyone is here looking for the prince, it will be him. He knows your face. I'm not allowing you to go."

"This is ridiculous," Sigrid cried out, throwing her arms into the air. "You've not given me a single—"

"*No*," Anam said. "I said no. Send Cualli if you must, but the answer is no. If you want enough respect to have responsibilities, then you will need to learn to take orders."

Sigrid wanted to turn Anam to ash. Their eyes met and bore into each other, neither willing to flinch from their position. Only Brigid's hand on Sigrid's shoulder tore her attention away.

"Maybe she's right," Brigid said.

"What?"

"If it is that Commander Gorm, then he'd recognize you."

"And if it isn't?"

Brigid shrugged. "There will be other things for you to do. This is not the battle to fight."

Sigrid looked back to Anam with defiance heavy in her chest. "Fine. I won't go."

Sigrid watched the crowd at the bar with steady, unflinching eyes. She had to remind herself every few moments to blink and not look too suspicious. Come on, she thought in frustration, you're not new at this. Stop acting like it.

"Hello," a man said to her, his eyes bright but nervous.

"Hello," she responded without interest, barely looking in his direction.

"Are you free? I'd love to buy you a drink."

"No," she responded, pulling her eyes from the bar to give him an apologetic look. "I'm afraid I'm not free for the evening."

"I've seen you around before. You usually are working."

"I'm waiting for someone," she responded, feeling the heat in her stomach and trying desperately not to snap at him. She had a mission for the evening, but that didn't mean she wouldn't return eventually for work. She needed to retain a kind, welcoming persona, but she wanted to brush the man off.

"Ah, of course." He sighed, giving her a nod and heading back to the table he'd been sitting at.

Finally, she thought, taking a breath and returning her eyes to the bar. A new person had arrived. The fan in her hand tumbled to the floor, and her body was flooded with ice. "No," she whispered.

Gorm.

She quickly bowed her head, allowing her curls to spill into her face. She hoped it was enough to hide herself, desperate not to be seen by him. Her heart raced in her chest, so fast she was certain it would burst through her ribs. It was a chore to keep her breath steady so that those at tables around her wouldn't notice.

Her eyes slowly turned up to look back at the bar. A sigh of relief escaped her throat. He was looking away and did not seem to notice her. He stood with a group, a few soldier-looking types and a couple of Heddish women she knew often worked the same spot.

She didn't want to think about Anam, but the woman's words crept into her mind. Worse, she thought of Brigid's pleading voice, how she begged Sigrid not to go. "You promised," she'd said, collapsing onto Sigrid's bed in frustration. "Sigrid, please, I am begging you. Not this time. Please."

But she'd gone anyway.

Hoping he was sufficiently distracted, she quietly slipped from her chair and began to hurry across the room. She repeated over and over again that she could make it, that he wouldn't notice her, but just as she began to reach the door, she heard his voice ring out over the others.

"You!"

She froze, every muscle in her body burning but locked in place.

"How lovely. Join us!"

He couldn't have been speaking to her. Looking around, she tried to find someone else, but when she peeked over her shoulder, she saw his eyes firmly settled on her. A smile was spread across his thin lips. A cruel, terrible, disgusting smile. Bile rose in her throat.

Turning, she forced herself to lift her chin and give him a steady gaze. He wouldn't do something in public, would he? Surely that would bode poorly for him.

"Me?" she asked.

One of the women he was with waved in Sigrid's direction, her pink lips spread in a glowing smile. "Sigrid! Come!"

Fuck. Now he knew her name. Every instinct in her body told her to bolt, but she couldn't make a scene. Instead she flicked open her fan, hid the bottom half of her face, and stepped toward the bar.

The woman who had so unknowingly given away such an important detail hooked her arm through Sigrid's. "Come! We were about to have drinks."

"Hilda, hello," Sigrid said, trying to keep her face free of any telling emotions. She hoped it was working. "I was just about to head home, I am sure you can handle these handsome men."

"Oh, there's plenty for us both," Hilda giggled, batting her eyelashes in the direction of one of Gorm's comrades. Perhaps she was wise not to be alone with Gorm. Perhaps the other one just seemed like a better mark.

Gorm's terrible smile never left his face. "A pleasure to meet you, Sigrid. Are you one of Hilda's sisters?"

"Yes, yes." She smiled, gesturing to the gold lotus on her forehead. "I've known Hilda for a few years, though we do not work in the same house. It is a pleasure to meet everyone. Are you new to the city?"

"Just arrived," Gorm replied, bringing a glass of wine to his lips. It looked like he was drinking blood, and it made Sigrid's stomach churn. "I've only been to this city a few times, and never have I had the pleasure of visiting this lovely place. Everyone has been so welcoming."

Hilda let out a charming laugh and slipped from Sigrid's arm to the arm of the soldier she'd been eying earlier. Gorm never took his eyes off Sigrid. The attention brought goose bumps erupting across her arms.

Sigrid batted her lashes, keeping that smile plastered on her face. She was aware of how painfully fake it must have looked, but she couldn't summon anything more believable. She just wanted to flee, to tell the others who had arrived. She wanted to beat her head against the wall for not listening to Brigid. How could she have put herself in this situation?

"Are you cold, dear?" one of the men said, trying to capture her attention.

"Hmm? Oh, no." She laughed, trying to brush the man off.

"Give her your coat," Gorm said loudly, gesturing for the man to remove his jacket.

"No, it's really all right," she replied hastily, lifting her hands between her and the soldier who had begun to remove the coat. "I'm feeling a little under the weather. I should be getting home."

"I understand," Gorm replied. "I recently had an encounter that left me in bed for a few days. I do hope you recover well ... Sigrid, was it?"

"That's it!" Hilda cheered.

Oh, beautiful, stupid, unknowing Hilda. Sigrid ached to slap her.

Sigrid fanned herself and laughed, slowly backing her way toward the exit. "It was a pleasure. Have a good evening!"

When she felt the cool air of the night on her back, she turned and bolted down the road. Rocks stuck in her sandals as she went, but she did not stop until she saw the unassuming door of the Collective's current headquarters.

CHAPTER TWENTY-TWO

She knew she should have gone directly to the headquarters, to Anam. Anam would want to know, wouldn't she? Sigrid paced around her bedroom. When she'd gotten back, Cualli and Zuma were dually entertaining someone, their door locked tight. Sigrid could hear them as she ran past the room, but the sounds were drowned out when she closed the door behind her.

"Fuck," Sigrid said, turning to her vanity and quickly lighting incense.

She dropped to her knees in front of her small Ata statue, suddenly wishing more than anything that she could visit the temple in Uruachi again. She wanted to speak with a priestess, to receive some sort of council. She wished she were with Chimalma. Her heart ached at the thought.

"Please, please, let something go in our favor," she pleaded beneath her breath, her voice barely a whisper. There were other gods to look to. She could call upon

Buluc for strength in battle, or Xilonen for luck. She could even call on Mihcutli, the god of death, to strike down Gorm before he could do any damage. But she didn't want their help. She wanted Ata's. She was the only one who had ever been there for Sigrid in her time of need. She was the only one Sigrid ever felt at all.

"I have lit incense for you since I was a child. I have sacrificed coin at your altar when I needed it the most. Please. Please let us gain an advantage. Your people need you. Please."

A breeze blew through Sigrid's window, but otherwise, it was silent. Tears welled in her eyes as desperation filled her chest. She wanted to scream, to tear her room apart. Part of her couldn't understand where all her emotions were coming from. She wanted to be rational, to sit down and look at things logically, but her mind raced anyway. Every possible terrible scenario played out in her mind. She could see her neighborhood burning down. She could see Agnar being dragged away and Baldr beaten in the street. Every gruesome scene she could think of played out in her mind, no matter how far-fetched. Her anxiety grew until it threatened to spill from her mouth.

"Sigrid?"

She looked up, surprised. Baldr stood in her doorway, watching her with concern in his eyes. She must look a mess, she thought. Mascara blackened her cheeks, the kohl around her eyes had smudged until she looked like a raccoon. There was lipstick on the back of her hand. When had she wiped her mouth?

Baldr did not wait to rush forward, his hands taking hers. "What's wrong? What happened?"

"Gorm, he's here," she hissed, her nails digging into his flesh. "I saw him. He recognized me."

"He's here?"

"Anam told me not to look into it, Brigid said ..." Her voice failed.

He shook his head. "I was visiting with my uncle to gather some maps. What happened?"

She recounted Cualli's story for him—or, she tried to, but her words were coming out jumbled. She cried out in frustration, pulling at her hair as Baldr's arms wrapped around her.

"It's okay, it's okay," he said, pulling her to his chest. His fingers brushed against her scalp as he took her by the back of the head, his other arm snug around her back. Sigrid sobbed into his shoulder as she found she no longer could speak.

She could not calm herself no matter how much she tried. Part of her was angry with herself, her thoughts calling her a coward for reacting so strongly to Gorm's appearance. Another part of her could only think back to the fight in the forest. She'd been so calm the next day. Why had she been so calm then, when now she could hardly keep it together? How had she survived such a dangerous situation only for such a tame one in comparison to bring her to her knees? She was desperate to understand.

"Hey, hey, hey." He patted her back. "Breathe with me." He inhaled slowly until his chest was full.

Sigrid followed his lead. Slowly, she sucked in a deep breath. She held it as he did and released it in sync with his. He led her through the exercise for several minutes. Once her sobbing had stopped and her breath was restored to normal, Sigrid found her words once again.

She recounted what Cualli had told them, and how they'd gone to Anam with the information. She told him about the evening at the restaurant and how Gorm had acted as if he'd never known her. "Then I was running home and … I've never felt so panicked in my life. So afraid. Even when I met him the first time, I didn't … I didn't feel like this. Why didn't I feel like this then?"

"Hey, stop," Baldr said, brushing hair out of her face. "It's okay. How you feel is understandable."

"I just don't get it."

"It's okay. You will have time to reflect on it." He rested his palm on her cheek and brushed tears from beneath her eye with his thumb. "Are you okay?"

"Now I am. Thank you."

"Good. Do you want me to tell this to my mother? If you need to stay and rest, I understand, but she needs to know."

Sigrid inhaled a deep breath and held it. "No," she said, releasing the breath. "I don't want to stay. I need to be involved. If I had never gone, he would never have recognized me. What if he figures out Agnar is here?"

Baldr's lips flattened into a thin line. "Well ... we cannot dwell right now. It doesn't matter what may have happened down another path. What matters is what is happening right now. We need to tell my mother. Do you think you can do that?"

"Yes," Sigrid said firmly. The shakiness she'd felt earlier was beginning to wane, and her confidence began to blossom once again. "I can do this. Just give me a few minutes to clean up and we can go."

Baldr nodded, his lips spreading into a smile. "Can I kiss you?"

"What?"

"To remind you that it's okay."

She blinked. "Yes."

Baldr leaned in and gently pressed his lips to hers. She held her breath, allowing herself to relax against his lips. His touch was soft, yielding, and he was careful not to push too far. She melted.

The Collective's headquarters were quiet when they arrived. "Are you sure she's here?" Sigrid asked.

"She's always here."

"Maybe she'll be at home?"

Baldr frowned and glanced sidelong at her. "She's not at home. She hasn't been at home for more than clothing in weeks. She's here."

Baldr ascended the stairs first, with Sigrid's hand resting in his. At the top of the stairs, the rooms were black except for the sliver of light coming from Anam's office. The knot in Sigrid's stomach was tight and grew tighter as they approached the door. Baldr reached out a hand and gently pushed the door open.

Anam looked up from her desk in surprise. Sigrid released a sigh of relief, though she was a bit surprised by her own reaction. The headquarters had just been so quiet.

"Mother," Baldr said firmly. Whatever terrible fear clutched Sigrid's heart, it did not seem to have its fingers in him.

"Is something wrong?" the elder woman asked, setting down the quill in her hand. "It's late."

"We know who those soldiers are." Baldr inhaled a deep breath, pulling Sigrid closer to him. He rested his hand on the small of her back. "Sigrid saw them."

"Oh." Anam's gray eyes cast over Sigrid. "I take it by the look on your face something rather unpleasant happened."

"Yes," Sigrid said. "I'm sorry. I was recognized."

Anam's expression didn't change. "Recognized?"

Sigrid nodded. "It was Commander Gorm. I went to the Rosewater to see if I could learn anything."

"And learn you did. Did anything happen?"

Sigrid shook her head. "He acted as if he didn't know me. Treated me like the rest of the entertainment."

"Is it possible he didn't recognize you?"

"Oh, no, he recognized me. He definitely knew it was me. One of the other workers knew me and said my name. There's no doubt he'll have information on me."

Anam tilted her head to the side, and Sigrid heard the sound of the bones in her neck cracking. She tilted her head in the other direction to the same effect. "I told you not to go. There was always a possibility, and you disobeyed me anyway."

Sigrid swallowed hard and felt Baldr's hand softly rub her back. "I should have known better. I'm sorry. Agnar is with me, he'll know where to go now," Sigrid said.

The elder woman nodded, her lips narrowing into a thin, taut line. "He'll have to stay somewhere else. We may even consider hiding him outside the city, at least until this Commander Gorm is gone. Where is Agnar now?"

"I'm ... not sure," Sigrid replied, her face paling. "I didn't see him at the Pearl when we left or when I got back from the Rosewater."

"Well, where could he have gone?"

Sigrid clenched her fists. "Perhaps he's out with Brigid? She had plans for the evening, but perhaps they ended early and they went for food or a walk. We'll find them."

"Good. Find him and bring him here. He needs to be out of there as quickly as possible. You will continue to go about your business as normal. Gorm already knows your name and where to find you, so you must act as if you have nothing to hide. If you are questioned, you left Agnar a long time ago."

Questioned? Sigrid did not like the thought of whatever questioning Gorm might think up.

CHAPTER TWENTY-THREE

As it turned out, Agnar had not been very far at all. When he strolled through the front door of the Pearl the next day with Brigid laughing on his arm, he was rather surprised to see the surly looks on his friends' faces.

"Ayo," Agnar said, waving his free hand at Sigrid and Baldr, who were huddled together in the front entryway.

Sigrid reached out suddenly and grabbed the man by his ear. "Do you have any idea how worried we were?"

"Ow!" Agnar flinched, letting go of Brigid in surprise as he tilted in the direction Sigrid was yanking his ear. "What are you talking about, Mother?"

Sigrid huffed. "We went looking for you. Both of you. We have news, bad news, and I thought ... By Ata, I honestly thought the worst for a while."

Brigid gasped. "What happened? We haven't heard anything."

Sigrid and Baldr looked between each other. It was Baldr that spoke. "It's Gorm. He saw Sigrid last night, and he knows her name. It won't be long before you're seen here. We are going to move you tonight since you've already walked through the door rather blatantly in the sunlight."

Agnar's pale face was stricken of color, and Brigid's went ashen.

"I don't think I heard you right," said Agnar.

"No, you did," Baldr replied. "Gorm. He's back. And he's going to figure out you're here if he hasn't already. My mother is preparing to hide you somewhere else. She even mentioned getting you out of the city—"

"No," Agnar interrupted. "I'm not leaving the city."

"But it might be best—" Baldr started but was quickly cut off by Agnar once again.

"I said no. I'll go somewhere else, but I'm not leaving. I made the decision to join the Collective. I'm here, I made my bed."

Sigrid opened her mouth to retort, but it was Baldr's hand on her shoulder that pulled her attention. "You'll still need to leave the brothel," he said flatly, careful not to betray his feelings. He didn't want to alarm Agnar any more than was necessary. "We'll hide you somewhere in the city, somewhere you won't have to be far from us. But we'll have to lie low. Sigrid, it probably isn't a good idea for you to be seen going anywhere Agnar might be, not for a while." The woman's lips flattened into a line, but she knew he was right. He continued, "Brigid, you may have to stay away for a bit. He doesn't know you yet, but he'll figure out who you are. We can't risk leading him to Agnar."

"No," Agnar protested, placing an arm in front of Brigid as if shielding her. "That's not fair."

"You're right, it isn't," Brigid said, pushing down Agnar's arm. "But he might be right. Unless ... I go with Agnar, to wherever he's being stored. I'll leave the brothel for ... however long we need, a few weeks maybe, and run errands for him. Get food, supplies. Whatever he might need."

Baldr swallowed. "I'll have to ask Anam."

"No," Brigid said sternly. "Anam will have to agree, because I *am* going with him. He can't be alone, and if he's going to be holed up somewhere, then he should be with someone he trusts."

Sigrid's eyes glanced between the three. "Let Brigid go with him," she said, though her chest clenched with anxiety. "Maybe it'll keep Brigid off his radar for a while too. Besides, Brigid, you've been saying you've wanted more time to study."

A light laugh parted Brigid's lips. "Ah, yes, I suppose I have been saying that. It will give me plenty of time to study the books the healers gave me."

It was clear Baldr did not like the idea, but he had been, for the moment, outvoted. He lifted his hands in submission. "Fine, fine. But we should go quick. Agnar, grab your things and throw a cloak on. We'll leave when night hits."

Sigrid stared forward at the edict plastered across the still-boarded-up temples. She didn't know what she'd expected. They had closed their temples; it had only a matter of time before they'd make another order.

"All shall pay tithe to a shrine of their choosing," she read before angrily ripping the poster from the door and crumpling it into a ball.

Voices filled her ears from every direction, anger rippled through the city. It was bad enough that the king had closed their temples. People had been forced to worship in their homes, many losing their closest communities for lack of places to gather. Now to demand the tithes they might have given to their own gods?

Sigrid spit in disgust. Turning, she pulled her hood over her head and made her way through the winding streets to the Pearl. The green welcome flag was on the door, beckoning in men as they passed by. She tore it from its hooks and slammed the door behind her.

"Has Baldr been here?" she said, turning to look at a startled Zuma.

Zuma closed the thick book in her thin hands. "He came looking for you for some meeting."

"And Cualli?"

"Went with him. It seemed serious."

Sigrid tossed the crumpled-up flag onto a cushioned chair and turned on her heel. Back into the city she fled, stopping only when she found the red door of the Collective's headquarters.

People gathered inside. The main room was packed full. At the head of the room stood Anam, with Baldr at her side. Sigrid looked through the crowd for Cualli's black halo of hair. She spotted it near the front. Pushing through the crowd, she placed her hand on Cualli's shoulder, but said nothing as she heard Anam begin to speak.

"This has been coming," she said. "You are angry. I can feel your fury. If we are to overcome this challenge, we must do so with calculated focus."

Murmurs spread through the crowd. Some nodded in agreement, but there were grumbles of displeasure. The energy in the room was hot, the crowd a kettle set atop a steady flame.

"So what is your plan?" Sigrid spoke before she could think, her voice sharp as it cut through the rumble of the crowd.

Anam's eyes darted about until they found Sigrid. Her thin lips pursed, which exaggerated the lines around them. "We have a list of demands, but they will not hear them until we make them. I am calling for us to shut our businesses to the Heddish. Do not sell to them, do not buy from them. Do not take your money to the shrines. We will bleed them and remind them of our power."

Someone called out, "That's it?"

Anam's jaw set hard. "Do not underestimate the power of collective bargaining. Do not let this opportunity slip through our fingers. We spent weeks demanding they reopen the temples, and this is their response."

"Why not take their temples from them?" a man shouted, a good part of the gathered people crying out in agreement.

Anam shook her head. "There are times when violence works, but this will not be one of them. If we retaliate and tear down their shrines, they will impose stricter penalties. No, we will starve them. They will resist, but eventually they will see."

Sigrid crossed her arms. Her thoughts were chaotic, and the hot air made her feel trapped. Was Anam right? Could they successfully starve out their oppressors?

She inhaled a deep breath and held it within her chest until her lungs were lit aflame. "What are our demands if they agree to meet with us?" she called out.

Anam regarded her for a moment as people shouted demands they wished to be added to the list. She held up a single hand, and the room fell silent. "We will demand they hand over control of the city to us."

Shouts began again, filling the room with chaos and heat. Voices rang in Sigrid's ears, clouding her mind. It was too soon, wasn't it? Uruachi hadn't yet sent anyone to aid them. Were they really going to provoke the jarl, and through him the king? Would the jarl give up power?

"Quiet!" Anam called out. Her voice went unheard, leaving the woman to simmer in her discontent. She called out again, "QUIET!"

This time the room fell silent, and the room now had the same eerie stillness that preceded a summer storm.

Anam's voice sliced through Sigrid's mind, forcing Sigrid's eyes once again on her.

"We have a chance, and we are going to take it. Go home and tell your families. Tell your friends and associates. Do not spend money in Heddish stores. Do not pay taxes if the tax man rings. Do not sell to Heddish culls. If you work in Heddish homes, do not go to work. We will take care of each other so that no one goes hungry. No one will lose their home. We will provide where the Heddish will not. Now go."

Anam turned, beckoning for the other Elders to follow, and stalked from the room. Baldr remained behind as the crowd began to disperse into the streets, his eyes pinpointed on Sigrid.

"Let me walk you home," he said, extending his hand to her.

Sigrid looked to Cualli, whose eyes fixated on the door. "Are you coming?" Sigrid asked.

Cualli shook her head. "No. Tell Zuma I'll be home tomorrow. I have people I need to deliver tonight's message to."

Sigrid nodded, curious to know exactly what Cualli had been doing. "I'll tell Zuma what has happened."

"Thank you." Cualli placed her hand on Sigrid's shoulder and squeezed. Then she was gone, leaving Baldr and Sigrid alone.

He took her hand, his calloused fingers rough against her own, and brought it to his lips. "I'll make sure nothing happens to you," he said, his voice soft as it wrapped around her, cleansing her mind of the chaos of the meeting.

Sigrid's crimson lips pulled into a smile as she opened her palm against his cheek. "I'll turn away every Heddish cull."

He nodded, turning to kiss the inside of her palm. "Thank you. You'll be taken care of. I promise."

"I'm not worried about myself," she said, the tension in her body slowly eroding as she touched him. "This is something I can do. I can turn away Heddish culls."

Together they walked to the Pearl, where he left Sigrid with a comforting kiss that didn't last long enough for her liking.

She only saw him once more before the chaos started. As soon as the Heddish caught wind of the Collective's scheme, they sent tax collectors to the door of every elf. They were turned away each time; the city came together in solidarity. After enough doors were slammed in their faces, the tax collectors stopped asking for tithe. They started taking it.

By the time the tax collector got to Sigrid's door, he was in a foul mood.

"I have nothing for you," Sigrid said firmly, moving to close the door in his face.

The tax collector's palm slammed against the wood. "By order of the jarl, you are to pay thirty percent of your month's wages. Now."

"No," Sigrid said simply.

"A whore like you must have coin lying around. It belongs to the king."

"I said no," she replied, opening the door and squaring her shoulders.

She was taller than him by several inches, and by the look of his spindly arms, she was far more used to hitting things than he. The tax collector shrunk back, giving her a look so foul she could feel his hatred, and he slunk off to the next home.

Another tax collector came the next day, then another the next. On the third day they had been so thoroughly refused by every elf in the city that they began approaching homes with guards in tow. Once the guards were involved, the city broke out into violence. The city enacted a curfew, but it was of no use.

Sigrid watched as the streets filled outside her home. The sun was beginning to set over the horizon. With every bit it sunk, the people of Copper City grew more agitated.

Sigrid took a seat to pull on her boots. As if having read her mind, Balder burst through the door, a heavy cloak over his shoulders. "No, not tonight, Sigrid," he said, pointing at her half-laced boots.

"What?"

"Tonight, I need you to stay inside."

Sigrid's heavy brows furrowed in indignation. "What? No. I'm coming with you."

"Sigrid, I need you to stay *here*," he said, his voice strained and thick. "Please. Tonight, I am begging you to stay."

"Why?" She dropped the laces of her boots, sitting back against the sofa cushions. "Why can't I come with you?"

Baldr chewed his bottom lip. His face was drained of color, and his hands were shaking. Leaning forward, she inspected his clothing. The knees of his pants were dirty and there was a cut on his cheek. He'd been in a fight.

"Gorm," he said. "Stay here, and I can make sure you're guarded. Please, Sigrid, I am begging you. Do not come into the city tonight. *Please.*"

She wanted to be defiant. Her mind itched to tell him no, to continue lacing her boots and push past him into the streets. The look on his face, though, she couldn't ignore. She'd never seen him so scared. Was he scared for her, then? Did he fear for her safety?

Tears welled in her eyes. Aside from Brigid, had anyone been scared for her in her life? When had anyone come to her aid that wasn't a fellow painted woman? Her heart melted. Of course she would do as he asked. She trusted him. That meant trusting him when he needed her to do something. Or, in this case, to not do something.

"Okay," she said. "I won't go."

He exhaled the breath he'd been holding and fell to his knees in front of her. "Thank you," he said, resting his forehead against her knee. "I may be gone for a few days. I wanted to see you before ... anything happens."

"Okay," she said, drawing her fingers through his silken hair. "But make sure you come back. I won't wait around forever."

"I know," he whispered. "I know."

And he was gone. The nights grew raucous, the sounds of protest and upheaval carried through the thin walls of the Golden Pearl. Sigrid's resolve to stay home began to wane, but she wanted to keep her promise to Baldr. He'd never requested anything of her. He'd believed in her, and she was going to show him she'd earned his admiration. Home he'd asked her to stay, so home she stayed.

CHAPTER
TWENTY-FOUR

"Hey," came a soft voice from Sigrid's door, startling her as she read a book in her lap.

"Baldr," she said, exhaling, her a hand over her chest. "You scared me. I didn't expect I'd see you tonight."

The man in the doorway exhaled a sigh, pushing off the hood of his cloak. He wore a guard's uniform. Sigrid wondered briefly where he'd gotten it.

"Sorry," Baldr replied, standing awkwardly in the doorway. His gloved hands fidgeted together.

"Anything interesting happen today?"

Baldr shook his head, his eyes darting toward the window that overlooked the street. "No. But I thought ... perhaps we could talk for a while. I came in looking like a guard, so I thought ... hopefully this disguise is enough not to attract much attention if I stay awhile."

Her lips parted in a smile, and for a moment she felt at ease. "I'd be happy for the company. It's been so ... weird with Brigid gone. Going about my day pretending things are the way they used to be. Not even that, because I don't have Brigid."

Baldr took a seat on her bed, his elbows settling on his knees. He continued to fidget, but he kept her gaze. "It must be hard not having her."

She nodded, sliding a folded bit of paper into her book to keep her place. "I mean, I was away from her for a while when we went to Uruachi. Now she is away from me. I should be used to her absence by now."

"You're allowed to feel lonely. I know I haven't been around much either."

A dagger split her heart open at those words. He'd read her so easily. "Well ... I am not the center of the world! And it is not forever."

Baldr frowned. She hated seeing him frown, hated seeing those lips pull into anything but a smile. Heat filled her body, and she fought back the urge to touch him. He wouldn't mind, she knew, but ... something held her hand back, kept her steady. They'd spent so much time together. Why had it become more difficult to be around him, not easier?

"You've been out every night. How's it been?" Sigrid asked, changing the subject.

"Better than I would have anticipated. The guards are at least not escalating things. Businesses were forced to close, and they are arresting some people, but so far all those people have been released the next day."

She sighed and stood, moving to sit next to him on the bed. Their knees met, and suddenly she wondered why she'd ever felt like she couldn't be near him.

Baldr, relaxing as she took her spot, reached out a hand and placed it on her thigh. "People are upset. That's good. They should be upset. All of this is unfair. Unjust."

"That's what the Heddish know. Injustice." She leaned on him, resting her head on his shoulder. The two of them cast their eyes out the window, where just out of sight she knew people were gathering. They could hear them, though. There were angry voices, but they weren't as loud as they had been some nights.

"They're getting tired," he said. "It's just so much at once. My mother ... says that is the point. Exhaust people. Take everything away, then give small things back to make it seem like you're generous. We hope people can keep this energy, but ... who knows."

"Is the Collective planning anything new?"

He looked at her, his fingers curling around her wrist. His thumb pressed against the soft underside, sliding up into her palm. "It is best if you don't know. We can't ... we can't risk Gorm trying to get any information out of you. I'm sorry."

Her heart sank, and she wanted to rip her hand out of his grasp out of spite, but she left it, letting the spite burn out in her chest like a flame burning through a piece of cotton. "I ... get it," she replied, understanding why they couldn't give her information but resenting it all the same. She'd traveled so far from home for them. Hadn't she earned more trust? Had one mistake ruined her standing?

"Hey," he said in his soft voice, a hand coming to touch her face. They sat so close, so intimately. It felt like a long time since they'd been that close. How many days had it been since the festival? A couple weeks, perhaps? "I know this doesn't feel good. It isn't forever. Just until we're sure this threat has passed. It is as much to keep you safe as anyone else."

Her gaze traveled to his. Those gentle brown eyes of his stared into hers, and she could see small flecks of gold in them. They were deep, shimmering pools of honey and light, and despite her frustration, she wanted to get lost in them. "Baldr ..."

He leaned in, pressing his lips to hers. She felt electricity shoot from the spot he kissed her, filling up every inch of her and lifting the hairs on her arms. This was what a kiss should feel like, she thought. Full of energy and affection. Her body melted into his touch, her mind filling with a warm haze that left little room to think of anything else. What had they been talking about? It didn't matter. Only he mattered.

His touch grew fiercer, and his hands came to hold her sides, his fingers pressing into her. The thin, simple gown she wore felt barely present. Blood rushed in her ears, deafening her, and as her eyes closed, all her senses homed in on him. He smelled of fresh wood and herbs, of the very soul of the earth. When he began to pull away, she grasped for him, not wanting to give him up.

"Sigrid," he whispered, a hand sliding around her midsection until it settled on the small of her back. "I ... have been thinking. A lot."

"I see," she responded, ice piercing her heart. All the heat she'd been feeling vanished, and she felt her veins freeze.

"That night when we kissed ..."

"Should we not have?"

"I'm tired of worrying. The longer this goes on, the more I feel ..." He paused, his brows knitting together as he searched her face for the right words. "We won't get a break anytime soon. I can continue to funnel all my energy, my emotions, into one thing, or I can open myself up. I want to open myself up. To you. You make me feel ... *insane*. I can't stop thinking about you when you're gone, and it is almost painful not to touch you when you're here."

Sigrid stared at him, not sure what to say. Relationships were so difficult for her, especially with people outside her job.

But he'd probably thought of all that, she thought. He'd known her for some time now. He would think over every detail. He'd probably been brooding over it. If there was anyone she trusted to have thought about this, it was Baldr.

"I ..." Her words caught in her throat, and her thoughts raced too quickly to focus on any single one. She shook her head. "I want you. You know I want you."

He responded by pressing his lips to hers once again. This time, she would not let him escape, would not let him prolong the moment with words. Her arms wrapped around him as she slipped into his lap. The fire in her core reignited as her chest pressed against his, forcing him back onto the bed. His breath hitched as she took her spot on top of him, and as her lips traveled to his throat, she could feel the speed of his beating heart.

Power surged through her. Confidence, aided by his confession, blossomed in her chest. Her hands grabbed his and pinned them above his head as her hips ground against his. He gasped, and a smile spread across her face as she kissed him.

She let that power take over. Her hands lifted the ugly guard's tunic from his body and haplessly tossed it aside, letting it fall wherever it may. She marveled at the strength of his body. His body was tight, his muscles clearly defined under his brown skin. Her fingernails dragged across the expanse of his chest, tracing scars so light they must have been from childhood. She wanted to kiss each one.

How often had she lain with a man and simply willed herself out of her body? Now, she willed herself to be present, to feel every inch of him. They rolled together, writhing on top of her bed, their lips barely parting for breath. The air in her lungs fueled an internal fire, fanning it until it threatened to consume her entire being.

They were stripped of their clothing, their bodies pressed together in the heat of the night. She wrestled for control, pinning him beneath her. She took in his body with her eyes, her lust glimmering. It was the most beautiful body she'd ever seen. She wanted to caress every inch, to kiss every exposed bit of flesh. So she did. Her lips traveled across him, journeying through the plains of his chest and down to his naval. His breath caught in his throat, and he tried to prop himself on his elbows to look at her, but she was instantly on him again, her lips crushing his. She was in charge.

Her eyes met his. "I want you," she said, reaching between his legs to grasp him. Her fingers wrapped around him, his body shaking, a soft moan flowing from between his plush, bitten lips.

He nodded, his lips falling open. "I am yours." His words were hushed, as if he were barely able to form words at all. "I promise you. I am yours."

The next morning was calm. Baldr's arms were wrapped around Sigrid, their naked bodies were pressed together beneath her blanket. At first, she basked in the embrace and the heat of his body, but as time passed, she squirmed. Wriggling out of his embrace, she tossed off the blanket to a rush of cool air. Baldr shivered and buried himself beneath the blanket, but she found herself too energized to stay in bed.

Moving to the vanity, she took a seat and inspected herself in the mirror. There were faint marks along her neck and chest. Her cheeks were flushed. She busied herself with her usual morning routine, her chest so full of joy it threatened to burst. She cleaned her face with a cotton pad and stared at herself in the mirror. As she applied her makeup, she took more care than usual, lining her eyes slowly. She willed time to slow around her and took a moment to simply remember every second.

She saw Baldr begin to stir as she glanced at his reflection in the mirror. She paused as she applied a black dot on her cheekbone, watching him sit up and look around for her. When his eyes finally found her, he seemed to relax, and Sigrid's heart fluttered.

"What time is it?" he asked, rubbing his eyes.

"Just after nine."

"We slept in."

Sigrid laughed. "A perfectly reasonable hour. Many men have spent the night and dawdled off at this hour, so you are one of many."

Baldr laughed awkwardly.

"Oh, I didn't mean it like that." She cringed. "I just meant ... you won't be noticed when you leave. Just another cull finally waking after a night of debauchery."

He stood, his body naked as he made his way to her. She watched him, shamelessly letting her eyes linger first on the hard lines of his stomach, then what rested between his legs.

His hand lifted her face by the chin, and his lips found hers. "I know what you meant," he said softly, brushing his thumb beneath her eye. "I have some business I need to do today. What are your plans?"

"Same as they have been: Avoiding attention. Looking normal."

Baldr sighed, taking a seat on the edge of the bed to pull his shirt over his head. "I'm sorry. I know this isn't fair."

Sigrid quietly applied rouge to her lips. "I just feel like ... I've proven myself."

"You have."

"Do others feel that way?"

"Sigrid. You are not being punished. It is unfortunate that Commander Gorm has his sights on you, but it won't last forever. Eventually, he'll take his search elsewhere. Until then, you need to lie low. You're lucky you haven't been dragged out in the street and questioned as it is."

He was right. She hated it, but he was right. This wasn't about her capabilities, as useless as she felt. It was about protecting the Collective. And Agnar.

"I just wish I could see Brigid," she said, opening her armoire. Her fingers slid across the fabric of the few dresses she owned, each handcrafted. Over the years she added beads and embroidery to patch holes, until most of the gowns were elegantly decorated. Gaudy, she'd heard Heddish women say, but she found them beautiful.

"I'll see what we can do. Soon." His hands slipped around her waist, and his lips found their way to her ear. "I need to go. I will visit more, I promise. Every time I can."

She turned in his arms and placed her palms on his cheeks. Even in the ugly guard's armor, he was handsome. It was almost painful to look at him. "I can't wait."

She'd considered going to the gymnasium. It'd been well over a week since she'd been last, and with how little she felt she was allowed to do, her body ached to do something. Anything. She had already put on a dress for the day when she decided she needed to hit something.

She was wearing far more makeup than she normally did at the gym. She hadn't bothered to wash it off, she had been more determined to quickly change into leggings and a tunic and leave than look appropriate.

There were eyes on her. She could feel them. Gorm wasn't being inconspicuous anymore. Maybe he never had been. Whatever the case, she knew someone was watching her the moment she left the Pearl's front doors. When she tried to spot them, she could not detect whose eyes were on her, who was following her through the streets.

At least, not at first.

Sigrid stopped to talk with a baker near the gym who she'd been buying bread from for years. That's when she saw him—a small man dressed so plainly he almost blended in with everyone else. That's probably what he'd been betting on, she thought. His pointed ears stuck out from beneath his hair, and he was very good at looking occupied, wandering from booth to booth to look like nothing more than another shopping local.

But he wasn't a local. This part of town was old, and the ties were deep. Sigrid knew everyone around here. She knew the butcher, who gave her a better selection than the Heddish one nearer the Pearl. She'd had a brief fling with the son of the baker, but the woman always liked her, and she was always welcome to whatever bread was left at the end of the day.

This man she did not know, and neither did anyone else. They regarded him warmly, assuming the spy was just another strange traveler that sometimes passed through town. It was safer for an elf to stick to elven neighborhoods when possible. His face was unfamiliar, and that was enough.

If only she hadn't seen him outside the Pearl when she left. If only she hadn't felt his eyes on her as she traveled the streets. If only he weren't so stupid.

"I'll see you later, Itzel." Sigrid smiled at the baker, giving the aging woman a peck on the cheek. "Tell Temoch I said hello and let me know how red his face gets."

She considered going somewhere else. Changing her path, spend the day shopping. He didn't need to know her routine. No, she thought. She'd stick to the lighter dumbbells and forgo touching any of the training swords. Sitting on a mat, she posed and stretched her body, trying to look as if she were not keeping her eye on the door.

Sigrid was perhaps more tired than she'd meant to be when she finished. Throwing her bag over her shoulder, she proudly exited the gym, pretending that she did not see the man in the distance. She strolled down side streets that she knew well, streets she'd played in as a child, and visited with old, familiar faces along the way. She stopped to say hello to a white-haired elderly woman sitting in a chair outside her home, and again to a little girl drawing figures in the dirt.

When she turned down an alley as the sun began to set, she was sure he thought she was just going to chat with others. She could hardly believe her own plotting. She'd never done anything like this before. Maybe that's why he got lazy and strayed a little too close. He didn't see her when she slipped around a building and hid behind a closed stall. It was quiet in the little alley save for his light footsteps.

He hit the ground hard. Sigrid was on top of him faster than he could fight back, and soon he was beneath her, and her arms wrapped under his pits with her hands clasped at the base of his skull. He fought back, but she was heavier than him. Stronger.

"Who are you?" she seethed through gritted teeth, holding on to him as if he were an angry bull ready to throw her from her saddle.

"Go to hell," he spit back, thrashing around to get out from beneath her.

"I'll take you with me." Sigrid felt a surge of confidence and held him tighter. She wasn't going to let Gorm turn her into a coward, sitting at home doing nothing while Baldr and the rest of the Collective faced the hard tasks.

If anyone heard them, they did not poke their heads out to investigate. Sigrid and the spy rolled around on the ground as he managed to get his arms free. A fist connected with her cheek, nearly knocking her off him. She fought back, her knuckles cracking his nose. The man screamed out in pain as blood spilled from his nostrils. "You bitch," he huffed, trying to grab her by the ponytail. She grabbed his hand as it reached, then slammed it back on the ground.

"Tell Gorm," she said, struggling with each word as he fought her, "to fuck off."

The man laughed. There was yelling in the distance, the voices urgent. Loud at first, the voices disappeared into the distance, as if people were running. An explosion was set off from somewhere in the city and panicked voices filled the air.

Sigrid gave the man a puzzled look. "What's happening?" she demanded, placing her forearm at his throat and pressing down.

The man struggled out another laugh. "Fuck off." He spit blood onto her cheek, his nails digging into her arm as he tried to push her off.

She did not let up. No matter how he struggled, she didn't let go. After a few painfully long minutes, the man beneath her finally went limp. His heart still beat in his chest and he groaned, but he was dazed.

He was light, she found. It was not too much to lift him, with one arm around his neck, and lead him through the streets. She hoped he looked like nothing more than a drunk cull being carried off for the evening. Sigrid inhaled a breath deep into her lungs and stepped out of the alley.

He seemed to grow heavier with every step, but once she was moving, she didn't dare stop.

Soon the Pearl was in her sights.

His breath was shallow and ragged, but she feared he would come to before it was safe.

Something was happening. Nobody even stopped to look at her as several people ran past her toward the center of the city. Others rushed in the opposite direction with children and pets in their arms. She couldn't make out the situation from their heightened voices.

Kicking open the door to the Pearl, she strode through without caring if anyone was there. She went straight to her room and tossed the man on the bed. From the chest at the end of her bed, she pulled out a set of silk ropes and bound his wrists and feet. A gag was placed in his mouth, should he wake and try to scream. Many men had been in that position before, but none had ever been like this.

"Stay here," she said to the unconscious man.

Outside her window she could hear the streets fill with people. There was angry shouting in the distance. Another explosion rocked Sigrid's senses, this one far closer than the first. Something was happening.

Sigrid's feet flew across the floor. Only stopping to lock her bedroom door behind her, she tore out of the Pearl like lightning.

CHAPTER TWENTY-FIVE

Smoke filled her nostrils. As she moved toward the center of the city, toward the palace, and people began to spill into the streets. It did not take long before she encountered a group of guards.

"You!" one of them screamed after her.

She did not so much as pause before darting off down an alley. There were footsteps behind her, but she disappeared into the crowd, ducking behind a tall elven man with a hammer in his hands. Suddenly he swung it, and Sigrid ducked, hearing the hammer meet something with a sickening crunch. A warm liquid sprayed her body. The scent of copper filled her nostrils, and she spared a glance behind her at whoever had been hit.

The guard who chased her had been closer than she realized.

"Thanks," she said to the massive man.

He shrugged, moving away from her toward the looming palace.

Sigrid darted down streets and alleys until she could see the red door of the Collective's headquarters. "Baldr!" she called out, busting through the front door.

Empty.

Nobody had been there in some time. Anything that had been there before was gone, nothing but dust and bits of random furniture was left. She wondered when they'd moved.

The knot in her stomach tightened. Baldr hadn't mentioned it. Perhaps he couldn't, she thought. But he should have. She'd risked her livelihood to travel with him to Uruachi. She'd put her life on the line for the cause he introduced her to, and he hadn't even bothered to tell her they'd moved, let alone to where.

She saw red when she turned and stalked out of the abandoned building. The chaos of the city faded around her.

They didn't trust her. Even though she had lain low, just like they'd asked. Even though she was one of them. They didn't take her seriously enough to trust. To them, she was just another painted woman with nothing to offer. It stung the worst when it came from her own people.

Had Baldr fought? Argued? Had he advocated on her behalf? He must have. All she could do was trust that he'd done just that.

Not knowing where to go, Sigrid turned back toward the brothel. Where else could she go if not home? It was not safe to be out without anyone, and she didn't know where to begin finding Baldr.

Turning the corner, she saw someone familiar gallop by on a horse. White hair. Anam!

Sigrid spun with a gasp, watching as the woman raced down the street. Two people on horses were behind her, but as soon as they were past, several more came running, each heading toward the wealthy Heddish district.

That's when it hit her. They wouldn't have hidden Agnar somewhere elves would have noticed him. He would have stuck out. The Collective had few friends in the Heddish nobility, but they did have at least one she knew of. The very same nobleman who'd given them horses for their journey.

Sigrid took off behind the running people. Through the crowd she darted, always keeping one person in sight. She came across a line of guards, each standing shoulder to shoulder the width of the entire street. They held shields in their hands and bashed their weapons against the crowd crying out before them. The men's faces shone in the light of torches, their gleeful, bloodthirsty eyes taking in the crowd.

Sigrid didn't have time to get caught in a battle. She watched a bottle fly, a rag hanging out the end with a fire lit. When the bottle hit the ground in front of the line, it exploded, lighting up the narrow street. People screamed and another bottle hit the ground.

Her eyes darted from side to side, desperately trying to find a way around. She spotted a ladder against one of the buildings next to a crate of paint. Darting to the side, Sigrid threw herself up the ladder and onto the roof. Below, she could hear the whinnying of the horses as they reared back, spooked by the explosive flames.

The distance to the next building was too far to jump. She yanked the ladder up the side of the building and dragged it to the edge. Hauling it over the side of the building, she laid it out so it created a rickety bridge between the buildings.

Screams filled her ears as smoke burned her nostrils. There was no time to dwell on what was happening below. She did not look down as she took her first step on the ladder. The wood held her weight, but it creaked beneath her as she walked. Her arms were held out as she breathed. One breath in, one breath out.

Flames shot up just beneath her feet. Her eyes were torn down to look at the scene below. Chaos reigned. The crowd was pushing back the guards, and Anam was at the head on her horse. The beast reared back but Anam held strong, her sword in one hand. As the animal's hooves met the face of a guard in front of her, Anam brought her sword down into the throat of another.

Sigrid swallowed hard. Steeling herself, she took another few steps across the makeshift bridge until her feet found the next building. She did not stop to breathe or take another look at the scene below before dashing across the roof. She nearly called out a blessing to the gods when she spotted stairs in the corner that snaked along the side of the building. Her feet flew down each step.

Almost every street that led to the Heddish district was consumed with as much chaos. She dodged swings from guards as she ran past, not stopping, not daring to catch her breath. Her feet encountered something soft, her body lurching forward as she lost her footing. She hit the dirt with a loud thud. At her feet was the body of a young elven woman, an arrow sticking out of her eye. There were no weapons around the body.

Letting out a scream, Sigrid scurried backward from the corpse. No, she couldn't be distracted, no matter how much the young woman's face drew her eyes. No matter how much she wanted to stare in horror at the stricken, surprised look on her young face, Sigrid had to keep going.

She lurched herself to her feet and kept running.

Soon, it was in her sights. Just in the distance she could see the estate. A carriage was out front, and guards were protecting the house from the confusion that loomed in the streets.

The door opened, and Sigrid's breath caught in her throat. Gorm strode out, a smile on his face so wide she could see it from the distance, his knife held to Brigid's throat.

Agnar exited next. Guards flanked either side of him. Both of his arms were tied behind his back. He pulled at their grasps, but his eyes were on the dagger glistening against Brigid's trembling throat.

"Gorm," Sigrid cried out, lobbing a fist-sized rock in his direction.

The rock hit at Gorm's feet, startling him. When his eyes settled on her, they grew bright. "Take the princess and her maiden to the camp," he commanded, shoving Brigid into the carriage. Agnar was pushed in next.

Sigrid grabbed another rock and flung it at Gorm's head. It missed, hitting the carriage instead. The man laughed, striding toward Sigrid with guards at his back. "The whore," he said, opening his arms wide as if for a hug. "We meet again."

Sigrid breathed heavily. Another large rock was cradled in her hand, ready to meet the side of Gorm's ugly head.

"This couldn't be a better evening if I'd planned it," he said cheerily.

"Did you?" she asked, her lips drawn into a thin line.

"The riot? Who can plan a riot?" He chuckled as if she'd told the quaintest joke. "I simply ... wished for the best."

"Let Brigid go," she said, her fist tightening around the stone. "You don't need her."

"Oh, but you see, I do! Our handsome princess here will only cooperate if she is safe. I need the princess, so, you know. I'll tell her you inquired, though."

The chariot lurched forward with that. Panicked, Sigrid threw the third rock. This time it slammed into Gorm's face, and she heard him cry out. He stumbled back, and when he looked up there was blood flowing from one of his eyes.

He drew his sword and lunged forward at her, one hand covering his damaged eye. She jumped out of the way as the sword came down, hitting the street beneath her.

Guards came running toward her, but Gorm turned and flashed his teeth in a snarl. "Leave her to me!" he barked, and the soldiers backed away in surprise.

Sigrid desperately looked around for some sort of weapon. She saw nothing but a broken piece of wood abandoned in the road. Grabbing it out of the dirt, she dove out of the way again as Gorm's sword nearly contacted her head.

He was bigger than her, but he was slow. As he raised his arm to swing at her again, she darted forward and stabbed the jagged edge of the wood beneath his arm. He howled and dropped his sword, releasing his eye just long enough to rip out the wood.

Sigrid tackled him to the ground. Kicking his sword out of the way, she pummeled her fists into his face, screaming into the night air. The soldiers barked their surprise, but she did not stop until Gorm grabbed her by the throat. He wrestled her to the ground, her fists still flying and connecting with his head.

His hands pressed down on her throat. She couldn't scream, and she gasped for breath, her hands tearing at him. She grabbed a handful of his hair and yanked, but he didn't budge. She desperately kicked her legs to try and roll out from beneath him, but his grip was too strong. The corners of her eyes began to grow fuzzy, and her chest burned.

Just as she was sure he'd won, she grabbed him beneath the arm and dug her fingers into the wound she'd given him earlier. Gorm howled in pain and released her.

Sigrid rolled away from him, the world a blur, and threw herself in the direction she'd seen the sword. Her fingers wrapped around the hilt, and as she twisted and swung, she felt the blade meet something hard.

The blade was lodged in the side of Gorm's head. His eyes were wide in surprise as he collapsed on his side, a pool of blood forming beneath him.

The soldiers he'd told off stood in horror for a brief moment before rushing forward with their swords drawn. Sigrid lifted an arm to shield herself from the incoming blow, but no blow ever came. Instead, she heard arrows whip through the air and bury themselves in the exposed meat of the soldier's necks.

Sigrid twisted to see who had come to her rescue. Collective rebels descended from the shadowy streets, some with bows, others with swords. Anam led the charge from on top of her horse. She'd lost her sword, it seemed, but a bow was in her hands now. Stars still danced in Sigrid's eyes, making the older woman look as if she were a deity.

"Ata guide me," Sigrid said under her breath, her hands covering her eyes in relief. She could have kissed Anam's feet.

Anam opened her mouth to speak, but a look of horror played across her face. Sigrid turned just in time to see one of the guards, an arrow lodged in his collarbone, shove a dagger into her stomach.

CHAPTER TWENTY-SIX

I t was too hot in the room. Every breath Sigrid took felt excruciating, but it wasn't until she tried to sit up that pain racked through her body. Groaning, she lay limp in the bed, her tongue so dry it felt like sandpaper in her mouth.

"Gods, thank you," Baldr whispered, his hot hand settling on her arm.

Sigrid opened her eyes and cast them at the man next to her bed. "Huh," she said.

"Huh?" He blinked. "You survive a stabbing and all you have to say is 'huh'?"

"Huh," she said again. "How ... how long was I out?"

"A few hours. It's almost afternoon."

Silence stretched between them. "What ... happened?"

"You got stabbed."

"I know that," she grunted. "I mean, what happened last night?"

He sighed. "Don't worry about it right now. We'll explain it later."

"Baldr," she snapped, cringing from the pain as she tried to sit again. "Don't—"

"You'll hurt yourself."

"Stop!" She clenched her fists tight. "Tell me what happened."

Baldr sighed. "Something exploded in the city near a group of guards and the crowd got violent. Things began to settle as the sun came out, but ... we made the guard flee the city, along with the rest of Gorm's soldiers."

Looking around, she realized she was not in her room. This was not her bed. "Where am I?"

"Our current headquarters," he said.

"Oh, good, now I get to know where it is. Very helpful now, Baldr."

He tensed, his lips drawing together. "I'm sorry," he said, his eyes tired and apologetic. "Things ... did not go the way I wanted. I went back to find you when things broke out, but you were already gone. I found some ... captive in your room."

Sigrid laughed, soon regretting it as pain shot through her abdomen. "One of Gorm's spies. He had been following me. I took care of it. Where is he now?"

"Alive," he said. "I almost let him go, but his broken nose led me to assume he was there for a more unusual reason. When you were stabbed, we went ahead and moved him, just in case. I figured he wasn't a cull."

"No, he's not." She sighed, looking at the ceiling with tired eyes. "So the guards escalated an already-tense situation and a riot broke out."

"Basically, yes."

"And I killed a … nobleman. A commander."

"That you did."

Silence swelled between them. When Sigrid did not say anything else, Baldr leaned forward and pressed a kiss to her lips. Though she was angry at him for choosing to keep things from her, for now she put aside her frustrations and melted into the kiss. His fingers brushed through her tangled hair, careful not to snag any knots. He was so delicate with her she couldn't tell if she enjoyed it or hated it. She wasn't some weak thing that needed to be coddled, but it felt good to be taken care of.

She did not press him for more details as she healed. In truth, since she was in no position to do anything, she didn't know how to broach how she felt. Would she have made the same choice in his position? she wondered. If her mother were the Collective's leader and Baldr's identity had been discovered by the enemy, would she have kept the Collective's whereabouts secret? She didn't know.

It was a few days before she was able to convince her nurse she could walk. It was not easy, but with a crutch, she was able to leave her bed. Baldr accompanied her around the building as familiar and strange faces milled about. Had their numbers grown, or were there many whose faces she'd never seen?

Nobody but Cualli and Zuma visited her. Nobody would, she figured. Brigid was ... gone. Kidnapped. Sigrid's mind was full of every terrible scenario she could think of. Images of a bound and tortured Brigid kept her awake as her stomach clenched in constant tight knots.

The new building they'd taken residence in was in the Heddish part of the city. Terrified of what would come next, a few noble families had fled in the chaos once the guards had been run out of the city. Sigrid had no doubt there would be tall tales across the countryside of savage elves massacring human children.

If Baldr was correct, few died in the riot. A guard died in the explosion that many assumed had been set by Gorm. There were the guards the Collective killed before they could get to Sigrid, and a few unfortunate souls who'd been killed by arrows as the guard shot into the crowd at random.

Destruction was abundant. Havoc had moved inward on the city, targeting the wealthiest Heddish homes around the palace. Some homes had been ransacked, while other households had played their cards right and invited the rebels in. Some caved quickly, pleading for the violence to end, and promised aid in exchange for safety. Others fled the city with their most treasured or easily transportable belongings. Whatever was left was quickly redistributed to wherever it could be best used—kitchenware to the community kitchens, beds to families, and clothing to those who lived on the street.

Sigrid wasn't sure how she felt about people being run off. She thought of Ivar, a cull who had always paid well but made her stomach churn. He'd never harmed her, but he'd always given her a sinking feeling in her gut. Where was he? she wondered. Had he fled? Or had he opened his home and his wallet to their cause to save his hide? Then there was Bjorn, a sweet young Heddish nobleman who had always been kind, but whose family disapproved of his attraction to elven women. His family surely would have fled.

"I'm not going to be working for a while," Sigrid said to Baldr, who was busying himself folding freshly washed sheets.

He looked up at her. "Do you want to work?"

She shrugged. "I ... have had to work for a long time. First I worked to survive, then I worked to remain comfortable enough to live. What will I do now?"

"The Collective will not let anyone go hungry if that is your worry. You didn't answer my question. Do you want to work?"

Did she? There were days where her job was excruciating. She could remember in vivid detail days where she wanted to quit, to do anything else; when working as a kitchen maid for pennies seemed preferable. But there were also days full of laughter, where she was joined by Brigid or any of the other women of their profession. There had been culls who were kind and whose company she enjoyed, even if those were rarer than not. It hadn't been a choice for so long.

She'd been brave enough to leave to Uruachi with Baldr, but when she returned, she also returned to work. Now, with such chaos, she did not know how to fill her days without culls or her greatest companion. "I don't know, I guess. What are my choices?"

She couldn't walk without her crutch, but she stood as tall as she could. Her chin held high, Sigrid strode through Anam's office. Baldr was sitting in a chair across from her desk, which no doubt had once belonged to some nobleman, and he gave her a nod of approval as she entered.

"It is good to see you doing well," Anam said, looking up from the papers on her table. "I've been meaning to visit you. I wanted to ask you about the Heddish commander you killed."

Sigrid's lips tensed into a flat line. "You had plenty of opportunities to visit me. He was going to kill me, so I killed him first."

Anam regarded Sigrid coldly, her dark eyes scanning up and down the younger woman's frame as if she could see right into Sigrid's core. "I would have as well. I was surprised to see you'd made it there before us."

"I know the city. People know me. How long have you lived in Copper City, Anam?"

"What?" The woman frowned, setting down her pen.

"How long have you lived here? Baldr's never said. I know he's only been here for a year, but how long have you been here?"

Anam's eyes narrowed. "Five years."

"You can learn a lot in five years. But you can learn a lot more in thirty. I made it there without knowing for sure if I would find the right place, because you'd decided I didn't need to know."

"You didn't. You are very clever, however. I'll give you that."

Sigrid glanced at Baldr. He shot her a soft smile and a quick nod. She turned her attention back to Anam, her fingers tight around her crutch. "You don't like me. I don't even think that you don't trust me, just that you don't like me. You let me go with Baldr because he trusted me, and I have a feeling you couldn't spare many more for such a journey. Not when you're spread between two cities. Honestly, you don't have to like me, that's fine. But you don't take me seriously because I'm a painted woman. That's what bothers me."

Anam's lips curled into a deep frown. "I have never said such a thing."

"You don't have to. It's fine, really. I don't expect everyone to understand my life or why I live it the way I do. It isn't for your judgment. But I have been useful. I helped convince Uruachi to send aid. I brought you your greatest ally yet. I killed an enemy. I have been far more valuable than you could have anticipated. I don't want to be left in the dark anymore. I want a seat at the table. I am every bit as useful as Baldr is, and I want that recognized."

Anam sat quietly for a long time. Her face was unreadable, but it was clear gears were turning behind those dark eyes. Finally, when she did speak, there was a slight upward curve to the corner of her lips. "You are very bold."

"I am."

"So, you want to take charge. I admire someone who stands up for themselves and goes for what they want. You're right—I didn't take you very seriously. Perhaps that was an oversight. If you want to be taken seriously, then I will give you serious jobs. I understand you apprehended one of Gorm's spies, yes?"

"I did."

"Baldr had him taken to a holding room. We've kept him healthy, but he's not speaking. Do you think you can get information from him?"

"Fine," Sigrid said finally. "I'll learn what I can."

"Good." Anam looked back down at the papers in front of her and began reading through them. "Anything else?"

Sigrid swallowed. Was that it? No argument? "I ... I guess not."

"Then you are dismissed."

Baldr stood and gave Sigrid a wide, toothy grin, and followed her out of the office. When the door closed behind them and they were sure they were far enough away, he pressed his lips against hers, his hands grabbing her by the hips. "That was something," he purred, settling his hand on the back of her head. "You were magnificent. She was impressed. I can tell."

Sigrid's heart beat as quickly as a hummingbird in her chest. She really had done it, hadn't she? "Maybe he'll have information. Maybe he'll know where they took Agnar and Brigid."

Baldr nodded, brushing a thumb beneath her eye and kissing the tip of her nose. "We'll get them, I promise. We've come so far. Nothing is out of our reach."

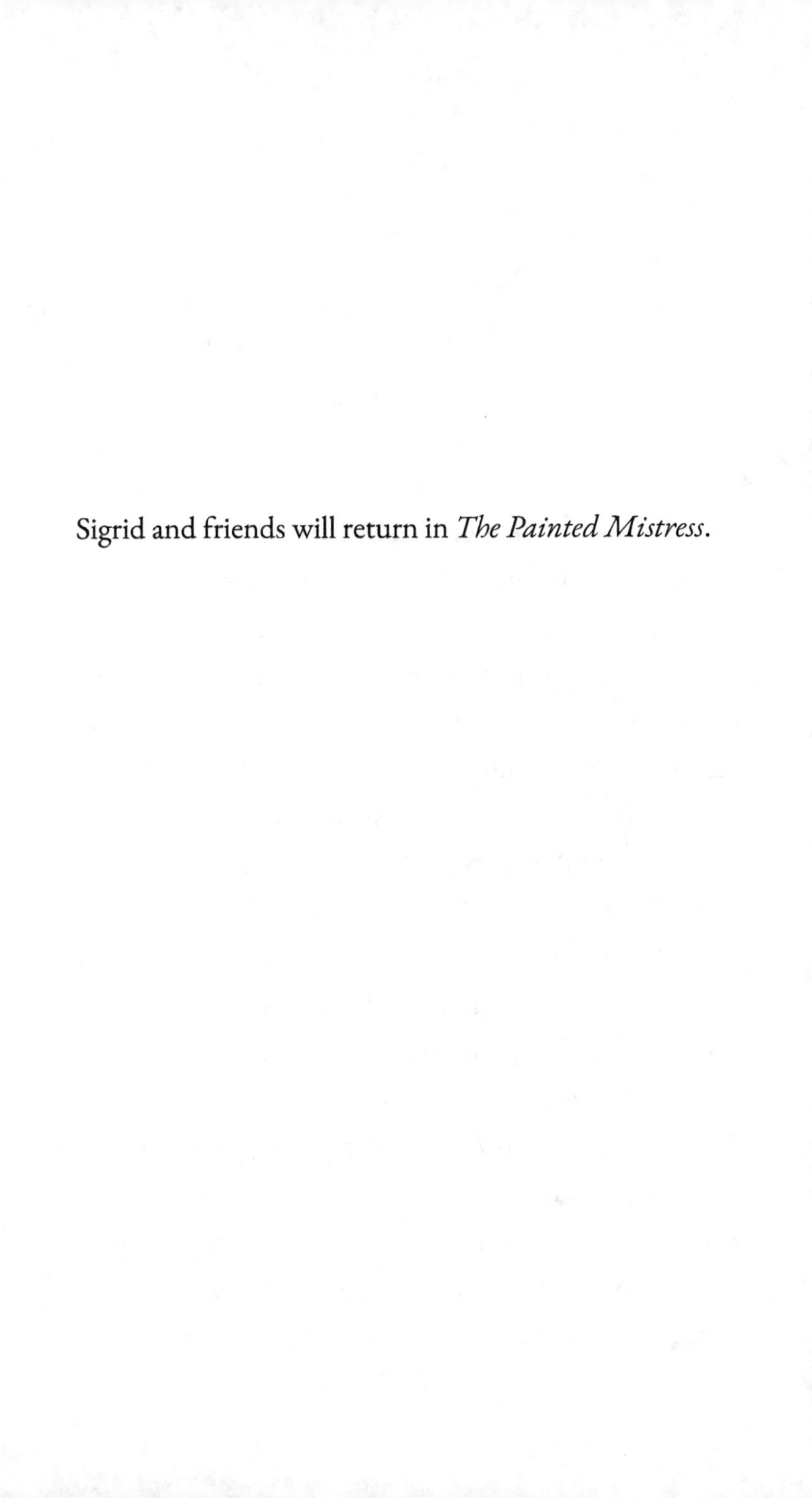

Sigrid and friends will return in *The Painted Mistress*.

ACKNOWLEDGMENTS

From its inception in 2018, The Painted Woman has evolved immensely, transforming from a portal fantasy to the rich narrative it is today. This journey of growth and change wouldn't have been possible without the unwavering support of my mother, Raquel. Born in Mexico, my mother tried her best to share her culture with her children, and this story is a love letter to the magic of my Motherland. Uruachi, in fact, is named for a small village in her home state of Chihuahua. She told me stories about this small town, so small it was basically a village when she was young, and I wanted to give the world of her youth the magic it deserves.

The indigenous people of Mexico, the people who are my cousins and ancestors, are the true inspiration of this world. The world of Hedeby, or the world it once was, is inspired by various indigenous tribes throughout Mexico, particularly my ancestral tribe, the Tarahumara. It is my earnest hope that this work honors their legacy and resonates with their spirit.

A special acknowledgment is reserved for the unsung heroes in our society – sex workers. Their history of activism, strength, and their often overlooked role in pivotal moments of change have been a guiding light in crafting this narrative. This book aims to challenge stereotypes and celebrate the full, complex humanity of sex workers, showcasing them as the heroines they truly are.